Protectors of the Crown

In pursuit of justice...and love!

As members of the Knights Fortitude of the Order of the Sword, Sirs Warin de Talmont, Nicholas d'Amberly and Savaric Fitz Leonard have sworn an oath of allegiance to one another and King Henry III. When faced with a new threat against the Crown, known only as the Duo Dracones, they must work together to find and bring the traitors to justice.

With each new lead, they risk their lives to get one step closer to the truth... But the biggest danger these three men are about to face is the women who are about to open their minds and steal their hearts!

Discover Warin and Joan's story in
A Defiant Maiden's Knight

Read Nicholas and Eva's story in
A Stolen Knight's Kiss

And now read Savaric and Marguerite's story in
Her Unforgettable Knight

All available now!

Author Note

There have been people of color living in England since the Roman conquest. Yet with new research, more people are believed to have lived in the medieval era than previously thought, especially in the main towns and cities such as London. And although their treatment would have been vastly different to the postcolonial era many centuries later, they would still have felt discrimination and bigotry.

It is against this backdrop that my hero, Savaric Fitz Leonard, a man of mixed racial heritage and a member of the Knights Fortitude, has to navigate life—within the murky, dangerous world at the court of Henry III. This, he does with the help of Marguerite Studdal, a woman he once cared for but ultimately spurned.

Can they find a way through the twists and turns of medieval England as they try to find the enemies of the Crown—the Duo Dracones? Can they also find a way back to one another and find the one thing that they've both denied and resisted for so long—love?

I hope you enjoy Savaric and Marguerite's story in the final climactic book of the Protectors of the Crown series.

MELISSA OLIVER

—

Her Unforgettable Knight

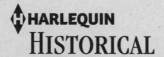

HARLEQUIN
HISTORICAL

ISBN-13: 978-1-335-72393-2

Her Unforgettable Knight

Copyright © 2023 by Maryam Oliver

For questions and comments about the quality of this book, please contact us at CustomerService@Harlequin.com.

Harlequin Enterprises ULC
22 Adelaide St. West, 41st Floor
Toronto, Ontario M5H 4E3, Canada
www.Harlequin.com

Printed in U.S.A.

Recycling programs for this product may not exist in your area.

Melissa Oliver is from southwest London, where she writes sweeping historical romance, and is the winner of the Romantic Novelists' Association's Joan Hessayon Award for New Writers 2020 for her debut, *The Rebel Heiress and the Knight*.

For more information, visit www.melissaoliverauthor.com.

Follow Melissa on:
Instagram: @MelissaOliverAuthor
Twitter: @MelissaOAuthor
Facebook: MelissaOliverAuthor

Books by Melissa Oliver

Harlequin Historical

Notorious Knights

The Rebel Heiress and the Knight
Her Banished Knight's Redemption
The Return of Her Lost Knight
The Knight's Convenient Alliance

Protectors of the Crown

A Defiant Maiden's Knight
A Stolen Knight's Kiss
Her Unforgettable Knight

Visit the Author Profile page
at Harlequin.com.

Women Life Freedom

Chapter One

Billingsgate Wharf,
London 1229

Savaric Fitz Leonard blew warm air into the palms of his hands before rubbing them together in an attempt to yield a little more heat into his chilled body. He had been standing for what seemed an eternity by the quay-side at Billingsgate wharf waiting for a cargo vessel, which had only moments ago pierced through the veil of dense fog that had wrapped itself around the mouth of the River Thames.

Thank God!

It had taken much longer than he had anticipated for this vessel, travelling from France, to reach its destination. Now at the witching hour it had arrived into the Port of London. And with it, Savaric prayed, crucial evidence that he, along with his Knights Fortitude brethren, Warin de Talmont and Nicholas D'Amberly, desperately sought. Savaric hoped that their informant in Paris had meant this particular vessel and not any other, otherwise the whole night would have been a waste of his time. Again…

It had been more than two years since the investigation into The Duo Dracones had stalled. The nefarious, traitorous group bent on treason, sedition, and the eradication of the Crown had dissipated once more before going underground. God, but when he thought about the traitors who worked tirelessly to conspire against the Crown it made his blood boil. It mattered not that Savaric and his Knights Fortitude brethren captured and cut down members of The Duo Dracones—they still managed to rally around their cause and come back more resilient than before.

And it did not help that they still knew far too little about the group and that each time the Knights Fortitude made progress and caught members of The Duo Dracones, they would choose death over revealing more about their organisation. Indeed, two years ago, the matter had once again come to a frustrating end when the few culprits who had not chosen death, and whom Savaric and the other member of the Knights Fortitude sought, had fled to France without a trace. This night however might bring about some much-needed change of fortune.

Or so Savaric hoped.

He melted into the shadows beneath a nearby arched doorway, as the flat-bottomed timber cog vessel gently lapped its way through the river to the dockside, with its single red-and-white sail flapping in the breeze before dropping down. Soon men hurled themselves off deck working together to spring the line into dock, hauling the vessel forward to the wharf, ready to moor.

Savaric pushed forward, weaving among the crewmen, grabbing hold of a spring line and blending in among the deck hands, whistling along to a ditty or two. The lines were soon tied, the vessel moored and the cargo carried, conveyed and deposited on the dockside. He threw himself into the thick of it, helping cart the heavy barrels and huge chests down as a man on the dock tallied each item. Wiping the sweat from his brow, Savaric pulled his hood low, flicking his eyes around the area until he caught sight of something that was not out of the ordinary but intriguing nevertheless. Indeed, it was what Savaric had been waiting for.

Two men, one of whom Savaric presumed to be the vessel's captain and the other presumably a merchant, richly dressed in expensive robes, looked as though they were about to make an exchange. He moved closer, watching as the merchant produced one leather pouch and then another from his sword belt, handing them over to the captain before the man pressed what appeared to be a vellum tied with a string into his hands. And from where Savaric stood the merchant appeared to have yet one more pouch tied to his belt.

Damn but he wished he could get his hands on both the pouch and the vellum, but it would be far too risky.

Savaric realised too late that it would have been best if he had not come alone. He could certainly have used the extra help from either Nicholas D'Amberly or Warin de Talmont, but they had been needed elsewhere. No, he would just have to manage on his own.

Bending down, he removed a slither of a blade that he had tucked away in his boots, before standing to his full height, expelling a breath before moving closer to the two men he had been watching. With his heart pounding Savaric lifted his head and adjusted his body, staggering back and colliding into them.

'Watch where you are going, you great big oaf!' The merchant barked, taking a step back as Savaric spun and stumbled.

'Beggin' yer pardin, sir. It's me feet, see,' he mumbled inanely, as he schooled his features to those resembling a simpleton. A necessity when acting the forementioned oaf. 'They're far too bigs for me legs. Or mayhap it's the other ways around. I do gets confused.' He swung his arms around in the air and bowed deferentially several times, relieved that the haphazard swipe of the wrist which Nicholas D'Amberly's wife, Eva, once a notorious thief, had shown him worked to perfection. He had deftly managed to appropriate the pouch by cutting loose the string attached to the merchant's cloak with the slither of the blade clasped in his fist. He wished he could also do the same with the vellum the man had given the captain. Again, he cursed his lack of foresight for being at the docks alone. Yet he had not envisaged this development. Although it might still amount to very little.

'Get off me, you fool.' The merchant shoved him away, making Savaric stumble back. He righted himself, doffed his hat and turned to move in the opposite direction, picking up his pace and weaving his way through the throng of people assembled along the busy dockside harbour, knowing it would not be long until the merchant realised the pouch to be missing.

Savaric acknowledged to himself the need to return with extra men in order to apprehend the captain of the vessel as well as the merchant. But for now, he needed to get away with the pouch, the contents of which were potentially far more important than anything else. Besides, he was one man against many assembled here.

Savaric glanced over his shoulder momentarily as he continued to move expediently before turning back and almost colliding with a young lad. His arms shot out, his fingers digging into the lad's shoulder to maintain his balance and prevent both of them from toppling over. The small hairs on the back of his neck rose and it was then that he knew something was amiss.

Savaric lowered his gaze, noticing first the flame russet hair hidden beneath a wide hood, the turned-up nose and lush mouth, before lifting his head and meeting the bluest eyes he had ever seen. Eyes that were staring back at him in shock and incredulity. Eyes which belonged to someone he had once known. He was jolted with recognition of this young woman dressed as a boy.

Marguerite Studdal...

What in God's name was she doing here? At this hour. And dressed as she was, in the guise of a...a young boy? The questions kept tumbling in his head but he could not shape the words, caught as they were at the back of his damn throat. Instead, he swallowed and continued to gape at her in disbelief, daring her to be an illusion. Hoping this to be a fanciful image that his tired mind had somehow conjured up at this very inopportune moment. Lord only knew how many times he had thought of her since the last time he had seen her.

He closed his eyes and reopened them, knowing now for certain that it was not his imagination playing tricks on him. She was here. Now. At the busy Port of London.

Surrounded as they both were by imminent danger. He expelled an irritated breath through his teeth and glared at the woman he had not seen for over two long years.

'Marguerite?' was all that he could manage.

'Good evening, Savaric.' She inclined her head. 'A strange time for a leisurely stroll I dare say.'

'What the devil are you doing here?' His fingers dug a little into her shoulders, testing that she was real before he dropped them to his side.

'Nothing that concerns you.' She glanced past him before returning her gaze to his.

His brows shot up, surprised at her curt rudeness.

'Oh, I rather think it does, especially in a place like this. Can you imagine if someone here also discovered that you are a young maiden?' He left out the danger this posed but the implication was there all the same.

'No one has, other than you, so please lower your voice,' she hissed.

'They must be blind to confuse you with a boy. In truth, why are you dressed...like this?' he motioned with a wave of his hand. 'And why are you here at all?' he asked again.

'I wonder at your inquisitiveness when you have troubles of your own, sir.'

'Never mind that,' he muttered in a low voice. 'It is dangerous, Marguerite. You should not be here.'

She bristled with indignation. 'How remiss of me, I should have remembered that I answer to you.'

Savaric blinked before answering. 'I did not say that.'

'I am glad.' She threw him a disdainful smile. 'Now, if you would be good enough to keep moving, we can then pretend that this unwelcome reunion never happened.'

Savaric could hardly believe his ears. What in God's name was wrong with the woman? 'Is this the thanks I get for coming to your aid a few years ago? This shocking incivility?'

He knew it was beneath him to bring up the past but couldn't quite help it. His remark might be flippant but it hid the horror and panic that had gripped him two years ago when Marguerite had been in mortal danger, being held ransom by enemies of the Crown—The Duo Dracones.

Savaric would never forget that harrowing memory of Marguerite being held by one of the bastards, with a dagger pressed so hard against her throat that a trickle of blood ran down her slender neck. He could recall even now the rage that ripped through him at watching the innocent woman caught in the middle of it all. An innocent woman whom he'd embroiled in all their problems after he had snatched her from London and escorted her to Guildford Castle. Indeed, Savaric had become too invested, too interested, and altogether too beguiled by the diminutive woman. It had been wrong in every way. So he made Marguerite believe that she meant nothing to him, other than being honour bound to ensure her safety.

But in that long-ago moment when her life had been threatened, his true feelings for her came to the fore. It made him feel raw and exposed and with that dagger piercing Marguerite's delicate skin, he had never been so helpless or so powerless.

It had been then that Savaric remembered who he

was and what he was expected to do as a member of the elite group of the Knights Fortitude—to be a damn Crown Knight, an experienced soldier and warrior. And Savaric had been just that—he had saved her life. Yet none of it had assuaged the guilt he felt for getting her involved in the first place. And for having intentionally made her think that he felt nothing for her other than indifference.

'No,' she said, bringing him back to the present. 'I have not forgotten.'

'Good, because I hope you are not courting trouble?'

He tried for a little levity but his comment missed the mark and sounded more impertinent and dismissive. And it was no surprise that her eyes flashed with anger.

'I have little time for this nonsense. And if you do not have the sense to leave, then I shall.'

Before he knew what he was about to do, he reached out and seized her wrist, gazing down into those fathomless blue eyes. 'Wait.'

'Let go of me, sir, if you will.'

'Not until you answer my questions.'

'I think not.'

'Marguerite?' he whispered as he released her wrist, feeling a little burned by such an innocuous touch.

She looked behind his shoulder again. 'You really do need to leave this place *now*.'

'You would have me leave you? Here? In this place, and at this hour?'

'Yes,' she hissed. 'I can look out for myself as I have for many years. Unless you want to get both of us killed?'

'I cannot abandon you here. My honour will not allow it.'

She gave a short hollow laugh and shook her head. 'Ah, yes, that infamous honour and valour of yours. Well, you must know that it is unnecessary. I am not in need of your protection.'

'Marguerite…'

'You would do well to listen to me, Savaric, especially after openly stealing that pouch you have buried somewhere on your person. It seems that you are the one *courting trouble* at this moment.'

The woman must have noticed his surprise because she sighed deeply before continuing to scold him as though he were a child. 'Do not forget that I lived with Eva and know every trick she deployed. You must also realise that those men you stole from will notice it missing shortly and come after you.'

'I cannot leave you here,' he muttered through clenched teeth.

'Go. Before it's too late.'

From somewhere behind there was a commotion and suddenly he heard a man bluster and cry. 'There's the bastard! Stop that man!'

'Marguerite…'

'Go, Savaric…*please.*'

'Stop him! Stop that man.'

Savaric needed to move. And he needed to move fast. He glanced at Marguerite for a long moment as uncertainty and hesitation gripped him, holding him back.

'Halt! Someone stop him from running away!'

A man to his side tried to grab hold of him, but Savaric pushed him away and quickly made his way through the crowd of crewmen and deck hands, cursing himself for leaving the maid there.

Damn, damn, damn!

What a disaster, and yet he could never have contemplated such a reunion with Marguerite Studdal again, however *unwelcome* it might be. Especially at such a place. And at such a time.

Savaric sprinted down a narrow cobbled lane in an attempt to lose the men who were now hard on his heel and then turned into the path on his right, rushing to take the next left pathway, passing vagrants, tavern drunks, merry dock workers, and barely attired women selling their wares. He came to an abrupt stop.

God's breath, but he could not do it. He could not just leave *her* there. He had to make his way back to the docks and get back to Marguerite. She may have been wearing a loose-fitting tunic, hose, and a tabard with a deep hood hiding her glorious red hair, but when one truly looked at her there could be no denying that she was a maid—and a beautiful, comely one at that. The thought of an innocent woman alone in a rowdy dockside, with many unsavoury characters milling around, made his blood run cold, especially while he was running away. It went against everything he believed in—everything he stood for. And if the woman found his honour and valour so distasteful then that was regrettable but it would have no effect on him or what he knew he must do.

Dragging his hands across his face, he took a deep breath before turning and making his way back. But as soon as he moved into the pathway to his right, a man punched him in the jaw, making him stagger backwards. He rubbed his jaw before unsheathing his sword from its scabbard and pointing it at the assailant who had struck him.

'I would advise against doing that again,' he drawled. 'Otherwise you will find yourself cut from here to here.' Savaric pointed his sword from the man's throat down to his stomach.

The man laughed as he groped for his sword, drawing it out and lunging forward. 'I doubt that, friend, and I wouldn't look round if I were yer. For you are now surrounded.'

Savaric looked over his shoulder quickly and saw another man draw out his sword and run towards him. In a quick succession of moves, he managed to manoeuvre himself so that he was now facing both of the men. Much better. He was used to this, fighting two and sometimes more men at the same time. And he needed to make quick work of this situation in order to make his way back to the dockside and ensure Marguerite's safety. The question surrounding her strange appearance at the docks was still on his mind. And it was just as troubling.

He continued to parry with the first man as his accomplice threw himself into the fray. Savaric fought both at the same time, blocking and counter-attacking, surprising them both with his quick hands and even quicker feet. He might be fighting against two men but Savaric was bigger, stronger, and far more experienced than these two, who no doubt worked for either the merchant or the captain, or mayhap both. The intriguing question, however, was whom *those* men worked for. Savaric would wager everything he had that it was The Duo Dracones. After all, a tip-off from their informant in France led him here, to wait at the docks for more information. And Savaric believed that the contents of the pouch he had stolen might be the key to what he sought.

He blocked one man's thrusting manoeuvre and countered it with a swipe of his sword in a riposte attack. Striding forward towards the man, he took him by surprise with heavy blows, clashing his sword down and across. Over and over switching from one man to another, Savaric relentlessly pushed them back, overwhelming them both with his sheer will and intensity.

'You ain't gonna win, no matter how good at fightin' a man such as yer is!' the man sneered. 'Others'll come 'ere even if yer best us.'

The man panted, wiping the sweat off his brow.

A man such as he… Savaric raised a brow as he lunged forward, having heard it all before.

'Much as I appreciate your consideration to a man such as…er, me, you should allow me to worry about that, eh?'

He swung the sword across, catching the other man and sending him falling to the dirt-covered ground, relieved that he had just one more assailant to tackle before he could get back to Marguerite.

'Yer won't win, I tells yer, but mayhap it's coz yer a simpleton and donna understand much.'

'Mayhap it is,' Savaric said with a wry smile on his face.

'Would'na expect much from a man with skin the colour of dirt—the same dirt and filth that lies beneath me feet.'

The smile slipped from Savaric's face. Oh yes, he had certainly heard it before. 'Is that so? Well, it's your friend who is there in the dirt and filth. And never fear, you will soon join him beneath *my* feet.'

'I don' think so.' The man looked over his shoulder and smirked. 'Told yer. I dids try to warn yer.'

Even without turning around Savaric knew that some sort of reinforcement had come to the man's aid. Damn but this was turning out to be a far more difficult night than he had envisaged.

He pointed his sword and turned carefully, noting that there were not one but two more men positioning themselves against him.

Ah, wonderful!

There were now three of them coming at him with their swords raised, pushing him back against the wall.

God's breath!

If only one of his Knights Fortitude brethren were here by his side there would be no question of the outcome. But even now Warin de Talmont and Nicholas D'Amberly were on similar missions to his, waiting at various ports along the Thames, just as he had done, seeking to gain vital information regarding The Duo Dracones.

However, at this moment Savaric was beginning to find a slither of doubt creeping under his skin, which was never a good thing. Not when engaged in combat. And however inexperienced these men might be, they outnumbered Savaric now considerably.

He lunged forward and caught one of the men by surprise, managing to disarm him, as the other two decided to come at him with an attacking strike. Holding them back was becoming more and more onerous. Savaric needed to think and he needed to think fast.

The men were gaining on him but he still managed to hold them off with his silky moves. It was then that Savaric felt something sharp against his sword arm and knew instantly that he had been struck. A sudden sting of pain spread through his arm but he had to push it out of his mind. He had to keep going. Exhaling through his teeth, Savaric realised that another man had joined the onslaught to his right. He felt an overwhelming sense that he was falling into something that he might not be able to crawl out of. God, but he could not hold them off for much longer.

And it was then that it happened. One man fell to the ground and then another seemingly struck from behind, and with what appeared to be a dagger hissing through the air before hitting its mark. Whoever had thrown the weapon had hurtled it with precision. Savaric used this brief opportunity of reprieve to strike one of the men and dispatch another as he moved forward, towards the diminutive figure at the end of the pathway who had come to his aid. Who in heavens was it?

But he did not have to wait long before the answer was revealed to him when the hood lowered slowly.

He narrowed his eyes, trying to discern his rescuer. *Marguerite...?*

Savaric rubbed his eyes with the backs of his hands. It could not be.

'Yes, I suppose it must shock your sensibilities, but, it is *me*.' She looked in both directions. 'However, we haven't the time to tarry here. You must leave now.'

'I will not be going anywhere without you, Marguerite. So do not ask it of me. I refuse to leave a lone woman in a place such as this—whatever new skills you might have recently acquired,' he muttered, nodding at the hilt of her dagger.

'Not this again! We have no time for this.'

'And yet I am unmoved.'

'Oh, believe me, Sir Savaric, that can be arranged. In truth, I would like nothing more than to leave you here to fend for yourself.' She leant in. 'But then I would rather not suffer the wrath of Hubert de Burgh.'

What?

He stilled. 'What did you say?'

'I believe you heard me. Now, come, I am escorting you.'

'You? Escort me? Where exactly?'

'Wherever you wish, Savaric. Your lodgings or anywhere else you would prefer but somewhere far from here. I have two horses with my page but we must make haste.' She stood with her hands on her waist and tilted her head to the side. 'Ah, I can see this is difficult for you. Do not say that you are one of those men who finds it difficult to accept aid from a mere woman.'

'I did not say that,' he ground out through gritted teeth.

'Good, because I would otherwise call this behaviour far less becoming than anything you might have accused me of. And for a man so evidently honourable and gallant, especially after I just saved your hind.'

'Are you mocking me?'

'No.' She sighed deeply. 'But a little gratitude would not go amiss. And you're hurt, Savaric. That cut needs to be tended to, and soon'

'Apologies, you are quite right.' He made a deep bow. 'I thank you and am in your debt, Marguerite.'

'Think nothing of it. After all, you did the same for me two years ago, as you reminded me earlier.' She shrugged dismissively. 'Let us say that whatever debt was due has now been duly paid. We part on even terms now.'

Who was this woman, who looked like Marguerite Studdal and even spoke in the same voice? For the words coming out of her mouth were the antithesis of the memory he had of the young maid from two years ago. Back then she was guileless, gently spoken, and timid. Nothing like this fiery, aloof, and confident woman.

He gazed at the woman before him and nodded. 'Yes, I suppose we do.'

'Good, now, let's get to the horses. You may lean on me if you really must or better still my page.'

'I believe I can manage.' A wry smile twisted at his lips. 'But tell me, how did you learn to do that with those daggers?'

'How does anyone learn to do anything? With perseverance. Now come.'

No, it seemed that he did not know who Marguerite Studdal was any longer.

Chapter Two

Marguerite spent much of that morn running through everything that had happened only a few hours ago. In particular the shock of seeing Savaric Fitz Leonard after these past few years. Heavens but she had not expected to be reunited with the man the moment she had arrived back on English soil. Not *that* soon. And not before she had readied herself for such an encounter.

Marguerite had spotted Savaric on the crowded dockside at the Port of London, while she was blending in, weaving in and out of the crowd, dissembled as a young boy. She had arrived earlier that day on a different vessel that she had boarded in France, only a few weeks earlier. Knowing, as she had right from the beginning of the journey, that the cog ship was bound for the kingdom that she had once fled. And yet nothing, nothing had prepared her for the full force of seeing Savaric Fitz Leonard again.

It had been two years…

Two years since she had last seen him. Two years she had been left heartsick and confused by Savaric. Two years since she had moved on and never looked back. Two years since she had decided to approach Hubert de Burgh, the man Savaric and other members of the Knights Fortitude had sworn fealty to, with a proposition—one which the great man had eventually agreed to. That she would gather information at the French Court and somehow attempt to find a connection to The Duo Dracones—the group that almost ended her life.

Indeed, Marguerite had discovered the captain of the recently arrived cog ship, the very one whom Savaric had stolen from, in a Paris tavern passing a leather pouch to a member of The Duo Dracones who had also fled England earlier than she had. *Renaisser...* A man who she still had nightmares about. A man who frightened her so much that she had been unable to breathe when she had encountered him there. But the man had disappeared from the busy tavern, leaving her with only one alternative—to follow the captain in the hope of discovering more. This had led her to discover that the captain's vessel on the coast at Honfleur was due to leave for London just as she was about to embark for England herself a sennight ago, which had been puzzling in itself. In any case, Marguerite had had just enough time once she had reached London to get back to the port to await the arrival of the captain and his vessel, which naturally brought her to a man she had not believed she would meet so soon—Savaric Fitz Leonard.

Marguerite had hoped that she would have time to ready herself before her inevitable encounter with the man but that was not to be. And the initial spark of joy that had coursed through her had been visceral and yet extremely painful. It was quickly replaced by her resolve hardening as a defensive wall wrapped itself around her heart, as she remembered everything that had come to pass between them. Rejection and indifference. But never again. She would not allow for such foolishness again.

Marguerite stopped and expelled a breath, standing perfectly still on the cobbled pathway that she had been walking along. In truth it had all been her own fault. It had been Marguerite who had misread and misunderstood the situation. It had been Marguerite who had believed two years ago that a kiss they had shared and their closeness meant far more than it actually had, and it was Marguerite who had foolishly allowed herself to become enamoured by Savaric Fitz Leonard while he had escorted her to Guildford Castle. All those days and nights together had woven a certain spell on her, captivating her in a manner she had never known before. Yet the man had never felt the same and had made his feelings perfectly clear, explaining that there could never be a future between them.

Foolish indeed...

But it mattered not. The humiliation she had once felt had long dissipated—her life now was so entirely different to the one it had once been. As was she.

Marguerite was no longer that innocent, guileless woman. No, she had learned to change and adapt to survive, becoming the woman she was always destined to be. Strong and resilient.

She paid the toll at London Bridge and meandered across, taking in all the familiar sounds and smells of the thoroughfare heaving with people even at this early hour. Customers haggled before exchanging monies with vendors from their timber-clad buildings that housed the various guilds of craftsmen, from mercers and haberdashers to fletchers and bowyers, all trying to sell their wares. She smiled to herself and took a deep breath of the toil and sweat into her chest. God, but she had missed this—missed the hustle and bustle of London and its instantly recognisable haunts. And while she loved the vibrancy and refinement of Paris, it wasn't home.

And it was here on this very bridge that Marguerite had first set eyes on Sir Savaric Fitz Leonard, and was instantly mesmerised by his unusual looks, huge stature, and striking amber-coloured eyes. Not to mention his large-rimmed leather hat, adorned with plumes of feathers, that he always wore. On any other man, the hat would have seemed far too flamboyant, but on Savaric it was distinguished and incredibly attractive. He had fairly taken her breath away. And while their meeting had been portentous and under peculiar circumstances, Marguerite had felt drawn to him from the first.

Her chest tightened as she reflected on that far-away feeling of excitement, recalling that lopsided smile of his, and the gorgeous glint in his eyes the first time she had seen it. She immediately stopped, chastising herself for her reckless lapse of judgement. God, but what was wrong with her? If she was to see the man again, as she would do this morn, she had better take care and forsake everything that had gone before.

She stepped inside the Chapel of Thomas à Becket, the imposing stone-bricked, castellated building standing proudly in the middle of the bridge, passing worshipers and pilgrims on their journey south to Canterbury. After dipping her finger in the holy water and making the sign of the cross, Marguerite moved with purpose along the aisle and into the vestry, grabbing a flamed torch from the metal sconce before descending down the damp granite spiral steps. She stealthily made her way along the large, cavernous lower chapel, reaching the under-croft with its rib-vaulted ceiling and quickened her pace, her long cloak flapping at her heels.

Walking to the furthest corner, she slid aside a hidden wooden panel that looked remarkably like an ordinary tall livery cupboard and pressed down the third stone inside on the bottom right-hand side, which released the back panel. She pushed it lightly, making the back open rather like a door, and stepped inside. Securing this by bolting it, she resumed her progress down the hidden passage towards the muffled noise coming from inside the chamber at the end.

Opening the latch, she let herself inside quietly without alerting the man with his back to her—*Savaric*... He was sat on a wooden table, stripped to the waist, engaged in a heated argument with his fellow Knights Fortitude, Nicholas D'Amberly and Warin de Talmont. They were all so engrossed in their conversation that they had not noticed her entering the chamber. Marguerite fell back, hiding in the shadows, and watched as Nicholas D'Amberly carefully sewed the long wound that Savaric had received on his arm the previous night. His huge arm glistened with sweat as he clenched his teeth in pain.

'Hell and damnation, Nick, just get on with it,' he hissed. 'Please.'

Marguerite instinctively wanted to go to him but held herself back.

'Apologies, my friend, I am going as fast as I can.'

'Here, have some more of this.' Warin de Talmont held out a flask, which Savaric took. 'You were saying…'

'That I saw *her* again. Can you imagine the shock of it after all these years?'

Ah, so their discourse must be about her?

Interesting…

'Yes, but why would you care that your paths crossed last night?'

'I never said that I did.' Savaric pulled back and dragged his fingers through his hair. 'Only that the woman was there at the dockside, waiting just as I was, but did not seem surprised to see me.'

Yet Marguerite had been…exceedingly surprised. It was just that she excelled at hiding her true feelings behind a mask she had fashioned for herself.

'There's more besides,' he continued. 'She tracked my movements and saw that I had filched the pouch from the captain of the vessel. The woman had seen the whole thing.'

'I cannot see the relevance?' Warin de Talmont muttered, looking away.

'Can you not?'

'Allow me to fetch you more ale.'

'Yes, it is rather good.'

'I do not want any more damn ale.' Savaric bit out, looking from one man to the other. 'What in God's name is going on? Marguerite not only seemed to know about us but mentioned de Burgh and how she did not want to "suffer his wrath".'

'I doubt anyone would.'

'Indeed, our liege lord is known for his displeasure when he is in one of his fits of temper.'

'I swear one of you had better talk and talk swiftly,' Savaric hissed, narrowing his eyes. 'For on my oath, I shall show you far more than a fit of damn temper.'

'Why would you believe I have the answer you seek?'

'You might not, de Talmont. But he does.' Savaric pointed at Nicholas D'Amberly. 'He has that shifty look in his eyes when he is hiding something.'

'You wound me,' Nicholas said wryly as he made the last and final stitch on the man's arm. 'There, it is done. I swear my stitch-work can rival any lady bent on such fine intricacy.'

'True, I have always believed you would fit in well in the bower chambers, D'Amberly.' Warin grinned.

'Indeed, you have my thanks, Nick, as well as my apologies after the trying evening I have had. Even you would be as testy as I am.'

'Possibly. What is it that you believe my eyes—shifty or otherwise—betray, Savaric?'

'Tell me everything that you know about Marguerite Studdal.' Savaric stood up and pulled his tunic gingerly back on. 'After all, your wife is a close friend of hers.'

Nicholas raised a brow at the mention of Eva's name. 'What precisely is it that you wish to know?'

'I would like to ascertain why the woman was there, alone, by the docks in the first place. I cannot believe it was coincidence. And what has she to do with Hubert de Burgh?'

His two friends exchanged a look, neither able to answer for a long moment before Nicholas broke the silence.

'We do not know why Marguerite was at the port Savaric, however…'

'However?' Warin repeated.

'However, Marguerite has been expected back in England, or rather in London.'

'Indeed? And exactly where has she returned back to England from? And how is it you know this information?'

'Ah, as to that.' Nicholas rubbed his forehead before turning to Warin. 'A little help here, if you please.'

Warin sipped his ale and grinned. 'You are doing quite well on your own.'

'Good God, Nick, do not tell me that you have known where Marguerite Studdal has been all this time?'

'Believe me, I would like to attest to that but I… I, er, cannot.'

Savaric looked from one friend to the other, standing with his hands on his hips. 'Hell's teeth, man, why was I never informed?'

Neither of his friends spoke for a long moment, the silence punctuating the tension.

'Why the interest, Savaric?' Warin de Talmont muttered gently. 'Why does it matter now?'

A very good question…why would Savaric care one way or another?

'Mayhap it was all done and done for the best,' Nicholas D'Amberly said, patting Savaric on the back.

'And mayhap it wasn't,' he snapped. 'Am I to believe that you have both known where the woman has been for the past two years but thought it best not to tell me?'

'Come now, Savaric…'

'Why?' he growled low. 'Why the hell would you keep something like that from me?'

Marguerite stepped out of the shadows and took a deep breath. 'Because I asked them to.'

She had decided to take Nicholas and Warin into her confidence and asked them to keep Savaric from knowing where she was for a number of reasons. Firstly, she did not truly believe he cared where she had gone. And if he had done, then it mattered not a jot. After parting ways with the man, Marguerite had wanted all ties between them to be severed completely, especially since she had been nursing a bruised heart.

Savaric spun on his heel and turned to face her. His chest rising and falling. His bewildered gaze penetrating into her. The man certainly did not look happy to see her here. Well, good, neither was she.

'What in heaven's name are you doing here?' he said through gritted teeth, a muscle ticking in his jaw. 'Or mayhap my so-called friends might be able to answer that?'

'I believe you should ask the lady herself.'

'And on that, de Talmont and I will push off to The Three Choughs. And should either of you need a friend, so-called or otherwise, you know where to find us.'

The two men slapped Savaric's back and nodded a greeting in her direction before quickly making their way back through the many passages out of the chapel and onto the tavern on the bridge that bore the coat of arms of Thomas à Becket. But Savaric did not acknowledge this or anything other than her presence in this chamber, which Marguerite presumed had always been reserved for clandestine meetings for the Knights Fortitude. Until now…

'Well, are we going to just stare at one another, or shall we proceed with the interrogation?' she said, lifting her chin.

The man did not respond but continued to watch her for a long moment. The silence between them was pierced by the crackling fire spitting in the hearth and the torch lighting the chamber. Yet nothing managed to dent the icy tension emanating from the man who stood in front of her.

'So,' he said finally. 'We meet again, Marguerite Studdal, and so soon after last night's escapade.'

'Yes, and it promises to be just as delightful an encounter.'

The man raised a single brow in answer. 'I am glad that you find this so amusing, but I fail to appreciate it myself.'

'I do not, Savaric, and in truth you are making me feel a little nervous.'

'How careless of me.' He leant back against the table and watched her with narrowed eyes. 'I would never dream of causing such a thing, especially for someone who only recently saved my life. Tell me, Marguerite, is this what you expected?'

She frowned. 'What on earth do you mean?'

'Oh, come now…let us not be coy. After all, it is not a coincidence that you are back here in London or even present in this secret chamber.'

'No.' She lifted her head. 'It is not. But if you are implying that I planned any part of this…this reunion, I did not.'

'Well, that is heartening to hear,' he said sardonically. 'Yet hardly enlightening.'

He pushed away off the table and prowled around her in an attempt to intimidate her but she refused to oblige. Instead, Marguerite made sure she stood perfectly still. She would not allow him to see how he affected her so. How her pulse quickened, just by being near the man again.

'You believe I should enlighten you?'

'I would be obliged if you should tell me the truth, Marguerite. I would also be obliged if you should tell me why you are here in this chamber?'

She opened her mouth in response, but nothing would come out.

'It has something to do with Hubert de Burgh, has it not?'

'Yes.'

'And pray, what might that be?'

She raised her eyes to meet his. 'As I said to you last night, I do not answer to you.'

'That might be so, mistress, but if you could be so kind as to *oblige me*,' he said again through gritted teeth.

She took a deep breath before answering him. 'I work for him.'

'You do *what*?'

'Surely that must have been your summation. After all, I am here in this secret chamber, as you have so eloquently reminded me.'

Savaric looked like thunder. Really, she would do well not to rile the situation further and yet she could not help herself.

'So, you work for de Burgh?' His smile did not reach his eyes. 'In what capacity, may I ask?'

She sighed, feeling a little weary of the man's intensity. 'In the same capacity as you, Savaric. I collate information for him.'

'I see,' he said. 'And where might you be doing this… this work?'

'Much as I am flattered by your interest in my movements, sir, I cannot see what it might have to do with you.'

'Humour me, mistress.'

'My work continues here in London but for the past two years I have been based in Paris.'

For the past two years any information that Marguerite had gathered at the French Court had been sent back to de Burgh, in particular anything that might prove useful in connection with The Duo Dracones, which up until now had been very little. However, in that time she had ingratiated herself with many of the French nobility and courtiers alike, and more recently King Henry's mother, the Dowager Queen Isabella.

In truth, it was with the former Queen of England's entourage that Marguerite had travelled back to England the previous day, after the illustrious lady had a sudden need to see her son. Which admittedly had been rather odd given the King's estrangement from his mother and her enmity with Hubert de Burgh, after he had confiscated her dower lands for marrying without the Crown's permission.

'So, you were in Paris? All of this time, and working for de Burgh?' Savaric muttered an oath under his breath and shook his head. 'Unbelievable.'

'How so?' She lifted her head to meet his gaze. 'Because you cannot believe that I would be capable of such a feat?'

'I think that last night would put doubt to that assumption, but I cannot pretend that all of this is not preposterous.'

'Oh, and why might that be?'

'I would say that was fairly evident.'

'Indeed? Well, I am at a loss to comprehend you, sir. Unless you are mistaking the woman I once was for the one I am today?'

Something flashed quickly in his eyes. 'I am not.'

'Good, because that woman no longer exists,' she muttered softly.

'Seemingly.' He absently raised his good arm, his fingers reaching out to touch her before he must have remembered himself and dropped it abruptly to his side.

'What are you really here for, Marguerite?' he whispered. 'Why would you even consider becoming involved in this…this danger?'

'Are you seriously asking that?'

'I believe I am, yes.' Even his stance, with his legs apart and his hand on his hips, was beginning to annoy her.

'It was not for *you*, if that was your meaning.' Marguerite instantly realised her mistake, but it was too late. The words that spoke of their previous connection fell out of her lips before she could catch herself.

Savaric pinned her with his gaze as a flush crept up her chest, neck, and face.

'I did not presume it was.'

'Good.' She looked away. 'Because that would be the

height of arrogance when my motives were altogether different.'

'I have no doubt they are, mistress, but what I cannot account for is why you would want to embroil yourself in this after everything that happened two years ago.'

'You mean after you abducted me and held me for ransom until my friend complied with aiding the Knights Fortitude?'

Marguerite watched the colour leach from his face and knew she had struck a raw nerve. He felt the guilt keenly, even if that had not been her intention. And yet Marguerite had known even two years ago after being foisted onto Sir Savaric Fitz Leonard that he would pose no danger to her. Instead, she had felt protected—safe. Indeed, they had forged an alliance of sorts until it had all gone awry. Not that any of that mattered now.

'All of which makes me puzzled as to why you then decided to work for Hubert de Burgh?'

'Because, Savaric—' she lifted her chin and met his gaze '—after you embroiled me in this world, I thought to use everything that happened to my own advantage and get what I have always sought.'

'And what would that be?'

'Justice—justice for my father and for my family. This was the only way that I could make my bargain with de Burgh and exonerate my father's name and return the land confiscated by the Crown after his execution. I agreed to work for de Burgh to collate useful information, in exchange for the justice I seek.'

Marguerite remembered the first time she had visited London with her father when she was a small maid, and how she had been in awe of the sights and sounds all around her. Everything new, and so thrilling. But it had been a fallacy. London was far from being the glittering city famed for being paved in gold. For, lurking beneath the surface, there was artifice and trickery. It was present around every corner if one knew where to look. From the intrigues at the Royal Court to the dirt and stench of its infested, grime-ridden streets. One misstep and one could find oneself in peril.

'And this…this work you have undertaken was the only way to exonerate your late father?' Savaric lifted a brow as he crossed his good arm over his chest.

God, it really did feel that she was under interrogation. Her rancour rose. How dare he? How dare he question her in this manner? It was nothing to do with him. In truth, Marguerite answered to no one, save Hubert de Burgh. And only until their arrangement was at an end. Until she had proved herself to the great man and gathered enough information to help put an end to The Duo Dracones. In return, de Burgh promised that he would bring about justice and posthumously absolve her father's name as traitor to the Crown, with all of her father's lands which had been confiscated when he had been executed for treason returning to her young brother as his rightful inheritance.

'I fail to comprehend why this is any of your concern, sir, but since you ask, yes. It was and still is the only way.'

He did not respond but watched her intently with a cold, inscrutable gaze that made Marguerite want to squirm.

Eventually he spoke, his voice low and steely. 'So, you have been engaged in this work in Paris, you say?'

'Yes.'

He shook his head in disbelief. 'And yet this is the first that I know of it.'

'Yes,' she said again.

'Why? When it seems that my friends Warin and Nicholas, and I'd wager their wives, have known where you were? Why would you want to keep this information from me in particular?'

It was a question that she was reticent to answer. Not to Savaric anyway. He did not need to know.

'Does it matter?'

'Not especially.'

'Well then. There is no need for me to address it.' She raised a brow and started to move, feeling a little restless.

He reached out and stilled her, his large hand encircling her arm, holding her in place. 'I would like to know all the same, if you would oblige me.'

'Ah, but I am under no obligation. Not to you, Savaric.' He seemed to flinch at that. 'And why would you care? When all matters between us were resolved. When all ties between us were cut. We parted and that was that. All I did was to ensure that it remained so.'

A muscle leapt at the corner of his jaw. 'Yet I find that I would like to know more, if you would indulge me.' He took a step towards her. 'Why would you not want me to know where you were?'

Marguerite lifted her head and looked into the depths of those amber-gold eyes of his, and wondered what he was thinking. Was he concerned for her? Had he missed her? Did he ponder over the time they spent together and how he had rejected her, albeit gently? And after Marguerite had embarrassed herself by declaring her feelings to him. It had still been a rejection all the same. And yet…yet sometimes when she was alone with only her own company, her mind would wander back to that time. Those snatched moments. An unexpected connection that had surprised them—caught them both off guard. Did Savaric do the same? Did he remember the aching sweetness of their kisses or had he forgotten it all?

Almost as soon as these musings swirled around her head, Marguerite pushed them away, annoyed with herself. Why did she care what he thought of her at all? It had all happened a while ago—what felt like a lifetime had passed since she had last seen him. These reflections were as futile as they were inconsequential.

'I did not inform you, Savaric, as I believed it to be of no importance for you to know. You went your way and I went mine. And nothing more.'

Chapter Three

Savaric gaped at the woman standing across from him, her chin lifted in the air, her eyes defiant and a small challenging smirk on her lips. He clenched his fists at his sides, incredulous that this was the same woman who had needed his protection two years ago. A woman whose life he had saved.

Indeed, this prickly, imperious woman was certainly not the same as he remembered. The confident manner in which Marguerite had wielded the dagger so effortlessly had confirmed that notion. God, but who had taught her *that*? In truth, everything Marguerite had once been—gentle and compassionate—seemed to have been stripped away, leaving the hard shell of a woman standing in front of him. Savaric itched to do something that might snap her out of it. But mayhap the woman he had once known, and had been beginning to care for deeply, no longer existed, as he had just been informed.

Yet to know that all this time, *all* of his friends, indeed even his liege lord, had known where Marguerite Studdal had been and what she had been doing, but had refrained from telling him because she had requested it… Well, it was like a punch in the gut, similar to the physical blows he had received in the alleyways near the Port of London the previous night. And to make matters even worse, the woman had been working… working for de Burgh in the same murky, dangerous world that he did.

Hell's teeth.

'Allow me to comprehend this,' he said in a clipped tone. 'You intentionally kept your whereabouts from me, as well as everything you were doing for de Burgh. Yet consider—had I known about you, Marguerite, then last night's disaster might have been avoided.'

She tilted her head and gave him a withering glare. 'I could also say the same thing, sir. Had I known that you would be at the docks, the disaster that then unfolded might have been avoided and I could have been spared from having to save your hind.'

'Just so.' His lips twitched despite the fact that he found this woman intensely irritating. 'It seems that both of us have been ill-served by this…this lack of knowledge about one another.'

'Yet I would wager I would make the same decisions now as I did back then.'

God, she was aggravating. 'Would you now? Interesting.'

She scowled, her brows furrowed in the middle. 'How so?'

'Well, mistress, if you would change nothing about the decisions you made in the past…' He took a step towards her. 'It would also suggest that you would change nothing that…er, happened between *us*, between you and I.'

'I did not say…' She flicked her cold gaze in his direction.

'Did you not?'

'No.' She stepped away from him. 'God you are insufferable.'

'I dare say I am.' He inclined his head. 'And yet, I cannot help but feel a deep sense of disappointment that you failed to trust me and then continued to make matters worse by insisting my friends keep this truth from me. It was badly done of you, Marguerite.'

It was more than that. Savaric could not help but feel an ache somewhere in his damn chest—not that he did not deserve it. He had treated the woman badly two years ago.

Something akin to regret flashed across her eyes before disappearing just as quickly.

'I can offer no apology as there is none to give.' She took in a shaky breath. 'And as I said, I felt it best to sever all ties between us after everything…everything that happened.'

Yes, well, she had him there…

Two years ago, he had done everything in his power to turn Marguerite away from him, in the hope that she would understand that there could be nothing between them.

Their acquaintance, such as it was, had started badly, as both Marguerite and her friend Eva had hurtled into their world after conspiring to steal an important missive from Nicholas D'Amberly and the Knights Fortitude. And while D'Amberly dealt with the woman who had stolen from him to find out who had hired her prodigious talent as a thief, Savaric had been tasked to more or less abduct Marguerite and keep her away from her friend to ensure that Eva would comply with their investigation.

It had all gone to plan except for the fact that Nicholas had surprisingly ended up falling in love with his thief and marrying her. And as for Savaric and Marguerite? Well, their tenuous connection had been equally surprising but far more complicated. They had gone from mutual dislike to being friends of sorts as they opened up to one another. And while Savaric enjoyed Marguerite's company far more than he should, their growing closeness and the simmering attraction had become far more difficult for Savaric to contain.

He had wanted Marguerite with a ferocity that had shocked him to his core. He had never in his life felt as though he might be unravelled that easily, and by a woman no less. It was as unbelievable as it was unthinkable. Savaric had always managed to contain everything in his life and yet this small, beautiful woman, with eyes the colour of woad and hair that resembled every blaze and flicker of a damn flame, had managed to upend his world. The situation had become even more untenable after he had kissed her, giving in to a passion that had left him breathless and longing for more. That was when he knew that he had to put a stop to everything before he fell even deeper into the treacherous mire that would become too onerous to navigate.

So Savaric did what he had to, and pulled away from Marguerite, making her believe that he had never cared for her. He had done everything he could to convey his unsuitability and even welcomed Marguerite's gradual change of heart, turning whatever she had felt for him to intense dislike. Savaric had wounded her—not something he had been proud of causing but his actions had been necessary. But then had come the sad inevitability of the acceptance of losing her once she had disappeared from his life.

And it seemed that Savaric had been successful in convincing Marguerite and even his friends of his indifference. All of this time. Yet he had been far from indifferent. Savaric had acted swiftly knowing he had little choice but to end things before they truly began. It had all been for Marguerite's own good, as a connection with him could never work. It would never be accepted. For Marguerite, born to a wealthy landed knight, and a man of dubious origins like Savaric, it was impossible to be anything more. Especially with additional difficulties, such as the difference in the colours of their skin…

And although Savaric, as a knight, and backed by one of the most powerful men in the realm, was fortunate and held an important standing as a member of the Knights Fortitude, it was still a tenuous position to be in. One that was a constant battle to navigate. He would prefer to be thrashed a thousand times than to have Marguerite subjected to the kind of insults and intolerance she would, doubtless, be subjected to, were she attached to a man like him. It was done and done for the best.

But now that Marguerite was in the same chamber as him, the intensity he had always felt whenever she was near was present once more. Even now, he had to fight to keep from reaching for her, despite the fact that she was far removed from the woman he knew and would probably punch him for his troubles. It mattered not. The underlying attraction that hummed between them was still there after all this time apart. And still just as unwanted.

'Yet here you are again, mistress. Those severed ties apparently tethered back together again.'

'Only temporarily and certainly not of my choosing.'

He frowned. 'Nor mine.'

'In truth, I would rather restrict how often our paths cross, if you don't mind.' She matched his sardonic gaze, looking him up and down.

'Certainly.' He shrugged. 'I cannot see why we would have the need of further discourse after this day.'

Her spine seemed to stiffen at that. Good… How in heaven's name had they come to stand this close facing one another? How was it that he was looking into the depths of those blue eyes of hers trying to fathom answers that he sought? And how was it that his whole body was now thrumming with unfettered desire noting the rise and fall of her chest? Her sweet floral scent wrapped itself around him and pulled him closer. God, but how could this small, fiery woman still have such a hold on him, even altered as she now was?

'*Marguerite…*' he whispered softly, dragging his knuckle along the soft sweep of her face and down the slope of her neck covered with a cream lace necktie. He had missed her. Not that he had any right to. 'What happened to you?'

Savaric dipped his head as Marguerite leant into his touch, his fingers caressing her skin, and the fullness of her lips, taking in all those gorgeous little freckles on her nose, when Marguerite suddenly snapped her head back, his question seemingly jolting her out of this brief stupor.

'Nothing in the least.' She frowned and took a step back away from him. Instantly he dropped his hand, clenching it by his side. 'And I agree, there will be no further need for us to see one another again.'

His nostrils flared. 'No need whatsoever.'

They both stood there, glaring at one another so intently that they had failed to realise that someone had quietly entered the small secret chamber and was listening to their exchange.

'I am afraid that will not be possible.' A voice from the shadows broke through the tension.

Savaric stepped away and swiftly turned on his heel. Damn. He came face to face with Hubert de Burgh lurking in the shadows. First Marguerite, now de Burgh? Lord above but were there more surprises waiting to pounce on him from those damned shadows in this chamber this morn? The ordeal from the previous evening had made him a little careless. Or mayhap it was because he had come face to face with this tempestuous woman who had scattered his mind.

'Forgive me, my lord. I was not aware of your presence here,' he muttered, inclining his head.

'I am quite aware of that, Savaric.' The older man returned his greeting as he took a step towards them, turning his attention to Marguerite. 'I am happy to be reunited with you, my dear. I trust your passage by sea was less than arduous?'

Marguerite dropped to an elegant curtsy before de Burgh raised her back up by the hand to stand before him.

'I thank you, my lord. My journey to London by sea with the Dowager Queen and her ladies has indeed been less than arduous.' She flicked her gaze briefly to Savaric. 'However, since then, it has been most trying.'

Savaric bristled, a muscle twitching in his jaw.

De Burgh smiled as he patted Marguerite's hand. 'I am aggrieved to hear that and trust that will no longer be the case now you are back. Do you not agree, Fitz Leonard?'

'Of course, my lord,' Savaric ground out through gritted teeth, feeling as though he were a child, chastised for his petulance.

'Good. Now that it appears we have managed to settle our…well, *differences*, I can come to the reason you are here at my behest, mistress.'

Marguerite pasted a benign smile on her lips as she tried to take in what Hubert de Burgh was saying, and yet all she heard was dull noise in her ears drowning out the man's voice.

All she could ponder on was what had transpired between her and Savaric only moments ago, and how the man had pervaded the carefully constructed wall around her heart. He had touched her. He had almost kissed her. And she would have foolishly allowed it—welcomed it even. God, but she had been foolish indeed!

What happened to you?

The effrontery of the man for uttering such words as he gazed into her eyes made her want to kick him in the shins. Could he be so ignorant to what had happened to her? Mayhap he really did not know, but everything

she had become was as a result of the events that occurred after they had last parted ways. Yet it was more
than just the danger that she had been exposed to. She
had opened herself up to him, like a flower in spring-
time, but it had all been for nothing as Savaric had never
wanted her, save for a stolen kiss or two. It had meant
nothing to him.

In truth, it had all been a timely lesson for her, as
she had discovered how woefully lacking she had been.
And apart from her friend Eva, Marguerite realised
that she could never again put her faith in others. She
had to be the one to protect and defend herself, and so
had recruited Nicholas D'Amberly—Eva's husband—to
teach her the basic principles of hand-to-hand combat.
Marguerite learned quickly that because of her sex and
her size, a weapon such as a dagger was one that she
was best able to master and wield with precision after
hours of much-needed practice. And practice she did,
diligently, over and over again.

She acquired other skills as well, honing them relentlessly and with dogged determination, until she was
ready to make her proposition to Hubert de Burgh. And
in doing so, Marguerite had known she was offering
the man something that he did not already have in his
Knights Fortitude—*a woman*.

A woman who looked as unassuming and benign as
Marguerite did but was just as cunning and ruthless as
any one of his men. And she could penetrate areas of
the court that the Knights Fortitude could not.

Indeed, her association with Hubert de Burgh had
been fruitful when all was said and done, but it had not

come without its losses. For one, Marguerite was beginning to forget who she once was…

She shook away such notions, reminding herself of the reasons she had been doing all this work for de Burgh and the Crown in the first instance. And her plans had begun when she had last seen Savaric Fitz Leonard. He had after all lured her, inadvertently, into this world. She'd just decided to stay there, for once taking charge of her own destiny.

De Burgh's voice suddenly pierced through her musings.

'I am sorry, my lord?' She blinked.

The man frowned briefly at her. 'I was saying to Fitz Leonard here that I am glad you have both smoothed over your differences.'

'Yes, well, now that I am aware of Mistress Marguerite's…er…many activities, sanctioned by yourself, my lord, I can see no reason why we cannot be civil to one another whenever our paths might cross.'

Marguerite raised a brow knowing that he wished just as much as she that their paths would be permanently severed, even if her heart ached at the thought.

'You are too gracious, sir.' She inclined her head, meeting Savaric's gaze. 'And now that we have established the bounds of civility, may I have a word with you, my lord? Alone.'

She noted Savaric glower at being summarily dismissed as she addressed Hubert de Burgh.

'Certainly, my dear, and would this have anything to do with the reason you are back in London?'

'It would.'

'Then in that case there is nothing you can say that

cannot be said in front of Fitz Leonard. He's one of my best men and I trust him implicitly.'

Marguerite glimpsed Savaric grinning slowly and rolled her eyes, trying not to allow her annoyance to show.

'I am honoured, my liege,' Savaric said, turning to address Marguerite. 'You see, mistress, we have no secrets between us Knights Fortitude and our liege lord.'

Which naturally implied that there were such secrets between her and de Burgh.

'That is most encouraging, sir.' Marguerite tapped her chin. 'Which brings to mind the need to adjust some of our plans now, my lord…after last night.'

'How so?'

'Well, naturally after what happened at the docks with the situation going awry, I presumed you would want to make those necessary changes?'

Hubert de Burgh turned to Savaric. 'To what is the lady referring, Fitz Leonard?'

'Oh, I apologise, sir,' she said innocently, before Savaric had the chance to answer. 'Only I believed you had already passed on your information since there are no secrets between you?'

Savaric threw her a murderous glare. 'I have not had the opportunity to apprise my lord of the events from last night.'

'And what were those, Fitz Leonard? Please do not say that there are more failures as far as The Duo Dracones are concerned?'

'Not quite.' Savaric kept his eyes pinned to Marguerite as he spoke. 'But let us just say that last night did not run as smoothly as I would have liked.'

'No,' she murmured. 'Certainly not as smoothly as, say, resolving our differences.'

'Just so.'

'Well? Can either of you please explain what happened then?'

Savaric dragged his gaze back to de Burgh before recounting everything that had happened the previous night. Marguerite was slightly surprised that he did not omit how she had come to his aid.

She nodded her thanks, deciding to return the favour by reaching inside her cloak, untying the leather pouch and holding it up.

'However, Sir Savaric removed this dextrously from a merchant who met the captain of the cog ship, my lord. The one I informed you about. And I would wager that it is of considerable importance.'

'Wait one moment. Are you saying that it was *you* who provided the information about the captain of the vessel and the possible ports at which he might dock his ship?'

'Yes.'

'Then that must mean it's *you*. You are our informer from France.'

'Yes,' she muttered again. 'I am.'

Marguerite heard a small intake of breath as realisation must have dawned on Savaric. He shook his head in disbelief, recognising that it was, indeed, Marguerite who had seen the bastard again—*Renaisser*. The man who was at the heart of The Duo Dracones. The man they had all wanted to capture ever since he evaded them two years ago.

It was on the tip of her tongue to say more about the

encounter but she refrained from doing so. She did not want to dwell on *him*, nor explain that since that time, Marguerite had difficulty sleeping at night from the terror that sometimes gripped her because of the men who had threatened her life. God's bones, but it had all been too close two years ago. Far too close. And had it not been for Savaric and the other Knights Fortitude, it was doubtful she would be alive today.

'I am sorry,' he whispered, so only she could hear. 'I am sorry that it was *you*.'

She nodded, understanding his meaning, her hand reaching around her throat instinctively, remembering the sharp blade of the dagger that had once pressed against it. Since that time, she always wore a lace wound tightly around her neck, to conceal a scar from the dagger drawing against her skin, cutting it—a permanent reminder from that dreadful time. She noted Savaric following her movements and cursing under his breath.

'Indeed, yes.' Hubert de Burgh nodded absently, not the slightest bit aware of what had passed between them. 'This altercation at the dock does change things, however. But I believe it would still be a rather favourable solution, when all is considered.'

'My lord?' Marguerite frowned, wondering what the older man was about to suggest.

'I think now that you are back in London, mistress, and in light of what happened last night, it might be prudent for you both to work together in your endeavours.'

And just like that, the brief moment of concern and understanding was broken, giving way to misgiving and uncertainty.

'Oh, now, wait, my liege,' Savaric spluttered. 'Would

that be such a wise decision? After all, Mistress Marguerite is hardly one of *us*. Not that I would like to disparage her…numerous skills, especially her talent with the dagger.'

'And while I may not be so illustrious a person as to be a member of the Knights Fortitude, I would have to agree with Sir Savaric on this matter. You know, my lord, my preference to work alone.'

'Yet I believe that this could prove to be a far better arrangement, as well as beneficial to both of you.'

'I rather doubt that,' she muttered quietly. 'My liege, I would ask for you to reconsider.'

'No, mistress, I remain unmoved on this decision despite both of your reservations about such a scheme.'

'But my lord…' Savaric started, but was silenced by the older man holding up his hand.

'I will not hear another word on this. With Nicholas D'Amberly soon for Eltham, Warin de Talmont departing for Surrey, and Thomas Lovent in Salisbury, there is no one apart from Mistress Marguerite and you to work together here in London, for the time being. And I need everyone to do just that, Savaric. This is our chance finally to catch The Duo Dracones. Once and for all! So I expect that both of you will join forces and work together. With you at court as part of the Dowager Queen's ladies, mistress. And you, Savaric, discovering more regarding this merchant and captain of the cog ship whom you encountered at the port.'

Savaric turned to Marguerite and shook his head in frustration before looking away in dismay.

God, but this was a disaster. How on earth was she going to work effectively with this man? And more importantly, how on earth could she possibly survive it? Having to see him, converse with him, rely on him and even *trust him*...

There was only one way. By making sure that she remained impervious to Savaric and her unwanted attraction to him. For Marguerite could not afford to make that mistake again. God...no. Her heart could not endure *that* again.

Chapter Four

Savaric swirled the ale around in his mug before tossing it back and wiping his mouth on the back of his hand. He had been waiting at the rear of The Three Choughs tavern on the bridge for most of the afternoon. And it was now growing late. Not that his new *associate* had graced him with her presence yet.

Marguerite had acquiesced to Hubert de Burgh that she would work with Savaric that morn before promptly leaving the secret chamber in the depths of the Chapel of Thomas à Becket, promising to meet later at The Three Choughs to discuss their way forward.

He knew that she was just as reluctant to work with him on this venture that had been foisted on to them as he was with her, but there was little choice in the matter. His liege lord had decreed it, so Savaric would somehow find a way to do his duty.

He lifted his head and expelled a shaky breath as he watched Marguerite from under his hat as she finally arrived at the tavern. She meandered inside, stopping to say something to her page, who nodded and sat at a nearby table, before making her way towards him.

God's breath, but the woman was lovely. She was wearing a long green woollen kirtle over a simple cream-coloured tunic and a short hooded cloak, not a stitch was out of the ordinary. Yet she was, as always, so very striking. And still affected him in a manner that was frankly incomprehensible. Indeed, she still had that hold over him. Savaric's chest constricted at her nearness, which was damned frustrating. How the hell was he supposed to stay composed around her? How could he attempt to be immune to Marguerite Studdal, when he was forced to spend time in her company? The whole situation was intolerable. As was his attraction to her.

'Good afternoon, Savaric. I hope you have not been waiting too long for me.'

'Not at all. I have only just arrived here myself.' The lie fell easily from his lips. 'Please, will you not sit?'

'Thank you.' She perched on the edge of a wooden stool and lowered the hood of her cloak. Her magnificent hair was tied back and hidden under a loose-fitting veil.

'Will you care for some ale?' He held up a jug of ale in one hand and a clean mug in the other.

'Please.' She nodded, accepting the mug.

Their fingers touched briefly, sending a jolt of awareness through his arm, but then again it was his injured one. Mayhap Nick D'Amberly's stiches were a little too tight. Mayhap he should get them checked again. Mayhap they should also examine his head while they were at it.

'Now that we have got the pleasantries out of the way, mistress, what say you regarding this difficult situation that we find ourselves in?'

He took a sip, watching her over the rim of his mug, his eyes falling to the drop of ale left on her plump lower lip after she had taken a swig of the drink. The woman then licked it with the tip of her tongue and sucked her lip into her mouth. Savaric groaned inwardly. Damn but he was not going to survive this with her.

'Yes, I have also been giving the matter a great deal of thought.'

He cleared his throat. 'Good.'

She frowned. 'The more I think on it, the more I realise that de Burgh never actually specified how we should work together, did he?'

He narrowed his gaze. 'What is it that you are alluding to, mistress?'

'Only that this predicament is just as unwanted and insufferable for me as it must be to you.'

Savaric nodded, unable to take his eyes off her damn lips. 'It is.'

'Something neither of us would desire.'

Desire? Lord above but must she use such a word?

Marguerite Studdal could not have used a more ill-judged word than she presently had. He shifted uncomfortably on the wooden bench and licked his dry lips.

'No.'

'It would be troublesome.'

'Vexing.'

'Arduous.'

'Inconvenient.'

'Infuriating.'

'Would it?' he drawled, raising a brow. 'Infuriating?'

'Yes, of course.' Her brows furrowed. 'Would it not be?'

'Certainly.'

'As it would be insufferable.'

He took a sip of ale. 'You have already said that.'

'Have I? How careless of me.'

'Indeed.'

'In truth I cannot see how you and I are supposed to work together.'

'With great difficulty.' He leant forward.

She made a single nod. 'And hence, the need for an alternative solution.'

'I am afraid that there is none. If de Burgh has demanded that we work closely together, than that is what we shall do, mistress.'

She sat back on her stool and studied him for a moment. 'Do you always do as you are instructed?'

'My training as a soldier and a knight demands it. So yes, always.'

'Interesting.'

'Not really. Every knight in the kingdom serves to honour the sacred codes they have sworn to.'

And especially Crown Knights, such as Savaric, and his fellow brethren of the Knights Fortitude and the Order of the Sword.

Pro Rex. Pro Deus. Pro fide. Pro honoris.

Indeed, their small elite group of knights held their motto at the heart of everything they did and along with Hubert de Burgh served King and country above all else.

'How steadfast of you.' Her lips curved slightly at the corners.

'I am glad we meet with your approval, mistress,' he muttered wryly, raising his mug at her. 'And yes, we take the solemnity of our vows very seriously.'

'I am certain that you do.'

'Honour, valour, faith, and loyalty. These are qualities that I hold very dear, Marguerite. Without them, I am nothing but one of those treacherous cutthroats I had the misfortune to meet in the alleyway last night.'

'Not every person who lives on the streets is as faithless as that, Savaric.'

'I do realise that.'

'I am glad because for one, there's Eva,' she said, mentioning Nicholas D'Amberly's wife. 'And another… myself.'

'I would hardly count Eva nor the daughter of a landed knight such as yourself, Marguerite.'

'Yet my esteemed father was executed as a traitor and, like Eva, I lived on those dirty, treacherous streets of London exposed to all manner of crime, depravation, and ugliness before I met you. We may not have had the same codes that bind you to your brother knights, Savaric, but we too had loyalty to those who earned it rather than by virtue of being born into such a position.'

Savaric scowled at her, irritated by the truth in her words. His own father might have been a nobleman, but his mother had been a woman of dubious birth and unknown origin. She had also taken silver coin in exchange for him when he was a mere infant. As such, he was the last person such sentiments could be applied to. Yet he knew well that he belonged neither to the streets nor the exulted heights at court. He belonged nowhere and to no one, except perhaps to his Knights Fortitude brethren. Yet just as Savaric was not allied to the streets, neither was Marguerite despite the fact that she had run away to London sometime after her father's execution, where she had met Eva and, through some providence of fate, to him as well.

'Very commendable.' Savaric hoped his smile did not betray how her words were turning over in his head. 'But I would wager there are few on the streets who would not put their own needs before those of others. And as for trust? I doubt it exists beyond something flimsy that can be swiftly severed.'

'Unlike the bonds made between knights, I dare say?'

'Precisely,' he said without elaborating further.

'Ah, so it seems that my suspicions were quite correct regarding you, sir.'

'Oh? And pray what are those?'

She tilted her head to the side and considered him. 'That you do not trust me.'

'No. I have no reason to, but then there are few outside my circle whom I do. You are no exception to that, Marguerite.'

'I see.'

He pinned his gaze to hers. 'But I would wager that I do not have your trust either, mistress.'

'No. I do not give my trust blindly to just anyone but bestow it to those who have earned it. Just as the streets of London taught me.'

'I doubt I have ever done anything blindly, but I do get your point.'

'Do you? Because for us to work effectively together, we do need to be able to trust in one another.'

'I agree. Mayhap it will come in time.'

'It is nevertheless a problem, Savaric. This mission, if you will, is more important to me than you can imagine.'

His brows furrowed in the middle. 'As it is for me.'

'I cannot have anything or anyone getting in the way of its success. My family's name, my brother's inheritance—it is all wholly dependent on me.'

'Then I hope you are commended for everything that you are attempting to achieve.'

'My brother is not aware and it matters not until I can deliver everything that I hope to achieve. But this is the reason that I prefer to work alone, unencumbered, and reliant on no one. Because if mistakes are made, they would be mine and mine alone.'

'How fastidious of you, mistress. I, on the other hand, prefer the opposite and work with men I can trust wholeheartedly.'

'Your Knights Fortitude brothers, Warin de Talmont, Nicholas D'Amberly, and on occasion Thomas Lovent, I assume?'

He blinked in surprise that she knew of such information regarding Thomas Lovent, who no longer worked just as a Crown Knight and had since risen to more auspicious heights. But then again Marguerite had been working for de Burgh. Something he still had difficulty accepting.

'You assume correctly, and, unlike you, I find it imperative to have those whom I can trust implicitly and know will always have my back work alongside me.'

'How fortunate.'

'Indeed.' He gave her a speculative glance before continuing. 'So now, in view of what you have said, how do you propose we move forward?'

Marguerite's eyes glittered, clearly delighted that he had deferred to her.

'I am very glad you have asked me this question for

I have been pondering on this since de Burgh made his demands.'

'Have you, now?'

'I have. And I would propose that we commence collating information on our own but then share our findings with one another and form a strategy on how to proceed with the mission.' She took a deep breath. 'That way we can contain the amount of time we spend with one another.'

Marguerite omitted saying that she would rather it was as little as possible but the implication was there all the same.

'Am I to understand that you would prefer to be in your own company, while collating information, as you put it, rather than have the pleasure of mine?'

'As I mentioned earlier, I do seem to work better on my own. I find it less distracting.'

'Well, then I am shocked and outraged.'

'No, you are not.' She chuckled softly, surprising both Savaric and mayhap even herself. God, but when was the last time he had made a woman—rather, this particular woman—laugh?

'Ah, so you claim to know me, mistress?'

'Not in the least.'

'But you do find me distracting?'

The laughter dried on her lips as she snapped her head up to meet his gaze. He noted the flush of her cheeks, which seemed to spread down her neck and along the expanse of her chest before disappearing under her clothing. His whole body was now taut, his tunic a little too tight as he pondered where the delectable pink blush might have spread to.

'I do not believe I said that *you* were distracting, sir.'

He clasped his chest with both hands. 'You wound me.'

'I rather doubt it.'

'Do you?'

She glared at him. 'You are being intentionally vexing, Savaric.'

'Along with many other epithets.'

'I merely meant that working alongside anyone would prove to be a distraction for the both of us, which neither of us need. Besides, you shall be gathering information around the city while I shall be doing so at court.'

'True.' He shrugged.

'In view of that, I would also ask you not to question the methods I might deploy in gaining information.'

'I would never dream of doing so.'

'Good, I am glad to hear it. After all, we are both sensible, and pragmatic. Indeed, there should be no reason why we cannot attempt to work together...despite our reservations.'

'Indeed,' he muttered wryly.

'Then I take it that you are in agreement with these terms.' She leant across the table again. 'I for one will not adjust any of this, whatever Hubert de Burgh demanded.'

'Oh, I rather doubt you would refuse him anything. After all, he is the key for you to obtain all that you seek. Is he not?' He took a sip from his mug and inclined his head. 'But I admit your terms seem acceptable... reasonable even.'

'Then you agree to them?'

'I do.'

Her shoulders visibly sagged in relief. 'Very good.'

Except that it was not good. Except that Savaric was somewhat uneasy about Marguerite's safety while she went about gathering information on her own in a manner of her choosing. And although he could acknowledge that she must excel at her work to be in de Burgh's employ, he remained apprehensive. Not that he could readily voice this, since the termagant would view it as interference. Yet he needed to consider how best to protect her, and as discreetly as possible, now that she was back in London.

'On one condition, Marguerite. That if you ever need my assistance in any matter, however big or small, you will get word to me through the tavern here or through the chapel we met at earlier. I will then come to you, at any time, or at any place, mistress.' He also leant in towards her. 'I warn you that I too am immoveable on this. So, what say you?'

She did not say anything for a moment, mayhap turning over *his* terms. But then she nodded, evidently coming to a decision. 'Very well, I accept.'

Savaric held out his hand. 'Then let us shake on it.'

Marguerite reached out and clasped his hand and that was when everything changed. That was when the moment stretched, as everything and everyone around them in the tavern seemed to melt away. It was as though there was only him and her and no one else. They continued to stare at one another, unable to move away. Savaric's gaze fell to the vein along her throat just above the lace collar that she wore, throbbing wildly. He itched to touch it. He wanted to desperately. For one mad moment he wanted to pull her gently towards him so that he could run his tongue along her elegant neck before nipping and sucking on that delicate vein. Instead, he turned his hand in hers so that he now held her hand, his thumb pressed into her wrist, taking her rapidly beating pulse, knowing his was racing just as wildly. His fingers caressed, played and entwined with hers, over and over again. Their touch made his blood quicken, licking a flame that rushed along his arm, through his body, pooling in his groin.

Christ.

And he was only touching her damn hand.

It was mayhap a very good thing that they had just agreed to work independent of one another in an attempt to restrict the amount of time they spent together. For him, it was not merely avoiding such a distraction—it was a way to maintain a semblance of sanity. Otherwise he would run mad.

He studied her small hand in his and looked away. What on earth was happening? Savaric had no answers but felt just a little dazed. Mayhap the punch to the face the previous night had knocked some sense out of him. Whatever it was had to cease immediately.

Savaric needed to remind himself why he had not allowed matters between them to become more two years ago. He needed to remember that the situation was just the same then as it would be now, if he allowed the attraction between them to grow. He could never allow that. He could never allow Marguerite to be exposed to the same vile prejudices that he faced for being different. And Marguerite would have to face such intolerance if she was his. That was the reality of the world in which they lived—hostile and unforgiving.

He let go of her hand and gently set it down on the

table, moved away, and watched as Marguerite blinked several times in confusion.

She suddenly stood and gave him a curt nod. 'I shall leave you now.'

'We can reconvene tomorrow just after vespers. Here at this very tavern and at this very table.'

'Very well, until then,' she muttered without meeting his eyes.

'Marguerite?' he called out as she turned to leave, not knowing what he wished to convey.

'Yes?'

A part of him wanted to rush forth and touch her, hold her, bury his head in the curve of her neck and rip away that damn laced collar which she constantly wore. His fingers clenched and unclenched at his side as he remained seated on the damn wooden stool.

'Take care as you make your way around the city.'

'I would remind you to do the same, Savaric,' she muttered over her shoulder before walking out of the tavern.

Chapter Five

Marguerite spent the next few days at court among Isabella of Angoulême, the Dowager Queen, and her ladies, whom she had travelled back to England with. Watchful and alert, Marguerite tried to gauge the true nature of the former Queen's return to a kingdom that had always been largely hostile towards her.

In truth it was only recently, while Marguerite was at the French Court, that she realised all was not quite as it should be with the Dowager Queen and her ladies, indeed her whole entourage. It was more than the usual whispers and rumours at court and something far more sinister. It had started with the death of a young courtier, found with her throat slit in the Dowager Queen's chambers over a month ago—eerily suggestive of the manner in which The Duo Dracones often dispatched their enemies. All very strange. As was the timing of this precipitous visit to England, which Marguerite did not believe to be coincidental. Especially since the arrival of the captain of the cog ship, had been on the same day.

Marguerite closed her eyes and took a deep breath,

filling her chest with the scent of late-blooming summer flowers before opening them again, blinking in the dappled sunlight. She resumed strolling alongside the Dowager Queen's ladies, who had originally travelled from Lusignan, where the Dowager lived with her second husband. And as well as her ladies, Lord Richard de Vars had also accompanied the Dowager, just as he accompanied Marguerite and the tittering ladies on their stroll around the gardens at the Palace of Westminster and the Old Yard that morn.

God, but she needed her wits about her with a man like Richard de Vars, who was not only a consummate flirt but thought nothing of touching and having his hands roam inappropriately over her person. It was a job in itself trying to avoid the man's stale breath when he leant in too close or those dreadful hands of his. Still, she pasted a smile on her face, giggled and simpered and acted the ignorant maid, in an attempt to learn more about the man and why he had also returned to his native England after so many years in France and Lusignan. Or mayhap about the man's friendship and allegiance to the Bishop of Winchester, Peter des Roches, whose enmity with Hubert de Burgh was well known.

Marguerite did not know what it was but there was something about Richard de Vars that made her a little uneasy, far more than just his revolting hands. At least the man made her deploy her quick senses and stopped her from brooding about a certain knight who made her heart trip over itself.

God, but her head was still reeling that in a short amount of time Savaric had managed to weaken her resolve to such an extent that she would have permitted him to take any liberties that he wished to. Just as she had at the tavern a few days ago. And the man had only been holding—nay, caressing—her hand. Marguerite had, however, felt that soft caress in every part of her body. And what had made it far more mortifying was that he knew perfectly well the effect he had on her. All of which meant that Marguerite had to tread carefully when he was near her.

Indeed, since their last meeting, she had stayed away from the tavern or any other place that she might encounter Savaric despite her promise to meet the man. She could not do it. Not yet. Marguerite was aware that she needed to work effectively with him. She knew that she would have to seek him out for that very purpose. But she also needed a few more days until she could understand all these bewildering feelings before she needed to push them away. Before she felt confident that her defences would be properly erected whenever she was around him.

Their small party meandered towards the sheltered sunken gardens, and just as they turned the corner around a beautifully sculpted topiary hedge, the very man she had been reluctantly pondering on appeared on the path, blocking it with his large imposing frame.

And just like that her pulse hitched, and her heart raced in an altogether annoying fashion.

He removed his far-too-flamboyant hat and bowed elegantly as the women all curtsied.

'Sir Savaric Fitz Leonard, as I live and breathe.' One of the Dowager Queen's ladies, Anais de Montluc, sighed as she turned her head and smiled up at him. 'What a pleasant surprise, sir! Do you remember when you escorted my lady Queen and her daughter to Angoulême a few years ago? Do not say that you have forgotten that I accompanied the entourage. Do not say that you have forgotten me, Sir Savaric?'

'How could anyone ever forget you, Lady Anais.' He stepped forward and pressed a kiss to the back of the woman's hand. 'I do hope you are well, my lady?'

'All the better for seeing you, sir.' She giggled, making Marguerite want to wipe that smile off her face. And just as swiftly she felt a pang of guilt at her sudden unexpected burst of jealousy.

'Will you not introduce me to your friends?' he drawled, without taking his eyes off the woman. Mayhap Marguerite might prefer to direct her pent-up frustration at the man himself. By stamping on his feet!

'This gentleman is Lord Richard de Vars.'

Savaric inclined his head. 'My lord.'

'And my Queen's ladies—Ann, Agnes, and Alice.' She leant towards Savaric, her bodice brushing against his chest. 'My lady Queen calls us her Four Precious A's.'

'Does she, now?'

'Yes, and she says that she can never manage without us.'

'How could anyone?' Savaric smiled. 'And what of this lady?'

'Ah, yes, this is Marguerite Studdal of Studdal Castle, lately arrived from France.'

'Delighted to make your acquaintance, mistress… ladies.' He looked so impossibly handsome, so impeccably splendid in his court finery. 'May I join you on your turn about the palace gardens or do you wish to keep all these lovely ladies to yourself, my lord?'

The women bar Marguerite giggled as de Vars nodded curtly. 'By all means join us, sir.'

They continued to walk along the pathway that became narrower, forcing their party to walk in twos. Savaric dropped back and stilled her arm indicating for Marguerite to do the same.

'What are you doing?' she hissed.

'Talking to you, of course. What did you think?' he whispered.

'Yes, but as you made a great show about being introduced to me just now. This familiarity is a mistake.'

'We could pretend to be old lovers,' he said ruefully.

She stumbled as Savaric's hand shot out to steady her. 'I am not jesting, sir,' she muttered from the side of her mouth.

'Is everything well, mistress?' Lord de Vars said over his shoulder.

'Quite well, my lord. Sir Savaric and I were just discussing the difference between English and French... er, cuisine.'

The man's laughter carried back. 'There is no comparison. French cuisine is infinitely superior.'

'Ah, but as a soldier, I am a man of simple tastes, so will have to disagree with you, my lord.'

They continued to stroll alongside one another with Savaric clasping his hands behind his back. 'And there is no familiarity, by the by, unless you make it so obvious, mistress,' he said in in a low voice.

'That would not be my doing but yours,' she hissed.

'I think not. You are the one flapping about like a

mother hen,' he whispered before raising his voice for Lord de Vars's benefit. 'Ah, but pottage is good whole-some food that satisfies the bellies of all hardy men. Makes them strong, sturdy, robust.'

Lord Richard de Vars, who was ahead of them with the Queen's ladies, stopped a moment and glanced back at them. 'Shall we wait for you to join us, Mistress Marguerite?'

'I would hate to inconvenience you with my slow ambling. By all means continue, my lord.'

'It is of no inconvenience. I would hate to leave you to amble…aimlessly.'

The manner in which the vile man spoke with such disdain, ignoring Savaric and warning against walking alone with him, made her want to reach for the hilt of her dagger. Lifting her head, she schooled her features benignly and batted her eyelashes instead.

'I will be there shortly, my lord.'

'Do not worry, my Lord de Vars, I shall return her back to you and the Precious A's after I show her…er, these delicate blooms here.'

But then again Savaric Fitz Leonard could try any-one's patience.

'Delicate blooms?'

'Indeed, apart from hearty foods, I am immensely fond of flowers, trees, bees and what not.'

'I had no notion of your interest in such things, sir.'

'Ah but you do not know me, my lord.'

'I know you only by reputation and believe me, it most definitely precedes you, Sir Savaric,' the man sneered.

'Glad to hear it.' Savaric had gone back to acting the

giant simpleton, albeit a vain knightly one. 'Then you should know not only of my simple taste in food but also how keen I am on nature's bounty.'

The man shook his head as he looked Savaric up and down.

Marguerite fixed a smile on her face. 'Please continue on your walk with the ladies, my lord. I would hate to detain you further, but I shall make haste anon, once I have humoured Sir Savaric for a short moment with his love of "nature's bounty".'

'Indeed, do not forget the flowers, trees, bees, and what not.' He bent down and picked a couple of the pink carnations at the stem and pressed flowers into his nose. 'Is it not splendid? And such wondrous scent.'

The older man rolled his eyes and nodded. 'Very well, we shall meet with you soon, my dear.' He nodded at her and smiled before grimacing at Savaric. 'Sir Savaric.'

'It was a pleasure, my lord. Wait…behold, have you seen anything so magnificently…pink anywhere in France? For I will not believe it.'

'Until later, my lord. And no, Sir Savaric, pink is not a colour that is only the preserve of the English,' she said loudly before lowering her voice so only Savaric could hear. 'What are you doing, Savaric?'

'Admiring nature's bounty, mistress. I believe we have just established that.'

'And the meaning of all this nonsense?'

He waited until Richard de Vars turned down the narrow pathway, flanked by shrubs and hedges with the ladies on either side of him, vying for his attention. As soon as the party was out of sight, Savaric's whole demeanour changed as his golden-amber eyes narrowed.

'This *nonsense*, as you call it, would not have been necessary had you met me at The Three Choughs as we had originally planned, Marguerite.' He turned and prowled towards her, making her take a few hasty steps backwards, until her back was pressed against a particularly spiky coppice.

'And you could not wait until we met later?'

'No,' he said, all humour gone from his face. 'I waited just after vespers as agreed and three nights thereafter, yet you failed to arrive, mistress. So, now I have come to *you*.'

He stopped to pick a few stems of carnation. His big, powerful fingers rubbed the soft petals absently and reminded her of how they had been caressing her own hand the last time she had seen him. Marguerite swallowed hard and exhaled a shaky breath at the memory. It was shameless of her to even acknowledge it but for the past few nights she had tossed and turned pondering on the other parts of her body that Savaric Fitz Leonard's large sensual hands could touch, caress, feel, stroke…

'Marguerite, are you attending?'

She blinked, opening her eyes, surprised to find that she had closed them. 'Yes, of course. I was just breathing in the heady scent of these…er, pink flowers.'

'Were you, now?' He smirked. 'It must be why you are blushing the same shade as this carnation, mistress. The heady scent.'

'Mayhap you should stick those flowers in your damn hat with all that feather plumage.' She exhaled through her teeth in exasperation. 'And I rather doubt that you have followed me here to the pleasure gardens to discuss your taste in food, the lovely shade of pink carnations, or even their scent. And certainly not the way in which I may or may not blush, Savaric. Unless it is to reminisce with your good *friend* Lady Anais—she of the Three Precious A's.'

'Four...'

'I beg your pardon.'

'I would hate to contradict you, mistress, especially when you are blustering so vociferously and so loudly, but I do believe the lady said there were Four Precious A's.'

God, the man was insufferable. 'I can think of many words that might also begin with an *A*. Let me see now... There's *annoying*, *aggravating*, and my particular favourite, *arrogant*.'

'*Argumentative* is a rather apt word, do you not think?' His lips twisted as if he was trying to control his mirth. 'However, my preference is for a different word. One that embodies your behaviour perfectly.'

'Oh, and what is that?'

'*Avoidance*. You have been avoiding me, Marguerite.'

'I really do not know what you are referring to.'

'I believe you do.' He stopped strolling beside her and crossed his arms over his chest, the pale pink carnations dangling from his long fingers. 'And you are not very good at lying.'

'Surely that is a blessing?'

'Regardless. Have you forgotten that we are supposed to work together? That we are supposed to share our findings with one another? Which by the way we are supposed to do every day, as agreed? It was your proposal to which I agreed by the by.'

She shrugged. 'There was merely no point in coming to the tavern when I had nothing to disclose or discuss. You already know from all the reports I sent back to Hubert de Burgh that I suspect someone among the Dowager Queen's ladies and entourage.'

'Yes, and even the Dowager Queen herself. But that,' he muttered, 'is simply not the point.'

'I rather think it is, Savaric. I am only trying to do my work, which by the way you are obstructing by meeting me here at the gardens at Westminster, harping on about pottage and pink carnations. What if Lord de Vars becomes suspicious of my motives here? What if he realises that I am not who I am pretending to be? That I'm not like the other ladies?'

'Then you get word to me immediately,' he growled.

'Very well.' She sighed, shaking her head. 'But you must leave, Savaric. We can talk anon.'

'Not before I have said my piece.' He rubbed his jaw. 'Can you not appreciate that we promised to do better in this situation, Marguerite?'

'I realise that.'

'And do not forget that we spoke of how we can begin to trust one another the other day. I have to say that this is a poor way to start, especially when we have much to discuss. In particular the contents of the pouch I filched at the docks.'

The man did have a point. Marguerite *had* been avoiding him, preferring not to acknowledge her blatant attraction. But it simply would not do. Neither would she have this mission fail. Especially when she was so close. The only way forward was to collaborate properly with Savaric.

'You are right.' She sighed. 'In truth, I would like to make this joint partnership succeed.'

'As would I. Do not forget that we shook on the agreement.'

It was best, however, if she could try and forget that particular handshake.

'Very well, I shall meet with you tonight.'

Savaric stepped forward and placed his large hand on the side of her waist, pulling her gently towards him.

'What…what are you doing?' she muttered.

'Hush.' He placed a finger to her mouth, making her lips tremble, and moved forward, his head bent close to hers. That was when she heard it. A twig breaking underfoot somewhere nearby. There was someone on the other side of the hedge. Possibly listening to their conversation.

'Giggle and simper like you were for Lord Richard de Vars,' he murmured, his lips brushing against her ear. 'Do it.'

Marguerite did as he commanded despite herself, as he leant even closer, his breath against her neck. 'Not tonight, not The Three Choughs.'

'Then where?' She felt breathless, dazed, and far too warm.

'I shall send word.' His head was dipped close to the curve of her neck. 'And I think pink does suit you after all, Marguerite.' He stood to his full height and took a step back, holding out the carnations to her. 'But I believe I have detected the source of the sweet floral scent. It's *you*…'

Marguerite blinked several times, taking the flowers

before lifting her head, the after-effects of his closeness slowly fading away.

But he was no longer there. The man had gone.

Marguerite waited a moment, exhaling slowly, trying to moderate her breath before she could possibly consider rejoining the walking party with Lord Richard de Vars and the Four Precious A's. Her whole body still hummed from Savaric's touch, his closeness.

How could she continually allow him to affect her in the manner in which he did? Mayhap she simply had to get used to being around the man, until it became mundane and ordinary. Yes, that might be the key. Indeed, she would endeavour to treat Savaric as she did his Knights Fortitude brethren, Warin and Nicholas.

Her eyes fell to the ground as she blinked, frowning. How strange. For there in the long grass by the bushel was something that glinted and gleamed as it caught the glare of the sunshine. Marguerite reached down to the ground and picked up the small item and straightened her spine, holding it out in front of her. A small shaving or clipping of silver. She could have sworn that she had seen something akin to this before.

Yes, strange indeed...

Chapter Six

Savaric's trail, which had begun with the contents of the pouch that he had filched from the merchant that night at the docks, took him to the great Tower of London the following morn.

The more he uncovered, the more he realised how potentially explosive his suspicions regarding the contents might be. It could change things irrevocably. Indeed, Savaric needed to tread very, very carefully. The whole matter confounded him as it also consumed him in his quest for the truth. But there was someone else who also consumed his thoughts.

Marguerite Studdal...

Every time he set eyes on the woman, she somehow managed to cloud his judgement and somehow pervaded his thoughts, making him constantly forget every reason he had pushed her away in the first place. If anything, Marguerite was more of a danger to him now than she had been two years ago. And that terrified him.

He needed to break away from the tumult that she caused in his damn head and remember that he had a mission, one which he had to carry out with Marguerite. It would be prudent to think of her only as an associate as he would his Knights Fortitude brethren, Nicholas and Warin, and even their wives, Eva and Joan. Indeed he respected and admired them—Eva for her tenacity and survival as a London thief and Joan for facing her diminishing eyesight with courage and grace. He needed to think on Marguerite in just the same way and nothing more. Yes, that would be the best approach, and Savaric would start by arranging to meet Marguerite to discuss any possible findings.

He particularly wanted to know whether Marguerite had discovered more at court regarding Isabella, the Dowager Queen, and her entourage, especially the reprehensible miscreant Lord Richard de Vars.

Savaric would wager that the man was far more than the vapid, pompous courtier that he presented. Indeed, the man's antipathy for Hubert de Burgh, was widely known. The English Crown, headed by de Burgh, had confiscated the Dowager Queen's dower lands upon her second marriage, as she'd entered into it without royal approval, and earned the enmity of both the Dowager Queen and all who supported her—loyal men such as Richard de Vars. And now they were all back on English soil...

Could they be conspiring against the Crown, and in particular involved somehow with The Duo Dracones? Marguerite certainly had her suspicions regarding them. Yet nothing currently tied them to the treasonous group, not that it could be discounted. As well as this, Savaric had been outraged at the way Richard de Vars had openly leered at Marguerite.

God's blood, but it made him want to punch the bastard hard in the jaw for his brash impudence. Yet all she had done in return was simper and bat her lashes enticingly. And even knowing the reason why she had invited this behaviour from the letch did not make it any more palatable.

It made Savaric want to protect her despite knowing that Marguerite was well equipped to look after herself. He did not doubt it after witnessing how she had effortlessly come to his aid that night on the docks. It was men like Richard de Vars whom he doubted. And it was because of this that he had a Knights Fortitude squire tail her every move, reporting back on any behaviour that might be deemed capricious. Marguerite would not appreciate his overzealous behaviour, which was why he was glad that she was not aware of it. Even so, Savaric could at least gain some peace of mind now that he had come to terms with her working for de Burgh.

And now that he had accepted her position within their group and had consigned her as an associate, Savaric would learn to work with the woman. Indeed, it was long overdue. After this visit to the main quarters of the Royal mint located within the enclave of the Tower of London, he would do so properly. Savaric would go and seek her at Nicholas and Eva D'Amberly's dwelling, where he knew Marguerite had been residing ever since she returned to London.

He hopped off the skiff that gently lapped the sides of the wharf close to the Tower and handed the oars back the boatman. Entering the city down river, rather than going through the city walls on horseback or on foot, was yet another precaution he had decided to take.

Savaric studied his surroundings as he made his way around the stone curtain wall and entered through the western gatehouse, along the pathway that led to the outer ward and into the inner one. He spoke to a sergeant patrolling the cobbled pathway and strode towards the heavily guarded small stone outbuilding and nodded at one of the guards who allowed him entrance into the quarter.

Here, Savaric was met with sweat, toil, and the clatter of industrious activity. The unbearable heat and noxious fumes from the furnace as well as the loud clanging noise of hammers beating down on the metal was overpowering.

A large burly man with a long blackened apron tied around him frowned as he approached him. 'Can I help ye there?'

'I thank you, yes.' Savaric reached inside his cloak and untied the pouch he had stolen from the merchant a sennight ago, holding it out. 'I would like to parley with the master, if I may.'

'You be speakin' to him, friend.'

'Good. Then in that case, is there somewhere, a privy chamber, that we can discuss matters? I would like to enquire about a few coins that I have, and would importune you to inspect them and ascertain their origins.'

'And whom might you be?'

'A Crown Knight working for my liege Hubert de Burgh,' Savaric supplied without adding that he was in truth a member of the Knights Fortitude. But then very few other than those involved would know about that.

The other man looked Savaric up and down as he awaited the inevitable question…

'You?' The man raised a brow. 'You are a Crown Knight?'

Savaric sighed, shaking his head at the usual reaction of doubt and surprise that *a man like him* could be a Crown Knight. After all, men with his colour skin were rarely knights of the realm. And despite the fact that he was used to this reservation, the niggle of annoyance at endlessly having to prove himself, as well as the resentment that went with it, were his constancy. He removed his seal tied to his sword belt and presented it to the man.

'I hope this meets your approval?' Savaric muttered sardonically.

The man looked a little sceptical but after examining the seal he must have concluded that it was genuine.

'No 'arm done, friend. We need to be thorough about who we let in here.'

'Of course, you do.' Savaric did not doubt that there were other prejudices at play but decided to leave it. He had other concerns.

'Follow me then.'

He followed the man, criss-crossing around the various stations of work, with his eyes peeled trying to take in the process of minting coins. At one end, in a seemingly restricted area, silver was being melted in the furnace before being hammered and beaten into thin sheets, which was then cut by hand into small coin-sized discs. On another table a tool was used to engrave the portrait of the King on one side of the coins. And it was the area that cut the sheets of silver into the small discs that particularly interested Savaric, something he watched avidly until he reached the rear of the work-room. They exited the building at the back, thankfully also manned by guards, down a narrow pathway and entered a smaller chamber.

'I must tell yer that you ain't alone in your enquiry, friend.' The man smiled as he ushered him inside. And there, apart from a fire in the hearth, a wooden desk, an assortment of other furniture, and a few scattered parchment ledgers was the one person he had put off meeting with—Marguerite Studdal, sitting atop a bench.

Oh, hell!

'Mistress.' He inclined his head. 'I had not expected to see you here.'

'A pleasure to see you again, sir.'

Savaric raised a brow. The woman looked anything but pleased to see him.

'What are you doing here?' she whispered as he turned to her, blocking the other man from view.

'I would wager that it would be for the same reason as you,' he muttered back.

'Well, good, good.' The master looked from Marguerite and then back to him. 'It seems the two of yer knows one another.'

'That we do.' Savaric indicated the bench with a single nod, making Marguerite scuttle along to allow him to perch beside her. Their shoulders and arms touched, sending a jolt of awareness through him. Yet he did not sever the contact. And neither did she.

'This makes it easier to answer you both at the same time, like.' The master returned to his chair on the other side of his large wooden desk. 'So how can I help yer?'

'Well, what I need you to see…'

'It's a peculiarity that…'

Marguerite and Savaric both turned their heads around in unison.

'Beg pardon. Please continue.'

'Not at all. Go ahead, sir.'

'After you.'

'No, I really do not mind.'

'And neither do I, besides you were here first.'

'Either way I…'

The master muttered an oath under his breath. 'If you can begin sometime soon as I ain't got all day…'

'Very well.' Savaric got his pouch and emptied the contents on the wooden table. 'Here, this is what I need you to verify.'

Marguerite nodded absently and brought out another small leather pouch, untied it, and did the same. There were fewer silver coins than in Savaric's pouch but they also looked to be of English origin judging by the engravings.

'I want to ask whether the coins were minted here.' Savaric said rubbing his jaw.

The master picked up a square slab of glass and looked at a few of the coins.

'Not sure, friend, but I'll 'ave a look in the daylight outside. If they weren't done 'ere then they would have been done at another site outside the city gates near Thorney Island, Westminster, or Canterbury.'

'Either way, I would like you to ascertain whether these are also English.'

Savaric tipped the remainder of the contents from the pouch he had stolen out onto the table. But these were not coins, but rather the edges of silver that had been cut, shaved or clipped, and evidently from coins…

'I have also come upon one of these silver clippings.' Marguerite held this out for the master to inspect. 'Are they what we believe they are?'

The man raised a brow and grimaced. He put them on scales and compared them with a few of his own minted coins before giving them a grim look.

'Yes. They may well be silver coin clippings.'

'Do you believe that they might be clippings that have purposely been cut from minted coins?'

'I do.' The man dabbed his clammy head. 'I believes that is just what they are, me lady.'

Savaric whistled low at the implication of what this could mean.

The man opposite shuffled about before speaking. 'I want you to comprehend, like, that I knows nothing about this.'

For a long moment neither Savaric nor Marguerite said anything but watched the master squirm in his chair. Eventually Savaric broke the silence.

'We did not say that you did.' He leant forward. 'Although I'm sure that you're aware that clipped silver is tantamount to treason, *friend*…'

The master swallowed hard and made a single nod.

Indeed, the practice of clipping minted silver coins was becoming a huge problem to the Treasurer and ultimately the Crown. It meant that the weight in the coins that had been tampered with was not just incorrect but that the clipped edges of the silver could be illegally melted down and made into anything, including bullions of silver, reused for possibly nefarious and seditious activities as well as flooding the market with counterfeit monies. And in a climate rife with conspiracy and treason this was indeed a concern. It seemed that the English treasury was being robbed, its revenue stripped without much detection. Until now.

'Well then, we had better find the source of this.'

The man nodded and walked out of the chamber with Savaric in tow. He turned the coins over in his fingers in the sunlight and exhaled sharply between his teeth.

'Well?' Savaric said as they re-entered the chamber. 'Can you tell us more about these coins?'

'Those are clipped all right and tight.' The man grimaced. 'And I is afraid to say that they were minted 'ere at the Tower.'

Savaric nodded, pushing down the bubbling excitement. This naturally meant that someone who had previously worked for or was still in employ here, at the Royal mint, could be the culprit clipping the coins. 'What about the other English coins?'

'Most were minted here and the rest in Canterbury.' He held out the coin. 'It's the small indented mark here, see, in the left-hand corner, that indicates the location of the mint.'

'Then the next question would be whether you have noticed any other coins clipped here? Anything that was suspicious or not quite as it should be?'

''Course not, otherwise we would have alerted the warden!'

'In that case we would need to ask you for the names of all your workers here.'

The man inclined his head. 'We'll do everything you ask to help the Crown.'

'I am happy to hear that.' Savaric flashed the man a quick smile. 'As that would help immensely with our enquiries. Incidentally, would you know whether any of your workers have been missing recently?'

The man rubbed his chin for a moment before answering. 'Come to think of it, yes. There's a young lad, an apprentice, name of Ned Lutt, who dinna show for work, so some of the lads he works with went to see him but he weren't there.'

Savaric frowned. 'I had always assumed that apprentices lived in dwellings together?'

'They did, they do.'

'But not this Ned Lutt?'

'No, he…' The man looked uncomfortably from Marguerite to Savaric. 'The lad preferred to be with his own kind.'

'I see.' Savaric's jaw clenched. 'In that case, if we could talk to these lads, that would be most helpful. And also the whereabouts of his abode, as well.'

'Of course.'

'In the meantime, you must alert the warden, and secure more guards for the time being. You cannot allow this to continue and above all, be vigilant and keep a look out. The security of the Royal mint is in your hands and from now, you will only report to Crown Knights and no one else.'

'Yes, sir.' The man bowed his head, with all of his earlier supercilious arrogance now gone. 'I will make sure that everything is as it should be.'

'Good, I hope for your sake that you do. And whatever you do, make sure you are extremely *thorough*… More so than you have ever been before.'

* * *

It was sometime after noon when Savaric and Marguerite left the Royal mint building after questioning all the apprentices and older workers, not that they had made any further progress. It was the one worker they needed to find with urgency who might possibly shed light on the clipped coins that had been found in the pouch that Savaric had stolen. The one who had failed to come to work for the past few days—*Ned Lutt*. And after learning the whereabouts of his dwelling, Savaric returned with Marguerite to the Knights Fortitude skiff that was waiting on the wharf for them.

Holding Marguerite's hand, he helped her on board, but released it just as quickly, feeling that brief touch down to his very bones. Sitting down across from her he clenched and unclenched his hand absently.

'I feel I should…'

'May I just…?'

They both started at the same time and instantly stopped. Marguerite's smile was a genuine one which seemed strangely abashed and somewhat knowing.

'I fear we may be forming a habit of this.'

He found it difficult to suppress the faint smile that twitched at the corners of his lips. 'I fear we might.'

'I believe I should also offer you an apology, Savaric.'

'What about?'

'In truth, I should have sent word to you about coming here.'

'As should I.'

'And also shared my findings. Indeed, I should not have been so evasive.'

'Neither should I.' He dragged his fingers through his hair. 'It seems that we have both been guilty of that.'

'Yes.' She nodded. 'You are right.'

'So, in the spirit of unity, tell me where you discovered the pouch you presented at the same time as I did mine to the master earlier.'

'From the captain of the cog ship, but unlike the merchant, he never realised it had gone missing. Not to my knowledge anyway.'

'I assume you filched it, then? But the question is when you would have had the opportunity.'

'After *your* thievery, actually.' She flashed him a brief smile. 'You had created quite a convenient discord on the dock after you filched the pouch from the merchant, and the ensuing mayhem gave me just the opportunity I needed to steal from the captain while he was none the wiser.'

'Very impressive,' he drawled, returning her smile.

'You were not the only one who learned how to steal from Eva.'

'So it would seem.' He crossed his arms over his chest and grinned. 'You took from the captain after I stole from the merchant, although it seems you were a better thief than me.'

'Did I hear you correctly, Sir Savaric? Did you just compliment my skills in thieving?'

'I did.' He rubbed his jaw. 'Well, the one thing this reveals is that this clipping of coins is far more widespread than previously thought.'

'There's more,' she added. 'I found a single clipping in the pleasure gardens at the Palace of Westminster.'

Savaric's eyes widened as he turned to her. 'When was this exactly?'

'The previous morn, when you happened upon me taking a stroll alongside Lord Richard de Vars and the Dowager's Precious A's. I found the clipped silver hidden among the grass near the bushel where we heard someone nearby step on a twig.'

'Interesting, very interesting. I hope you realise what this might suggest?'

'Yes. That someone at court may also be involved. And my suspicions are that it is among the Dowager Queen and her entourage.'

'Which is what we always hoped. A direct connection to The Duo Dracones from this unknown traitor at court to the captain of the cog ship, who you saw in a tavern with Renaisser.' He rubbed his jaw as he mulled over this new information. 'I just wish we had caught the captain or the merchant who gave him the pouches of these coins in the first instance. Mayhap we could have learned more about who these men are.'

'We shall,' she said, nodding. 'We shall find them.'

'I am glad of your confidence.'

She shrugged. 'At least we are making progress.'

'True, but there have been other instances when we have been close to apprehending the traitors. Even so, you are right, Hubert de Burgh will be encouraged by this. He has been under a huge strain to capture The Duo Dracones and those who wish to conspire against the Crown. They have targeted him from the start and although we have successfully scuppered every attempt they made with their every nefarious means, we have yet to seize any of The Duo Dracones.'

'Except for the one who got away.' She shivered, unable to say the hated man's name.

'Yes, except for *him*. And now they become bolder with their ambitions with these silver clippings.' He sighed through his teeth. 'Still, this progress, as you call it, will be welcome to de Burgh.'

'I imagine it will.' A long stray strand of her fiery red hair danced in the breeze, as she pushed it away from her face. 'And by the by, since you mention de Burgh, I meant to convey my thanks for informing him of my part in saving your hind that night at the docks.'

He waved his hand dismissively. 'Think nothing of it.'

'I think everything of it.' She pushed away the lock of hair as the breeze relentlessly kept whipping it back across her face. 'Not every man is confident enough to own up to mistakes as well as admit that a mere woman aided him when he most needed it.'

Savaric leant forward and reached for the glossy red lock, so satiny soft between his fingers.

'Most men are fools, Marguerite,' he whispered in a low voice and gently tucked the loose lock behind her ear. 'Never forget that.'

He stilled in the moment, unable to move. Unable to pull away from her. God help him but Savaric could not tear his hand away. He cupped her jaw and drew her towards him, his thumb slowly caressing the softness of her plump lower lip. He wanted to bend his head down to hers, replacing his lips with his thumb. To taste, just the once.

'It's to Thorney Island and Westminster first, sir, is it not?' his squire said, breaking this strange evocative interlude.

'Westminster?' Marguerite blinked several times before pulling away. 'Why would we need to go to Westminster first?'

'I believed you would want to get back to the Palace of Westminster—back to court where you can continue gathering information?'

Where those damned lecherous bastards at court could fawn all over Marguerite…flirt, entice, and mayhap even win her smile, her heart…

God, how pathetic were these musings. In truth, it did not escape Savaric's notice that it was just as perilous for a young, beautiful maid such as Marguerite at court with all those wolves circling around her as it was in the part of the city he was about to visit. Not that Marguerite was not capable of looking after herself.

She had done so for two years at the French Court, after all…

'Surely this matter would take precedence, would it not? Besides, I can continue with that later.' She eyed him with some misgivings.

'And what of the coin clipping you found in the grass? You might want to search for more.'

'That can also wait for now.'

'But do you not have suspicions regarding Richard de Vars? And the Dowager Queen and her ladies?'

'I do. Quite apart from my findings, it seems too much of a coincidence that they're here in London and only so recently after her dower lands were confiscated by Hubert de Burgh and the English Crown.'

'Which is more than she deserved after both she and her new husband aligned themselves to the French King.'

'And do you suppose that this betrayal to the French is felt keenly by King Henry?'

'She is his mother,' he ground out bitterly. 'How do you expect him to feel?' Savaric muttered an oath under his breath as he shook his head, shocked by his own outburst. Where the hell had that come from? It was so unlike him to allow matters of the state to personally affect him so. He was always so detached and rational, never allowing for more than was needed of him, that this was nothing short of surprising. But then this— the Dowager Queen's betrayal of her young son, King Henry—resonated deeply within him. Although it was nothing like the one carried out by the woman who had birthed Savaric. A woman he could never call *mother*, since she had traded him when he was only a young infant for a handful of silver coin. Not that he could even remember the woman or the far-away kingdom she had come from near the Holy Land. Nevertheless, it was still a betrayal and one that Savaric felt keenly.

'Are you…are you well, Savaric?' Concern was etched over Marguerite's face.

He lifted his head, and schooled his features to resemble his usual wry, nonchalant self.

'Of course.' He shrugged as he smiled. 'I do not know what came over me. Forgive me.'

'There is nothing to forgive.'

He quickly pulled his mind back to their discourse. 'All I meant was that the King is far more perceptive than the court gives him credit for.'

Marguerite was watching him warily. 'Of course. I can imagine that it must be difficult…for him.'

He shuffled uncomfortably, aware of her penetrative gaze. 'I am sure it is. And I, for one, do not believe this nonsense that the Dowager Queen's timely visit has anything to do with her wish to be reunited with her English royal children.'

She frowned. 'No, I do not believe that it does either.'

'Good, then we are in agreement. You can resume your furtive work in Westminster and at court.'

Marguerite stilled him with her hand. 'What is this about, Savaric?'

'Nothing, mistress, only that it might be wiser if we split up for you to continue as you were and for me to chase this Ned Lutt fellow. Besides, that part of the city is dangerous.'

It was not only a dangerous part of town but one which housed people very different to the ones that someone like Marguerite, who was now used to fineries of court, had probably seen.

'That would also be true of anywhere within the city, which is squalid, dirty, and filled with unsavoury characters. You forget that I lived in such places.'

'I do know that, Marguerite.'

Savaric had to persuade her not to accompany him as he went in search of the lad. He did not want to be with Marguerite more than was absolutely necessary. Indeed, he had already spent far too much time in the woman's company and it was making him feel quite exposed. It was almost as though he could easily lose the ability to think and behave rationally whenever she was near him. Even now he had almost lost himself— he had almost kissed her. He had certainly wanted to and would have had they not been interrupted. And to make matters worse he had almost opened up about his past regarding his birth mother of all people. A woman he never cared to discuss…least of all with someone as perceptive as Marguerite. He swallowed uncomfortably and changed the topic of their discourse, wanting these reflections gone.

'Speaking of which, mistress, how did you come upon these newly acquired skills? I had meant to ask you, since you surprised me at the dockside.'

She didn't say anything for a moment and then sighed before answering. 'Nicholas D'Amberly. I begged him to train me in combat.'

This seemed a far safer conversation, even with the sting of disloyalty for having this information about Marguerite withheld by his closest friends. It might still be a little raw but not acutely, as before. He may not like it, but Savaric had now come to terms with why Marguerite had insisted on this secrecy. Especially after the way he had treated her at the time.

'Nicholas taught you?'

'He did, along with Sir Warin.' She had the good sense to look a little guilty for employing both of his Knights Fortitude brethren while he had been kept in the dark.

'How on earth did you manage to secure their services?'

'Nicholas, of course, declined at first, but I was extremely persuasive. And I also had Eva on my side, so eventually he relented. Once he agreed to help, it was then much easier to also gain Sir Warin's help, with some persuasion from Joan, of course.' A faint smiled played at her lips. 'I remember how nervous I was, how lacking in confidence back then, as I trained with those young squires, but it was important that I had the rudimentary skills, so that I could defend myself when I had to.'

'You were obviously a good student.'

'Thank you. But it did not come naturally to me. It took time and slowly, slowly I began to improve. Eventually I found something I excelled at. Something that I was better at than those young boys—I realised that I was quite adept at hitting a mark with absolute precision and only a handful of daggers. I remember practicing for hours and hours, just throwing the weapon over and over again at a mark until I would hit it every time. Until the feel and shape of the weapon became part of me, like a second skin, an extension of my hand or arm.'

'Very impressive indeed.'

'I suppose it is for a woman.'

'It's impressive either way.' He leant forward. 'But I wish you had also come to me for…for advice and training.'

'You can understand why I did not,' she said quietly. 'Why I could not see you after…after everything that had happened.'

Savaric understood far better than she could imagine. It would have been too difficult and would have brought back all those emotions that he'd rather forget.

'But that does not mean that I do not have regrets about how it came to pass.' He covered her hand with his much larger ones and gave it a squeeze. 'I wish things had been different, Marguerite.'

She turned her hand around, so they were touching palm to palm. 'As do I.'

They sat there for a moment in silence, as he revelled in this touch, savouring the warmth of her soft elegant hand, wishing that it touched and soothed other parts of his taut, weary body.

In truth, Savaric wished for so many things but none as much as wishing that everything between them had not ended as painfully as it had. No, he could not rid himself of *that* regret. And although being thrust into Marguerite's company again was out of his control, as well as being difficult to navigate, it did bring with it the stark truth that he liked the woman—he still did, despite it all. Which would not do. He reminded himself again to think of her only as an associate and nothing more. He needed to for his own sanity.

He blinked, staring at their entwined hands, and cleared his throat, removing his hand from hers. 'And although I commend your skills, I still believe it might be prudent if you were to go back to court and the important work you're doing there, while I seek Ned Lutt.'

Marguerite sat back and raised a brow. 'And do you know what I believe, Savaric Fitz Leonard? I believe you might be correct—most men are indeed fools. Which is one reason why it is more prudent that I accompany you to find Ned Lutt.'

'I really do not think that is a wise course of action.'

She smiled inanely at him. 'Oh, I think it might be very wise indeed. After all, you never know whether those skills of mine might be needed again.'

Savaric ground his teeth together and looked away. God, but Marguerite Studdal could be infuriating. In every way imaginable.

Chapter Seven

Marguerite glanced at the man ambling beside her on the dirt-covered road from the corner of her eye and frowned, attempting to work him out. He had tried far too much to convince her to return to court. And the more Savaric attempted to dissuade her from accompanying him, the more convinced she became that she would have to defy his wishes. There was something he was being evasive about and she would wager that it had nothing to do with this mission. He was hiding something, not that Marguerite could ascertain what it might be.

They walked together in silence as the turgid stench of filth along the pathway became steadily worse and far more conspicuous. Marguerite noted the threadbare clothing falling off the urchins, the many beggars and the prostitutes across their way along with unscrupulous men hovering nearby. Indeed, this tableau seemed familiar, with the dwellings in such close proximity to one another, the poor quality of the buildings piled on top of one another, the thatched roofs decaying and offering little protection from the elements, and yet there was something a little different about the people living in this part of London. Marguerite glanced around and realised that there were far more people of colour settled here than she had initially perceived.

She stole a glance at Savaric's inscrutable face, a steely, determined gleam in his eyes, and wondered at the man striding down the pathway, seemingly wanting to put distance between himself and this place. She could hardly blame him but again Marguerite had a nagging feeling that there was more to all of this than she had first considered.

'Savaric!' a young boy called out. 'Over here. Savaric.'

The lad ran towards them along with a handful of other boys of differing ages from the derelict pile of timber and dirt that they had fashioned into a play area.

They halted as the children surrounded them. 'We are in a bit of hurry, Silas.'

The boy's dark brown eyes filled with confusion and hurt before it was replaced with a mischievous glint. 'Aren't ya gonna introduce us to yer friend?'

'Not on this visit.'

'Why not? You never bring anyone on yer visits.'

Savaric tried to move around the group. 'We haven't got the time for this, Silas.'

'Not that you come 'ere much, anyway,' the boy muttered as his friends nodded in agreement. 'Who'd wanna come to this hovel, though?'

Deciding to take matters into her own hands, she crouched beside the child. 'How do you do? I'm Marguerite. And I believe you must be Silas?'

The boy puffed out his chest. 'I ams. And this is Gil, Chumna, and Roddy.'

'I am happy to meet you all.'

'We be pleased too, lady.' The boy turned to the brooding man beside her. ''Ere, Savaric, why d'ya brings a fair 'damoiselle to these parts?'

'It doesn't concern you, Silas. And don't call her that.'

'Don't say you're hidin' some'fin.'

'In truth, we are searching for someone, Silas.' Marguerite smiled as Savaric gave her a speaking look, which she soundly ignored. 'Mayhap you have heard of him?'

Savaric glared at her before turning his attention to the group of boys. 'A young cove who goes by the name of Ned Lutt.'

Silas's eyebrows shot up as he grinned excitedly. 'We ain't just 'eard of the churl—we knows 'im! Keeps 'imself to 'imself, like. Moved into the neighbourhood recently and livin' 'ere, even though he gots a fancy job at the Tower.'

Savaric and Marguerite exchanged a quick glance. 'Do you know of his abode, Silas?'

'I can do more than that. I can shows yer. Not that I've seen 'im recently. Come, yer can follow us.'

They trailed after the lads, who ran ahead excitedly, taking them further down the pathway, criss-crossing from one road to another in the dilapidated maze of squalid settlements. They reached a tall, narrow dwelling with two floors precariously built on top of one another.

'Ned lives 'ere. Top floorin', like.'

Savaric smiled at the boy as he grabbed a few coins

from inside his pouch. 'Thank you, Silas. I would have difficulty locating him without you.'

'I likes to be of service. Besides, Ned's one of us. I'm sure the fella will 'elp if he can.'

One of us...

The boy meant that the young apprentice was also a person of colour.

'I am glad to hear it.'

The boy grinned, exposing many missing teeth. 'I'll comes with ya. Introduce yer, like.'

'Thank you, but that will not be necessary.' Savaric placed a hand on his slender shoulder. 'But tell me whether you know if there have been others who have come to look for Ned Lutt?'

The boy frowned and shook his head. 'Not that I knows.'

'If you do, you'll then remember to get word to me?'

'Verra well.' The boy chuckled happily at his luck as Savaric handed out more coins to each of them before they scampered away without another glance.

Savaric gave her a single nod, slowly drew out his sword, and stepped inside the ramshackle dwelling, with caution. Marguerite followed him, her fingers tightly gripping the hilt of the dagger strapped to her waist. They made their way up to the second floor of the building, taking in their surroundings, looking in every direction, and ascertaining that the area was secure.

They reached the small uneven landing that tilted at an angle and edged the door open.

'Anyone here? Ned... Ned Lutt?' Savaric walked inside the compact yet tidy chamber guardedly, as Marguerite followed, darting her gaze around and ensuring that there was no one else there ready to surprise them.

But there appeared to be no one there at all. The chamber had clean strewn rushes on the creaky wooden floor, and a narrow pallet in one corner with straw-filled bolsters and a coverlet neatly covering it. A plain wooden coffer was set against the timber-clad wall on the other side of the chamber, devoid of any personal items. There were a few empty metal sconces dotted around that might provide a little warmth. Other than that, there was very little else in the chamber.

All perfectly tidy, all perfectly ordinary. Yet it somehow felt as if someone had left recently.

Savaric looked under the pallet as her eyes flicked around the room and caught something glinting among the rushes on the floor. She moved to the other side of the room and reached out for it, holding it out in front of her, examining it between her fingers.

'Savaric. Here.'

The man got to his feet and strode towards her. 'Another coin clipping?'

'No.' Marguerite held the heavy medallion out in her hand. 'Come and have a look.'

It was small round metal emblem with two entwined snakes and a faint engraving on the edge. *Agneau*—lamb.

Savaric nodded as her eyes widened at the implication—The Duo Dracones, whose insignia was indeed the two identical snakes entwined together.

'I assume you know what this means?'

'Yes.' She nodded, feeling decidedly ill. 'It seems

that the apprentice Ned Lutt might have been involved with them after all.'

'Indeed.'

Dear God...

'What in heaven's name would draw a man like Ned Lutt, newly apprenticed to the Royal mint, for Christ's sake, to get involved with treacherous, murdering bastards such as The Duo Dracones?'

'I would wager it could be for many reasons, chief among them being that he might have been coerced into it. They do seem to be good at making people bend to their force of will.'

Savaric nodded. 'True, and judging from this chamber it seems that Ned Lutt has abandoned this dwelling and mayhap abandoned this medallion here on purpose.'

'Yes but where could he have gone?'

He frowned. 'I do not know, Marguerite.'

Just then they heard the muffled sound of footfalls moving away, down the crooked stairwell as though someone was in a rush to leave the building.

Could it be the young man they sought? Ned Lutt?

Savaric's eyes widened in surprise, seemingly having come to a similar opinion before he raced after whoever had just left the building. Marguerite followed after him, panting as she made her way out of the building and back onto the pathway. She looked in both directions and noted that Savaric had gained on the young man he was chasing, his longer legs eating up the distance far quicker. She ran towards them and by the time she had reached Savaric he had caught the man by the scruff of his cloak.

'Have mercy.' The petrified young man stooped to

the dirty ground, his legs shaking beneath him. 'Who are you?'

'Not who you think. We mean you no harm,' Savaric ground out. 'I presume you are Ned Lutt?'

The young lad looked from Savaric to Marguerite, gauging whether he could trust them before nodding.

'We seek only to ask you a few questions.' Marguerite hoped her smile gave him a little more assurance. 'About the work you do at the mint.'

The young lad's throat worked as Savaric held out his hand to help him back onto his feet. 'And also whether you recognise this.'

Ned Lutt faltered as the medallion they had found in his chamber was held out in front of him. The young lad attempted to make a run for it again but Savaric held on to his upper arm. 'Easy now, Ned, we only seek to ask some questions as we just explained.'

'Let me go,' the young lad muttered. 'I knows nothing.'

'Ah, but I believe you do.'

'I don't, I never wanted any of this.'

'Come now, Ned.'

The young apprentice glanced at the medallion and shook his head. 'You don't understand, messier, these people are dangerous. There ain't nuffin' they won't do to get what they want.'

'Is that why you are running away?' Savaric said. 'If so, we can look after you.'

Ned narrowed his eyes. 'Who are yer?'

'Friends. Savaric Fitz Leonard, and this is Mistress Marguerite Studdal, at your service.' He smiled reassuringly. 'Come with us, Ned. We can take you somewhere these people who have put the fear of God into you can never find.'

Ned Lutt nodded in resignation and just as Savaric let go of him, the young lad turned and ran in the opposite direction.

'Wait! Come back.' Savaric and Marguerite rushed after him but this time, just as Savaric reached Ned, she heard a familiar hiss through the air as a succession of daggers hurtled past from the opposite end of the pathway, and found their mark in Ned Lutt's chest.

No, no, no!

Marguerite reached them just as Ned slumped to the ground, and Savaric quickly surveyed the area around them, trying in vain to find the young man's assailant. But they both knew that whoever had thrown the daggers was now gone from the scene, since it had all been done from a distance.

Savaric turned back to her and shook his head, confirming what she already knew—that the assailant was gone.

Marguerite and Savaric knelt beside Ned Lutt as he gasped for air, seemingly attempting to say something.

'We have to help him,' she muttered. 'We must try and get him back to de Burgh, who might be able to do something for him.'

Savaric shook his head sadly, his face ashen, and she knew that there was very little they could do for him.

Ned looked up, sprawled on the ground as he clutched at Savaric's arm. 'Remember, the scriptures. What the priests always say.'

'What are you saying, Ned?'

'You must remember, *redimentes tempus, quoniam*

dies mali sunt,' the young lad said in between taking gulps of air into his lungs.

'I do not comprehend…'

'Time…there is so little time,' he whispered softly. 'For she shall be Queen.'

'Who, Ned? Who?'

'But you must stop it.' Ned clutched even tighter onto Savaric's arm. 'I pray that yer shall stop it.'

'Whom do you speak of?'

Ned shook his head with difficulty. 'The one they… they call *la femme immaculée*,' he murmured breathlessly before he coughed up a mouthful of blood, having said his very last words.

It was not long after the death of Ned Lutt that Savaric and Marguerite found themselves huddled opposite one another in a skiff that they had secured. And yet they may as well be sitting in different kingdoms, both wrapped in their own musings.

'Damn the bastards to hell,' he muttered, shaking his head in dismay.

She nodded. 'I cannot fathom that they managed to get to the young apprentice before he could reveal more.'

'He revealed nothing other than mere ramblings before his death.'

'Either way it shows that we are evidently on the right trail.'

He lifted his face to her. 'A trail that is proving far too dangerous, Marguerite. What if whoever killed Ned Lutt saw us with him? It would expose both of us in a manner that we cannot afford.'

'It was dark and we were well hidden in the shadows, Savaric, so do not concern yourself on that.'

'Everything concerns me. Everything frustrates and troubles me. All of it!'

She felt the same disappointment as keenly as he did but had to admit that despite it all they worked well together.

'I know but consider we must be getting close, despite this set-back.'

'Set-back?' His eyes flashed with an emotion she could hardly fathom. 'A young man lost his life because he had stupidly got involved with these people, who used him and then discarded him when he no longer served their purpose.'

'I know.'

'Another wasted life.'

'I know.'

'The most powerful people in the land, from the Bishop of Winchester to Isabella the Dowager Queen, along with their vassals and lackeys such as Lord Richard de Vars and many others—any one of them could be the conspirators. Any one of them could be behind this and countless other treacherous acts of rebellion in the kingdom. Indeed, any of them could be behind The Duo Dracones, and yet here we are after so many years searching, still seeking answers and trying to unravel the mystery surrounding the group.'

'I comprehend your frustration, Savaric, but it is not as bleak as that. We do know far more about them than in the past. What we found today could prove more useful than we envisaged.'

He dragged his fingers through his dark curls. 'While

I agree that this… Dispatching Ned Lutt might have been a way for The Duo Dracones to sever any ties that would connect them to the clipping of coins, with all the possible implications that presents in conspiring against the Crown, it still remains that we were too late to find out more. This has happened time and again, with the deaths of anyone connected to them. Even Nicholas's mother by marriage and his squire who had also become involved with the group two years ago were later found garrotted to death.'

Marguerite swallowed uncomfortably remembering the time when she first encountered the nefarious deadly group, who later attempted to ransom her for her friend Eva. God, but it did not matter how she tried to be impassive about that desperate time, it never failed to send a shiver down her spine. She had hoped to harden herself against them by now and face her fears but it still had the same effect. They still frightened her, especially the man who had nearly cut her throat and killed her like the poor young apprentice. And she still had the scars that the bastard had left behind on her neck…

'You are thinking on him again? The one who got away and who still lives.'

She shivered. 'How can I ever forget Renaisser.'

The distinguishing silver medallion, with two entwined snakes and an engraving on the edge, insinuated that the man at the centre of their trouble two years ago was quite high up within The Duo Dracones organisation. Those they deemed to be below, or as they had referred to them, *agneau* or sacrificial lamb, were disposed of when they were no longer needed…just as Ned Lutt seemingly appeared to have been.

'After that time, Renaisser disappeared and was never to be seen or heard of again, until you encountered him at the tavern in Paris with the captain of the cog ship recently.'

Marguerite might still be frightened of that time and in particular of Renaisser, but forcing herself to change and become involved in their capture was mayhap one way in which she was trying to assuage the horrors of the past.

'Yes, but don't you see this is precisely why we are close? They are getting careless, Savaric.'

'Not careless enough.' He sighed through his teeth and shook his head.

'We shall find out who did this.' She placed her hand on his and watched him under her lashes. 'But it is not just the progress of this mission that troubles you... is it?'

He rubbed his forehead. 'No. This game of divide, power and conquer has always been a tangled web, Marguerite, and yet it is men, rather boys like Ned Lutt, who get caught in its net when they become involved. And once they're no longer useful, they are always expendable. Always. It matters not to those in power as they are always deemed inferior anyway.'

Like me...

Savaric did not say it but the whispered implication was there all the same. What had the boy, Silas, said again? The boy who Savaric had paid far too much silver for information that they might easily have gleaned elsewhere?

He is one of us...

Savaric too had that same connection with these

young boys in the streets despite his exulted position of being a knight—and all because he was also a person of colour. It stood to reason that Savaric would be judged just the same as them.

For the first time, Marguerite could see the dismissiveness, censure and even intolerance that Savaric along with others like him might face. She had seen it first-hand from the likes of Richard de Vars, who looked down his nose at Savaric, to the master at the Royal mint's initial contemptuous manner.

And although Marguerite knew of the admiration, respect, and close bond that existed between Savaric and his Knights Fortitude brethren, she wondered whether Nicholas D'Amberly or Warin de Talmont were aware of the difficulties that their friend faced. Had Savaric disclosed any of this to them or did this proud man feel uneasy to discuss such matters? Did he bury it deep within himself, as he seemed to bury so much of his emotions? She did not know but wagered that he might believe it revealed a weakness that he could ill afford.

In truth, the man dealt with his situation with a quiet dignity and forbearance. He was everything that was honourable, chivalrous, and was so much more than what he believed himself to be.

Not only did the man rise in her esteem but Marguerite's heart ached for him.

'I cannot believe that anyone would consider the boy to be that. To be *inferior*.'

'Can you not, Marguerite? Then answer me this. Why would you suppose that a young man of Ned Lutt's standing, apprenticed to the Royal mint, for God's sake, did not reside with all the other apprentices on-site at the Tower? Aside from his chamber, which was tolerably clean, do you believe he chose to live in that squalid neighbourhood?' Savaric gave a hollow, bitter laugh and shook his head. 'In truth it was just the same for me when I had first been knighted. It caused much resentment and animosity that someone like *me* could rise to the hallowed ranks of being a knight, despite who my esteemed father was. It mattered not. I was judged before I had even reached for a sword, before I could prove myself as a warrior. There was no amount of scorn and derision that they could not constantly inflict on me. And from the first I was treated very differently to other newly knighted young men. From having to do the menial tasks that a squire would do, such as polishing the other knights' armour, tending to their mounts and such, to being made to sleep in the tents where squires and other servants slept on flea-ridden pallets, night after night. I soon realised that if I wanted to be accepted, if I wanted to succeed, I had to be better and stronger than anyone else. I had to work harder than all the other knights put together, just so I could prove my worth. It was what I had to do in order to earn that respect. But it never came easily. Never.'

'I am so sorry for it.'

'As am I, but it did make me into the man I am today.'

'Which is admirable.' She reached out and cupped his square jaw. 'Indeed, you have overcome much to get to where you are.'

'Evidently so,' he said bitterly. 'But at what cost? For every moderate success there are countless more fools like Ned Lutt, who also want to be more than their presumed worth. But I promise you this, Marguerite, I shall find them. I shall find the bastards who did this and make them wish they had never been born.'

'I do not doubt that you will gain justice for Ned Lutt and others like him, but do not forget that not every person holds the same views and intolerances.'

He held her gaze as she rubbed his cut and torn knuckle from the hand that he had punched into a stone wall in frustration earlier. She lifted his hand to her lips and heard him exhale slowly.

'Marguerite…' he muttered softly, as she turned his hand and kissed the centre of his palm.

Lifting her head she gazed into the depths of his golden eyes. God, but what she saw there made her weak at the knees. The intensity and unfettered longing was almost too much to bear.

Without thinking Marguerite closed her eyes and leant forward, gently pressing her lips to his and trembled from the touch. Savaric's lips were soft, warm, and utterly tempting. She had shocked herself and judging from his stillness, she had mayhap shocked him too. Marguerite knew she should not do it. She knew it was wrong to kiss this big proud man but could not help herself. It had been so long.

And though Marguerite might have stunned him with her actions, there was nothing for it. She desperately wanted to make him understand there was more than the hardship and difficulty that he had had to overcome in his life. She wanted him to realise that she would always stand by him. That mayhap she could show him a little tenderness in the cruel, unforgiving world that they both inhabited. In any case, it was just a kiss. An ordinary kiss, and nothing more.

And yet with everything that Marguerite offered, the man remained unmoved. Savaric seemed so taken aback by her surprising behaviour that he did not respond. He remained motionless, stiff, and coolly detached. And with it he was surely expressing his disfavour and disapproval.

Good Lord, what had she done? Marguerite had once again practically thrown herself at the man, when it was clearly most unwelcome. When was she going to learn that Savaric did not want this—even a chaste kiss, such as this was? What was wrong with her? Marguerite could feel the wave of embarrassment and self-consciousness assail her senses as she began to pull away. And that was when Savaric seemingly awoke from his apparent slumber and responded. His arms came around her, and drew her towards him, gently lifting her onto his lap. With one hand curled around her waist and the other around her head, Savaric pulled her close and kissed her back with such intensity that it made her gasp.

Good God, how did she ever think kissing him would be ordinary? Nothing—nothing—about Savaric Fitz Leonard could be described as *that*.

Chapter Eight

Savaric's heart was pounding so fast that he felt it
might tear out of his chest. God's bones, but when was
the last time he had felt this exhilaration, this thrill
coursing through him? His desire for her was one he
had difficulty reining in, and it had been there glaring
at him from the first time he had seen Marguerite again.
Not that he could have predicted *this* after the day that
they had just had. He could never have thought that
after such a day of ups and downs, he would be sat on
a skiff drifting on the Thames with a beautiful woman
in his arms who had only moments ago pressed her
delicious lips to his torn and bloodied knuckles before
kissing his mouth. And only after Savaric had foolishly
opened himself to her again, disclosing such intimate
personal memories which he had supressed, surprising
and appalling himself in the process.

Those memories were not ones he would ever want
to cling to. No, like many things in his life, they were
ones he would rather forget. Even if much of what happened to him shaped him into the man he had now be-

come. Indeed, his life had been so different before he became a Crown Knight and in particular before joining the elite, secret group of Knights Fortitude.

He desperately wanted to touch her, to brush his hands up and down and learn every curve and crevice of her lush body, but he would not do it. Savaric had initially pulled her onto his lap, had held her at the back of her head and at the small curve of her back but he had instantly let go. If he continued to touch Marguerite, to explore as he desperately wished to, then there would be no hope for him. He would be lost. And that small thin thread of control that he was hanging on to would snap altogether. So he allowed Marguerite to touch him, as was her wont, while he kept his hands at his sides and allowed his lips, mouth, and tongue do all the exploring in deep, sensually slow kisses.

His lips left hers momentarily as he grazed the sweep of her elegant jawline, the soft skin behind her ear, even kissing the soft lacy material around her neck before moving down to the modest neckline of her kirtle. He left open-mouthed kisses everywhere, wanting to devour her sweet floral scent and wrap himself in it before moving back to her lips. He deepened the kiss, tasting her and licking into her mouth.

Help me forget... he wanted to say. *Please...*

And she did. She seemed to understand what he was asking. After all, Marguerite had initiated the kiss, as she had reached for him unexpectedly. And while Savaric had tried to resist her, he found that the more she tried to coax a response from him, the more he was unable to withstand her. It was impossible and at that moment he could not recall why he would be so asinine as to deny either of them this.

Her hands came up around him, her fingers sliding into the curls at the base of his neck, clinging on to him. She kissed him with fervour, touching his tongue with hers, making him growl into her mouth. God, he could drown in this for ever. He could peel off all her clothing and lay her down naked, learning every part, every small dip and curve of her glorious body. He could give her the most exquisite pleasure. He could lose himself deep inside her warmth. He could…but he would not do any of it.

No, he could not. He would not. Even in that moment when his mouth was ravishing hers, his hands were controlled, restrained. And nowhere near Marguerite. If he touched her now, then there would be no hope for him with this woman. Savaric would unravel and then it would be impossible to hold on to even a piece of his sanity.

Yet he wanted to make this kiss last. Just a while longer. He wanted to hold on to this moment that pushed away all the hurt and pain from his past. He wanted to take what she offered. He wanted Marguerite Studdal. He wanted her just as he did before…

Damn.

It could never be. She could never be his. Not now, not ever. But how could he let her go when her mouth was soft, welcoming, and her scent enveloped him? He felt her lips part on a soft moan as he continued to rediscover everything that he had hoped to forget about this woman.

Savaric's eyes opened and caught the boat hand

watching him with a sneer curled at his lips. The man
tried to conceal it but Savaric had seen it all the same.
What the devil had he done? He should not have taken
it this far. In that very moment he realised his mistake. A mistake he should never have made. He should
never have exposed Marguerite to such censure from
the damn boat hand.

It was entirely his fault. He had allowed the intimacy
of Marguerite's embrace and the warmth of her lips to
fuel his desire. He had allowed his longing for her to
scatter all sense and reason and melt away his resolve.
He had allowed the failure to discover more about Ned
Lutt to cloud his judgement. He had allowed this mad-
ness, this stolen moment of weakness. He had knowingly allowed it all.

Savaric knew the way of the world. He knew that a
man like him and a woman like Marguerite could never
be anything to one another. He might be a knight with
the backing of the most powerful man in the land but
that was not enough. He could not hold off the scorn
of the world for kissing this woman, so very different
to himself in every possible way.

'We must stop this.'

'We must?' she whispered against his lips.

He pulled away, cupping her face. 'Yes, and we must
do that now.'

'We must...' she repeated.

He smiled faintly at her dazed state. It was so damn
endearing. 'Yes.'

Savaric wrapped his hands around her waist and
gently pulled her off his lap, returning her back to the
wooden seat in front of him. He watched her for a mo-

ment as her eyes shuttered open, blinking in confusion before coming back to herself. He watched her as a deep pink hue flooded her face, spreading down her neck and disappearing down the neckline of her kirtle dress. Tearing his eyes away he helped her right herself, smoothing her crumpled skirts, and rearranging her wispy transparent veil.

'I think I can manage, thank you.' She looked out across the Thames and exhaled softly.

'Yes, of course,' he muttered, sitting back in his seat and gazing in the opposite direction, watching all the different-sized vessels on the river.

They descended into an uncomfortable silence, both lost in their own musings.

'Forgive me.' He sighed, knowing that he somehow needed to address the kiss. 'It should not have progressed as far as it did.'

He noticed a small intake of breath. A moment where she squeezed her eyes closed. It was so fleeting, so brief, that he might have missed it had he not been watching her intently.

God's bones…

Savaric hoped his apology had not embarrassed her or hurt her feelings more, but he needed Marguerite to comprehend the folly in such intimacy between them.

He tried again as he reached for her hand. 'I am sorry.'

But not because I do not want you…

'As am I.' She pulled her hand away and placed it back in her lap.

He attempted a different track.

'Look around you, Marguerite,' he whispered. 'We

are on a skiff, in the middle of the river, where anyone could happen upon us. It is not safe here, out in the open like this, when we have much to do.'

And I have no right to kiss you senseless…

'Of course.'

'This, er…well, this…'

'Kiss?'

'Quite.' He raked his fingers through his hair. 'This, er, intimacy can only complicate matters, when we have no need for further complication, especially with the difficulties we already have with this mission.'

'Yes.'

'We have to work together. We have much to do.'

'You have already mentioned that. And you need not concern yourself. It was just a kiss—nothing more. But if you wish for me to forget it happened…'

'I did not say that.'

'…then I can forget that it did.'

God, how had it descended into this? Savaric was suddenly weary and tired from the events of this day. But he wished things could be different. He wished he could make her understand. He wished that he could make Marguerite comprehend that he did not want her to experience the same intolerance that he oft faced. That would be reprehensible in every way, as well as impossibly precarious.

'Very well.' He exhaled. 'It might be for the best if we did.'

Then why did he feel bereft and empty with that compromise? It was as though the earlier exhilaration that he'd felt had been drained away. And replaced with nothing. Nothing at all.

'Good. Then that is settled.' She turned away again and pinned her gaze out in the distance. Anywhere but at him.

'Marguerite,' he murmured softly. 'Look at me… please.'

She turned her head, but her eyes were steely and held nothing like the warmth they had radiated earlier. 'Can you possibly just leave this be, Savaric?'

'Yes, but I also want to ensure that what happened only a moment ago does not make matters…awkward between us.'

Like it had last time, he refrained from adding.

'Of course, because we have to work together.' Her smile was brittle as she repeated his words back to him.

'Yes.'

'And as you said there is much to do.'

'Indeed.' He inclined his head, wondering why she was repeating everything he had just said.

'In fact, we cannot risk the success of the mission.'

'No. That we cannot do.'

'Good.' She made a single decisive nod. 'Then we should alert Hubert de Burgh that our collaboration is no longer feasible. That for this mission to have a chance of success, we cannot work together.'

What…?

'That is not what I implied, Marguerite.'

'Mayhap de Burgh can arrange for me to work beside Sir Nicholas or even Sir Warin.'

'He would never entertain that. In truth he would be seriously displeased.'

'I would just explain that you and I are…incompatible.'

'Incompatible?' he ground out. 'I believe the opposite is true.'

'Or mayhap that we are unsuitable as associates.'

'Which he still would not look on favourably.' Savaric shook his head and sighed. 'Besides, I believe you and I actually work well together. I find that I appreciate your keen observations and insight, Marguerite.'

'You do?'

'Yes. As well as your deft handling of certain small weaponry.' He smiled. 'But other than what we have been tasked to do, there can be nothing more…between us.'

The relief that Marguerite had felt after disembarking that unbearable skiff, rippling with so much tension, had been palpable. She had wanted to scream her frustration at Savaric for having the sense to remind her once again of the error of her ways when she had decided to kiss him. It had been out of a show of compassion, that was all. But how quickly it had caught and sparked into a flame that burned through her whole body. How quickly it had changed into something far more potent.

She was mortified. Again.

She felt embarrassed. Again.

And this time, she had no one to blame but herself. She could kick herself for her wanton impudence, knowing full well that Savaric did not welcome such attentions from her. Yet she'd kept on pushing and coaxing him until he had lost the semblance of control and kissed her back. Why had she done that? Why?

Was it her vanity that had driven her to gain a response from him or something more? Either way she did not want to examine her reasoning, only knowing that it was a mistake. A grave mistake and one that could not happen again. How Marguerite had managed to keep that smile fixed on her face instead of screaming at him she would never know.

Savaric had escorted her back to Nicholas and Eva's dwelling just outside the city gates, in awkward silence, before arranging to meet with her, all the Knights Fortitude, and Hubert de Burgh at an appointed time. He would of course send a message as to the location of this rendezvous. Or mayhap Nicholas would. Or mayhap she did not care a damn as long as she did not have to endure more moments like this one. And thank God he had left shortly after, getting away as fast as he could, leaving her to make her way inside Nicholas and Eva's pleasant abode.

Savaric had the right of it, though. They had much to accomplish and would need to work harder than before. Especially now with the death of the apprentice and the consequences from that. Marguerite had to put her mind to this and only this so that she could finally gain the pardon that she had been working hard for. And once this was over, she would part ways from Savaric for good, but for now she would have to work with the man, making sure to put enough distance between them, so that she could prevent such a mistake from happening again. And for that, she would need to have her wits about her whenever the man was near.

'Marguerite?' Her friend Eva D'Amberly's voice called her back to the present. 'Dearest? You seem so far away.'

Marguerite blinked. 'I am sorry. I was pondering on all that had come to pass earlier today,' she muttered as she gulped down a mouthful of rich red wine after the pleasant evening meal they had shared earlier.

The two women were sat in Eva's bower chamber in a large and comfortable house on the Fleet near le Strand, which Nicholas had inherited after the death of his father. Since then, Eva had worked tirelessly to make this into a happy home and one that could be just theirs—hers, Nicholas's, and the babe she was carrying—not that Eva had yet disclosed that particular news to her.

'Yes, I can imagine that the death of the young apprentice must have been a shocking encounter.'

'It was a disaster, in every sense. The poor young man was cut down in the prime of his life. But we are close, Eva, to unravelling this. I can feel it.'

'I truly hope so. It has taken a toll on Nicholas as well as all the Knights Fortitude. The constant threats make it difficult to have a semblance of peace.' She continued to watch her friend over the rim of her goblet. 'But that is not the only matter at hand, is it?'

'What can you mean?'

'Nothing, I assure you. But you do seem different, Marguerite.'

She shrugged. 'Many things have happened in the past few years. It's only natural that such events change and shape a person. Look at you, Eva—you are very different yourself since I last saw you. You seem so happy and content with life.'

'I am, and only wish the same for you, my dearest one.'

She reached out and squeezed Eva's hand. 'We cannot all be as lucky as you. But know that I am very happy for you. Truly.'

'Thank you.' She laced her fingers together on her lap and smiled serenely. 'Tell me though, Marguerite, how do you get on with Savaric?'

'As well as can be expected. I respect his sharp mind, his judgement, his obvious skills as a knight, and the fact that he does not dismiss me for being a woman.'

'Very commendable.'

She shrugged. 'It makes working together much easier than I had first envisaged.'

'Good. That is very… good.'

'But of course, the man is still surly, irascible, maddening, and altogether vexing.'

'Apart from that.' Eva's lips twitched at the corners.

'And he has the most annoying habit of being right in most situations.'

'How thoughtless,' Eva muttered sardonically.

'Indeed. And when he is being insulted and derided, sometimes directly to his face, the man merely takes it in his stride and manages to stay so composed and unflappable. It's quite disconcerting really.'

'Some might say stoic, or possibly even remarkable given such a provocation. But I understand.'

'Quite, and must he be so understanding?'

Eva shook her head. 'Such inconsideration.'

Marguerite flicked her gaze to her friend. 'Are you mocking me?'

'Only a little.' She smiled. 'But only because you sound a little…er…'

'Ridiculous?'

'Mayhap, but I still love you.' Eva laughed.

'And I you. Indeed, there is no one in the world who can show me my own folly better than you.'

'Then let me say that I am glad matters between you and Savaric are better than you had first imagined. Well, despite the fact that he is surly, vexing, and annoyingly considerate, unflappable and even remarkable.'

'You said that, not I.'

'Ah, my mistake, forgive me. I did not realise that you thought the man to be unremarkable.'

'I would never say such…' Marguerite lifted her head and saw her friend's teasing expression filled with mirth and looked away, annoyed at herself for being taken in so easily. Honestly though, her nerves were in tatters this eventide.

'Don't mind me, I am just jesting with you.'

'I am happy that I can be of some amusement to you.'

'I'm sorry, Marguerite, that was badly done of me. And of course, your situation is far from being amusing. I am only glad that you are getting on well, despite…it all.'

'Despite his being as vexing as he is?'

'Despite that. But that was not what I meant.'

'If you are referring to everything that came to pass two years ago, know that it is forgotten. Those feelings that I once… Well, they no longer hold true.'

How Marguerite desperately wanted it to be so. And mayhap in time, after this was all over, it would be just that. She would no longer think of him again.

'If that is the case, then I am glad.'

'I had my reservation too, Eva. However, Sir Savaric and I have an understanding, and find that we actually work well together.'

As long as they both refrained from touching one another or, God forbid, kiss, she thought wryly.

'But while you are forced into each other's company, take care.'

Marguerite raised a brow. 'You cannot imagine that I would be in any danger now? Not after all this time.' She was not sure whether she was trying to convince herself or her friend.

'All I know is the reason that you left for Paris two years ago was as much to do with the work you were commissioned to do for Hubert de Burgh as it was for getting away from Savaric. You must know that I wondered whether you left with a broken heart?' Eva said softly.

Broken heart? Oh, God.

Marguerite opened her mouth to deny the nonsense, but the words were caught in the back of her throat. She swallowed uncomfortably. 'No, I assure you. I have never had the misfortune of enduring that affliction.'

Her friend studied her for a moment before inclining her head. 'If that is the case then take care for that to remain so. I would not want to see you endure such an *affliction*, as you call it.'

'Neither would I.'

Just then Nicholas D'Amberly strode through the doorway, making her shoulders sag in relief. She'd had quite enough of Eva's scrutiny and was beginning to feel a little self-conscious under her watchful eye. Indeed, her friend might mean well, but this particular discourse was far too exhausting. Marguerite had no wish to continually speculate and ponder on Savaric Fitz Leonard, his character, or whether she went to Paris for two years to tend to a broken heart. It was ridiculous even if it were true.

'Ah, so this is where you have both been hiding.' Nicholas bent over to kiss his wife and briefly place a hand on her belly.

Marguerite smiled inwardly. It seemed that she might have assumed correctly after all.

'How were your travails, Nicholas?'

'Well, I thank you. I have just returned from meeting with Savaric at The Three Choughs, and I must say that I hold the same belief as you, Marguerite.'

Marguerite felt her cheeks become a little warmer just at the mention of the man. Heavens above but what was wrong with her? It was as though she was losing her senses. Especially since it seemed that Savaric had spoken to his friend about her and given Nicholas her appraisal of the situation.

'Ah, so he informed you regarding what happened today?'

'He did. And I agree that although the young apprentice's death is a setback, we have actually learned a lot more than ever before. Progress has been made.'

'Not for the poor apprentice.'

'No, not for him.' He frowned. 'But know this. When we finally manage to apprehend The Duo Dracones once and for all, young men like this Ned Lutt will be saved from the same demise.'

'True.' She sighed. 'In any case, I hope you met with a favourable outcome in your findings?'

'Favourable enough.' This piqued her interest, although Nicholas seemed resistant to further discussion. 'However, I shall wait to disclose everything on the morrow, Marguerite. And now that Warin has also returned to London, we shall meet anon and decide the next course of action.'

Indeed, it was time that the treacherous Duo Dracones were caught. Marguerite could then fulfil this mission and gain justice herself by clearing her family name as well as reclaiming her family's confiscated lands. This was where all her attention, diligence, and efforts needed to be and nowhere else. Certainly not on Savaric Fitz Leonard. Beyond this mission, she needed to put the man firmly out of her mind.

Chapter Nine

Savaric flicked his gaze between his Knights Fortitude brethren, Hubert de Burgh, and Marguerite, who were all assembled in Nicholas D'Amberly's privy chamber at dawn the next morn. They sat around a wooden table that to his mind resembled the fabled table belonging to King Arthur and his knights, giving the impression of an equitable order to all, even though that was far from the truth with their liege lord present. But more than that, it was exceedingly practical since Savaric was able to see everyone who was there easily. Not that anyone presently in the chamber would even meet his eyes.

In truth, Marguerite had gone out of her way to ignore him ever since she had entered the chamber. She would not even glance in his direction, to the point that he may as well not be there.

'We are all come together to discuss our findings. And I must say that everything is now progressing tolerably well,' Hubert de Burgh muttered, raising his goblet of wine in the air. 'My hope is that now that we have gathered all the different pieces of the mystery surrounding The Duo Dracones, we can finally put them together.'

'And get the bastards,' Savaric added, raising his goblet as well.

'Indeed.'

'Now let us begin with everything we know so far.'

'Firstly, there was the discovery of the clipped silver coins in the pouches that the merchant was handing over to the captain, the night Mistress Marguerite arrived back on English soil.' Savaric nodded at her.

'Yes, and this was the same captain who I saw with my own eyes in discussion with a…a prominent member of The Duo Dracones when I was in Paris.' Marguerite seemingly made an effort not to mention Renaisser's name. 'However, I could not continue to pursue either the captain or the merchant as I was forced to abandon what I was doing and go to the aid of Sir Savaric.'

'Yes, I thank you for that much-needed intervention, otherwise I might not be here enjoying this wine with all of you.'

Nicholas raised his goblet in salutation. 'It is of no consequence, Marguerite, and although your trail of the captain was severed, I eventually managed to follow and track the merchant.'

Her eyes lit up. 'You did?'

'Oh, yes. I'm prodigiously good at finding people.'

'No one knows how he does it, but D'Amberly is exceptionally skilled at trailing and finding anything and anyone,' Warin said, slapping his friend on the back.

'I do seem to recall that.' Marguerite smiled congenially at him. 'And what did you do with the merchant? Have you interrogated him?'

'There was a slight problem there, unfortunately.'

Savaric groaned. 'Oh, no, please don't say that he was found to have met a similar fate to Ned Lutt.'

'I wish I could deny it.' He sighed, shaking his head. 'But I had the man dragged out from the bottom of the Thames, with his throat slit.'

'Dear God.'

'But there's more. We found the same round silver Duo Dracones emblem of the entwined snakes worn around his neck, with the word *agneau* etched in the corner.'

'Just like the apprentice.'

'Precisely. And not just that, but a few shavings of silver coin clippings were found clutched in the dead man's fingers.'

Savaric leant forward. 'It seems that those who have been involved with The Duo Dracones are now being picked off one by one.'

'Yes,' Warin interjected. 'And once they have fulfilled their purpose, they are being silenced before revealing anything about the organisation. Just as before.'

'Except for the captain of the cog ship,' Savaric said, rubbing his chin. 'If the man is still alive.'

'Which means that we need to man the ports, and look out for him, on the chance that he returns to England.'

'As well as…as Renaisser.' Marguerite interjected, instantly touching the lace cloth around her neck. 'Who was last seen in Paris.'

'And who could easily have returned to England by now.'

'He could, yes.' Marguerite tapped her fingers together, still refusing to meet Savaric's eyes. 'Then there is the person or persons that I have been suspicious about at court. In particular those among the Dowager Queen's entourage. This has lately been strengthened by a new finding.'

Warin looked from Savaric to Marguerite, as Nicholas raised a brow. 'What is this about a finding?'

Marguerite smoothed down her skirts. 'I found a small sliver of coin clipping in the garden of the Palace of Westminster, when I was on a promenade with the Dowager Queen's ladies and her entourage.'

'Who the hell could have dropped it there?'

'That is rather the point, is it not?' Marguerite said, raising a brow. 'The fact that someone did misplace or lose it there. Meaning that someone who is either at court, or visited recently, must also be involved with the coin clipping business and also The Duo Dracones.'

'So someone from the Dowager Queen's entourage?' Savaric pondered openly.

'The King's own mother?'

He shrugged. 'Possibly. Her enmity towards the English Crown is common knowledge. And since all her dower lands have been confiscated upon her new marriage, which was never sanctioned, her alliance is now no longer assured.'

'This is an extremely useful finding, mistress.' Hubert de Burgh tilted his head, bestowing one of his rare smiles on Marguerite.

'And what links all of these people, known or unknown, is these silver shavings or clippings of coin,' Savaric muttered.

'Yes. It does!' Hubert de Burgh slammed his fists

on the table. 'And it can mean one thing and one thing only. That these clippings of silver coin are being stolen, so that they can be melted down and used again. And think of what a huge amount of silver can purchase.'

'A mercenary army, for one.'

'Exactly.'

'That is the one thing I can surmise.' The older man stood and paced the chamber before turning on his heel and looking at each of them. 'And my suspicion is that it is to be used to finance a foreign attack on this kingdom.'

'I am of the same mind, my liege.' Warin de Talmont nodded.

'As am I.'

'And I.'

'There is more.' Savaric rubbed his jaw. 'The apprentice muttered words just before he died that I initially believed to be mere ramblings of a man who was breathing his last. But they were not that at all.'

Marguerite flicked her gaze to his finally and nodded. 'I agree.'

'What did he say?'

'Ned Lutt was particularly agitated about how little time was left.'

'Time?' De Burgh muttered.

'Redimentes tempus, quoniam dies mali sunt.'

'The apprentice said those words?'

'Yes, my lord.'

'Then the evil he refers to must be in relation to The Duo Dracones,' De Burgh said absently. 'Which means that they have plans to unleash it and unleash it imminently.'

'Hence the lack of time.'

'Yes, that would account for what Ned Lutt said,' Marguerite added. 'He also mentioned that someone would soon rise up to be the Queen.'

'The Queen? That is what he said, a Queen?'

'Yes, my lord. One whom they call *la femme immaculée*.'

Hubert de Burgh continued to pace around the chamber, his fingers pressed against his forehead. 'If we take the apprentice's words to be true, then I would say that he was referring to someone who is ambitious enough to be considered as the next Queen of England—and consort to King Henry.'

Savaric nodded. 'That was precisely my thought. And I would wager that this woman would be found among the Dowager Queen's own ladies.'

'As would I,' Marguerite murmured.

'Quite.' He dragged a hand through his hair. 'So it stands to reason that whoever this ambitious maid, this *la femme immaculée*, might be, she might have a bargain with The Duo Dracones.'

'Unless she is one of them.' Marguerite frowned. 'Which would mean that if they were to be successful in their endeavours, then a member of The Duo Dracones would snake their way into the Crown of England.'

'And, God forbid, become the mother of a future prince.'

'Hell's teeth.' Hubert de Burgh slammed his fists on the table. 'We shall never allow that to happen!'

Marguerite levelled her gaze at de Burgh. 'What would you have us do, my lord?'

'We need to plan. We need to mobilise but without

The Duo Dracones' notice. I will send word to Thomas Lovent and some of his men to meet his friend and one-time Crown Knight, William Geraint, Lord de Clancey to man the ports of Portsmouth and Southampton in the south.' De Burgh turned to Warin de Talmont. 'While you and Fitz Leonard secure the city gates and the Port of London, in case our friend the captain or even Renaisser returns, unless he is already here among us.'

The older man rubbed his brow before continuing. 'The Dowager Queen has expressed a wish to pay her respects and offer prayers at the shrine of Thomas à Becket in Canterbury, and then onto Dover Castle before returning to France. This may or may not be a ruse but we shall comply with her wishes and have the King and the court travel with her and give her the send-off she is accustomed to. But we shall remain vigilant. We shall use our eyes, ears, and brawn. And we shall be ready.' Hubert de Burgh turned towards Marguerite, addressing her. 'You, my dear, shall return to court and the Dowager Queen, her ladies, and even that toadying turncoat Richard de Vars, and travel with them to Dover, especially since you still suspect one of them to be this *la femme immaculée*.'

Marguerite made a single nod. 'Yes, my lord.'

'And you shall have D'Amberly here to accompany you at court and keep a watchful eye. He would be there if you need him.'

God's bones, no…

'My lord, if I may offer a different suggestion,' Savaric interrupted. 'It might be prudent if *I* were to accompany Mistress Marguerite, while D'Amberly works closely with de Talmont.'

'You, Savaric?' De Burgh looked suitably surprised. 'You have never enjoyed the, er…niceties at court. Not like Nicholas, who has always enjoyed courtly flirtations. Have you not always found such things trying?'

'Yes, my lord, but I find that as the only unmarried man in this chamber, it behoves me to throw myself in the midst of these courtly flirtations while I use my ears, eyes, and if necessary, my brawn and…' He turned his gaze to Marguerite. 'Keep a watchful eye on everything.'

Savaric did not know why it was so imperative that he was the one to be at court with Marguerite, only that it was. In truth, he should welcome this new arrangement that de Burgh proposed and put as much distance as he could between himself and the exasperating woman, but somehow it did not sit right with him. He needed to be the one to be there, just in case Marguerite had need of him.

'If I may, my lord, but I really do not think we need change your arrangements as they are. They make perfect sense to me.'

Of course, the woman might have other ideas about it.

'Do they?'

'Indeed, and I really do not think that it would be necessary to alter anything, my lord.' She smiled benignly as she addressed de Burgh.

'And if I may, my lord, I would say that while Mistress Marguerite is knowledgeable about the intricacies and customs of the French Court, she does not know the same regarding the English one. It has, after all, been a long time since she has been here.'

'Not that long, surely.' Her smile was unwavering, her response immediate. 'And besides, I would imagine that Sir Nicholas, as someone who is well versed in such intricacies, might be better suited to making me more accustomed to the English Court.'

She was certainly doggedly persistent about not having him anywhere near her at court. 'If I may, my lord…'

'This is highly entertaining,' Nicholas whispered to Warin. 'Who do you put your money on?'

'It is fair match here, but for loyalty's sake, mayhap Fitz Leonard?'

'That is where I am torn, as my loyalty extends to both,' he said on a cough.

'True, it is difficult to call,' Warin muttered quietly.

'*If* I may, my lord.' Savaric fixed both of his friends a quelling glare before continuing. 'I would also add that D'Amberly is well known at court.'

'True, I am…' Nicholas grinned, nodding.

'As I was saying, he is well known at court and so would rouse suspicion at being at the side of a woman who is not his wife and unrelated to him.'

'Ah, well done there, Savaric.'

'A point well made.'

God, but he was going to kill Nicholas and Warin.

Hubert de Burgh looked from Savaric to Marguerite and sighed. 'You are both as bad as my dear wife and I, when we have one of our rare marital differences.'

Savaric noticed Marguerite glance away, her colour rising.

'However, after considering both opinions here, I would say that although he has presented his case in rather a churlish manner, Fitz Leonard does make a good point, my dear. You would be better served with a man who is not too well known at court, and who is also unmarried.'

'Yes, of course, my lord.' Marguerite dropped to an elegant curtsy. 'As you wish. And if there is nothing further to discuss, I would take my leave.' With that she turned on her heel, her skirt flapping behind her as she left the chamber.

God's bones...

Marguerite continued to stride down the long hallway, cursing an oath under her breath. It made little sense after everything she had discussed with Savaric that he would then insist on being the one to accompany her to Dover with the English Court. Something she knew he hated. Surely he comprehended that once again they would be forced within each other's company. And unnecessarily so, when there were other feasible alternatives. The man would once again be a distraction—one that she could not afford, with so much at stake.

'Marguerite?' She heard his low voice reverberating around the stone walls as he called her name. 'Marguerite, wait. One moment if you please.'

God, but would he just leave her alone? For only a moment, to settle herself and restore her civility.

'Marguerite?' His voice was closer, his long legs making quick work to catch up to her.

She picked up her pace without actually breaking into a run. 'Can it not wait on the morrow, Savaric?'

'I shall not take up much of your time, mistress, and would rather say my piece now, if you please.'

She turned around and started back towards the man. 'No, Savaric, it would not please me at all!'

He caught up with her and stilled her. 'What in blazes is the matter with you?'

'Why would you intervene? Why alter the arrangements that de Burgh had made? Which seemed perfectly fine to me, by the by.'

'Because I believed that there was a flaw to it.' Must his answer seem so reasonable?

She sighed her annoyance through her teeth. 'I would have thought you would have welcomed not having to be my watchman. I would have thought after…well, after last night, it might have been prudent to agree to de Burgh's scheme.'

'What happened last night had nothing to do with it. I want to be assured of your safety.'

'Why? Why do you care?' She lifted her head and searched his eyes, wishing instantly that she hadn't. There was a quick flash of emotion there before it was masked over.

But she did note the small shaky breath. 'Do you really need to ask me that?'

Yes…no. I do not know…

She decided to ignore his question. 'I do not comprehend you.'

'Can you not see what we both stand to lose otherwise? I said before and I shall do so again—you and I work well together and make rather good associates, Marguerite. In truth, we need one another. We also need our wits, with the machinations of court around us.' He took a deep breath into his chest. 'And I believe that we can resist this mutual attraction between us, until we see this mission through, and then part ways.' She looked away, shaking her head. 'My hope is that this time we can even part amicably.'

'Amicably?' she repeated.

'Yes.' He nodded. 'As friends.'

Friends…? The notion seemed highly improbable. She rubbed her brow. 'I see.'

'Last night came about after the trail we were following halted, when we were both upset and fraught. But it was, as you say, a mistake, one that I doubt either of us will make again.'

'You seem very sure of yourself.'

And of me, she wanted to add.

Marguerite despised her weakness in regard to this man. She hated the unwanted attraction—nay, desire—she felt for Savaric.

'I admit that it is going to be difficult, Marguerite, but…' He tipped his finger beneath her chin and lifted her gaze to meet his, serious and brooding all at once. 'We have to put all our attention into the task at hand. It is what is required of me, of you… of all of us. We have to play our part at court.'

Yes, Savaric was right. The success of this mission was what mattered beyond all else. It always had. Indeed, Marguerite would do all in her power to bring it about. For one wrong step would spell imminent disaster. Besides, what else was there between Savaric and herself other than this unexpected redundant attraction anyway? Very little. And she would be wise to remember that it would always amount to that and nothing more.

'Very well. I shall play my part, as you play yours.'
She took a step back and inclined her head. 'Now if you
will excuse me, Savaric, I have much to prepare.'

Chapter Ten

It had not been difficult establishing herself back among the Dowager Queen and her ladies. Not nearly as difficult as being aware of Savaric Fitz Leonard's constant presence. Even when he was not in attendance, Marguerite could somehow *feel* him there. Whether he was actually there or not in person hardly signified. And between that and having to fend off the obsequious yet effusively boorish Lord Richard de Vars—he of the stagnant breath and the irritating habit of touching her as though it was within his right and however innocently—well, Marguerite had much to contend with. As well as being the prerequisite ears and eyes at court that de Burgh expected her to be.

Hubert de Burgh had been correct on the plans at court. As usual, he knew before any other courtier the arrangements that had been made for the tour. But then de Burgh was the most powerful man aside from the King, meaning he was also the most esteemed and the most hated man in equal measure. Indeed he had many enemies, especially in the heart of the court itself.

It had been decided that they would travel on a pilgrimage to Canterbury and then move to Dover, at the behest of the Dowager Queen. King Henry was happy to submit to his mother's requests, insisting that they all retire to Dover and give her a jubilant send-off. It amazed Marguerite that even with such a mother, who had aligned herself with France and married without royal consent, the King was still so willing to be courteous and forgiving. He was indeed everything a dutiful son could be—albeit a royal one.

With the preparations for their tour underway, Marguerite had much to occupy her and within a week it was time to say her farewells to Eva and Nicholas. God, but she hoped that the next time they all met again, *this* would all be over. All of it…

They travelled in a comfortable convoy, on large wagons with a procession of knights and the King's guards on horseback, making their way outside the environs of London and continued to make steady progress south.

Marguerite travelled on the same plush wagon that was conveying the Dowager Queen and her Four Precious A's on the journey. And while she had kept her ears and eyes open to anything that might be deemed suspicious, she had not encountered anything yet, only gaining a slight headache from the women's prattle instead.

Soon, the sunlight faded, and the men pitched huge elaborate tents to stay overnight before continuing on the journey the following morn at the break of dawn. One long day of travelling melted into the next, with their entourage entering the city walls of Canterbury on the fourth day.

They offered prayer and thanks at the newly built shrine of the martyred saint Thomas à Becket, in Canterbury Cathedral, for many long hours, and after mass, Marguerite found herself strolling through the cathedral's beautiful arched cloisters with the gardens in the centre of quads. She walked alongside Lord Richard de Vars and the Dowager Queen's Four Precious A's and spoke in hushed tones as she took in the heady scents of the flora that carried from the gardens in the quads. Her heels clipped on the stone pathway as they turned a corner and happened upon Savaric, who inclined his head as he approached them.

She had not met with him for the past few days, only catching a few glimpses of him sat on his magnificent destrier in all his knightly splendour, and topped with his signature wide-brimmed hat. Marguerite had to admit that it was somewhat comforting knowing he was here on this journey with her. In truth she was glad he had insisted on his accompanying her. Not that she would ever admit such a thing to him.

'Good day to you, Sir Savaric,' Anais de Montluc murmured as she fluttered her eyelashes.

'And a good day to you, Lady Anais, and to you, Lady Agnes, Lady Ann, Lady Alice, Lord de Vars, and of course Mistress Marguerite.' Savaric made a perfunctory bow as he took off his hat. 'I hope you are all keeping well?'

'Very well, now that we have happened upon you, sir.' The annoying woman giggled. She actually giggled at him when there was nothing of note to giggle about.

'And we always seem to encounter you in every manner of a garden.'

'That you do.' Savaric chuckled. 'As I mentioned the last time I had the pleasure of your company, my lady, I adore nature's bounty, as I am sure you do. And solitary contemplations are, I have been told, good for the soul. They are considered to be quite cleansing,' he added as he addressed the last part of his speech to Richard de Vars.

Why in God's name was Savaric intentionally antagonising the man? Was it that he hoped he might break through his façade so that the man might reveal himself?

'Yes, well, there are those whose souls would certainly need to be cleansed more than others.' Richard de Vars lips curved into a sneer, contorting his features.

Savaric raised a brow. 'You may have the right of it, my lord. Only one can never be too certain whose soul is so damned as to need *that*.'

'Indeed, but then there are others who have a better judgement on such matters than me. I am but a humble courtier.'

Savaric inclined his head. 'As I am but a humble knight, serving King and country.'

'And your fealty to your liege, Hubert de Burgh, of course.'

'Of course. But then we all do my lord, do you not think?'

Richard de Vars made a single nod before addressing Lady Anais Montluc, turning his back on Savaric, who looked a little pleased with himself.

Marguerite smiled inwardly at Savaric, who was

doing an excellent job of provoking the man, even though it might be considered a little reckless given the stature of a man such as de Vars. Indeed, Savaric was practically inviting the man to dislike and dismiss him in equal measure. Nevertheless, the approach did seem to have some merit. She would give him that.

It did manage to gain a reaction from Richard de Vars, and reveal the man's contempt for Hubert de Burgh, however much he tried to conceal it. No, Richard de Vars might be many things, but he was not very good at concealment. Which in itself was very interesting... For this man to be involved with Duo Dracone, he would surely need to be much better with skills such at concealment and deception, would he not?

Marguerite kept her mouth firmly shut and made certain that her face was as impassive as she could make it, showing little interest in Savaric or what was now transpiring between him and the ladies in waiting tittering beside him. No, she did not want to give the impression that they were acquainted beyond the last time they had all met at the pleasure gardens in the Palace of Westminster. Nor did she want Richard de Vars or even the Dowager Queen's ladies believing them more familiar with one another than they actually were. So, she adopted a bored, nonchalant stance, giving off a far haughtier demeanour, similar to one she'd seen on the Dowager Queen's ladies. Not that any of the women looked bored now.

'It is nevertheless good to see you on this pilgrimage and on this tour to Dover, Sir Savaric.' Anais Montluc beamed up at him, clearly uninterested in what de Vars was expostulating.

Savaric bowed his head. 'I must admit that I am privileged and honoured. Indeed, it is my first time here at this magnificent cathedral and I'm truly awed by its grandeur. And, of course, its wonderful gardens.'

She chuckled. 'It seems that you really are an admirer of gardens. Oh, forgive me, I meant "nature's bounty".'

Savaric smiled slowly and far too wickedly at the woman, recalling that nonsense he had spouted the last time they had all met. 'Quite. There are many things that I admire which could also be considered…bountiful.'

Oh, God, this flirtatious exchange between Savaric and the aggravating Anais de Montluc was as disconcerting as it was irksome. And while Marguerite knew that Savaric was simply playing his part, she was still somewhat vexed by it. Not that Marguerite had any right to be. She had no claims on the man at all, just as she had no right to succumb to a bout of jealousy.

'You are quiet, mistress,' Richard de Vars said, turning his attentions to Marguerite. 'I hope nothing is troubling you?'

'No, no.' She shook her head and smiled up at him. 'I was only pondering whether we might resume our promenade, my lord.'

'Mayhap you might wish to join us, Sir Savaric?' Anais giggled again. God, how Marguerite hated that irritating sound.

'I think on this occasion, I shall leave you to your walk. But allow me to say what a pleasure it has been to see you once again.'

'I hope we shall see more of you, sir,' Anais murmured before smiling coquettishly at Savaric.

'I am certain you shall, my lady.' He took off his hat and bowed once more.

They all took their leave, as Marguerite made sure not to glance in Savaric's direction. Not even once as they parted ways.

By nightfall, the large convoy made camp within the city walls on the royal demesne lands before they would embark on the last stage of their journey the following morn.

Marguerite sighed and continued to walk along the pathway outside the city walls, needing to clear her head with a little quiet and solitude after the past few days of constant chatter, not to mention her encounter with Savaric in the cloisters earlier.

There was yet another reason why she had sought refuge outside the city gates and needed time on her own. Marguerite needed to get away from Richard de Vars, who had made it his purpose to seek her at every turn and was beginning to prove himself to be a nuisance, especially after she had favoured him with a little attention. She would have happily dispatched the man far away but had to endure his presence in case he proved to be somehow involved with The Duo Dracones conspirators. But after today, Marguerite was beginning to doubt whether the man had anything to do with them. Not that they could rule him out just yet.

She inhaled deeply, taking in the cool night air. It was a beautiful eventide, with a full moon providing a silvery shimmer of light and a profusion of stars scattered in the cloudless inky sky. Marguerite had dropped to the damp ground and stretched her legs out in front of her when something caught her interest. There in the distance was someone with a dark cloak covering their head, a figure who moved with stealth and swiftness as they made their way towards the nearby woods.

Odd but it was skirts flapping at their feet, suggesting that the figure was a woman? Marguerite had moved between the branches trying to ascertain this when the figure stopped and looked behind them, with the long cloak they wore swaying in the light breeze. Yes, the figure was indeed a woman. How very strange…

The maid kept on looking over her shoulders as she hurried along in haste. Why in heavens would anyone, least of all a lone woman, travel outside the city walls and head to the woods at this time in the night? God only knew but Marguerite was determined to find out. She moved adjacent to the edge of the woods a distance away from the woman, weaving her way through the coppices and tall canopy of trees that thankfully hid her form, creeping closer and closer to her.

The woman stopped a short distance away from Marguerite, who was shielded behind a great oak, evidently waiting for someone. Slowly the woman removed the hood of her cloak and turned her head in both directions, presumably searching for whomever she had come to meet.

It was Anais de Montluc—one of the Four Precious A's. What in heaven's name was she doing here at this time? Could she be about to meet someone for an assignation? If so, why in such a furtive manner? Oh, God, was it Savaric? Could the blasted man be taking things so far with her to find out more information?

Marguerite's stomach plummeted at the thought. *Please let it not be so…*

Yet as the young woman made her way deeper into the woods, Marguerite noted something a little different in Anais de Montluc's movements. Indeed, the maid had always given the impression of being a simpering, silly maid, not to mention an incorrigible flirt. Yet there was something very different about her this eventide. She could not say what it was but Marguerite would hardly have recognised Anais or believed it was the same woman whose company she had been in all this time.

It was in the manner in which she moved, a sharp alertness, and the intensity of her gaze. In truth, she had dismissed Anais de Montluc as vapid and nonsensical. But could the maid have been feigning it? There was only one way to discover more. Marguerite would have to get a little closer to her and be the ears and eyes that she was required to be.

Marguerite crept further around to hide behind a tall bushel, which concealed her but still allowed her a better view of where Anais now stood. She lingered for a long moment, waiting for something, anything, to happen, dampening down her excitement, but nothing stirred. This could be it—this could be the moment Marguerite had been patiently waiting for all this time. A happenstance on this night that might somehow enlighten her to the questions she had been seeking for so long.

Anais de Montluc stood resolutely in the same spot, glancing around, seemingly waiting for someone to arrive. The breeze whistled through the branches of the canopy of trees, making the leaves rustle and dance in the night sky. Marguerite shivered as she hugged her woollen cloak around herself a little tighter. And then, just when she wondered whether her excitement had been misplaced, a tall cloaked man pulled a branch aside, allowing him to pass from the opposite side of the woods, and skulked towards Anais. She stood with her spine straight as the man approached her, while Marguerite watched on in anticipation.

'Ma femme immaculée, je vis pour server,' the man muttered reverently, before dropping to the ground and kneeling in front of Anais. 'I hope you have not been waiting long?'

Good Lord, Anais de Montluc was…was *la femme immaculée.* The woman whose name was whispered on the lips of Ned Lutt before he died. The woman who the young apprentice had implied would not only be queen some day but that she was the traitor who had been working with The Duo Dracones. Marguerite steadied her breathing, watching the scene more closely, as the man knelt at the woman's feet and bowed over her outstretched hand.

'Never mind that. It is of no consequence,' Anais said in a voice that was hard and steely and not at all like her usual one. 'Hold out your hand. Here, take it. You know what to do with it.'

She proffered what looked like a brown leather pouch, which the man duly took, bowing and lowering his head. 'My thanks, my lady. This will aid our cause against the enemy.'

'It shall, it will.' Anais then muttered an oath or a recitation that Marguerite had difficulty comprehending.

Who was the man? His stature and his low voice seemed a little familiar. Could it be the captain of the vessel whom she had followed from Paris to London, or a far more frightening prospect? Her hand unwittingly wrapped around her neck as she remembered the permanent scar and the man who had inflicted it there. Could he be... Renaisser? No, she could not allow him to invade her mind. Not when Marguerite needed her wits about her.

She took a step cautiously towards them, and then another, in the hope that she might learn more, while still concealed behind the coppice.

Crack...

The inadvertent sound of a twig breaking came from under her own feet.

Marguerite's pulse skittered as she held her breath, willing that they had not heard it.

Unfortunately, she was not so lucky.

'What was that?' Anais looked around before fixing her glare on the man knelt in front of her. 'I hope you were not followed here?'

'No, my lady.' The man stood back up and drew out his sword. 'But I shall investigate. Over there.'

Hell and damnation...

Marguerite quickly took a step backwards and then another before colliding with a wall. Her mind reeled in confusion as a sudden realisation hit her. There was no wall behind her. Before she knew what was happening an arm wrapped around her waist from behind, and a large male hand clamped down over her mouth tightly.

Oh, God...oh, God! Panic gripped Marguerite as she remembered the last time someone had come up behind her and snatched her in a similar manner. Her heart felt like it was in her mouth and her body was rigid with fear.

She was frozen, unable to move, unable to breathe. Marguerite thought she might actually swoon as she recalled that terrible moment from two years ago, when her assailant threatened her with a dagger to her throat. She could feel it again now—that sharp blade pressing deeper and deeper against her throat, that trickle of red dripping down her neck as the dagger cut into her. And that moment when everything stilled—when she believed her life was about to end at the hands of Renaisser. It did not happen, thank God, but nothing took that memory away.

Indeed, what happened to her two years ago had been so harrowing that it had stayed with her and moulded her into the woman she now was.

Even when she had seen Renaisser in deep discussion with the captain of the cog ship in Paris only a few weeks ago, the same feelings of helplessness had overwhelmed her. She had frozen, frightened with her heart hammering in her chest as the past had flashed across her eyes.

Could it be the bastard who had come to meet with Anais de Montluc? Could it be that it was he who had grabbed her again? Marguerite sent a silent prayer hoping that she was wrong. But either way she was not going to wait and find out. She might be frightened by the possibility that Renaisser might once again hurt her, but this time she would fight him. She could not allow this fear of the man suffocate and weaken her resolve. Not any longer. This was yet another reason why Marguerite had been working tirelessly for the Crown—to be able to prove to herself that she could fight the demons that had taken hold of her two years ago. To prove that she could defend herself and not be beholden to others by somehow slaying those demons herself.

Marguerite had to think quickly and remembered that she had a dagger strapped to her waist. She wriggled her fingers down trying to reach for it just as she was lifted up and carried from behind. She dragged her feet, kicking out, trying to stall whoever had hold of her.

'Stop it…' a voice whispered low in her ear from behind. 'Stop fighting me.'

Savaric?

Thank the Lord, but it *was* Savaric. The relief she felt was so palpable that she wanted to cry. God, what was wrong with her. Marguerite knew how to defend herself, skilled as she was with a dagger. And yet her fear of Renaisser was still strong enough to bring her to her knees. He still managed to reduce her to this weakness. One day she would overcome these fears, one day, she promised herself.

Marguerite's shoulders slumped as Savaric strode deeper into the woods before bringing her around, carrying her to the entrance of the city wall.

'You seem to know your way around those woods and Canterbury quite well. I thought you said you had never been here?' she mumbled, a little dazed at how quickly they were back to the city's gatehouse.

'I lied, Marguerite. And I have done quite a bit of that today.'

For a large man he was incredibly nimble and light on his feet and was far more careful about being heard than she had been. But then he was first and foremost a soldier and a warrior, more used to deploying the stealth and agility that would be needed in combat and in perilous moments such as this. Yet he carried her so gently, as though she weighed no more than a grain-filled hopsack—a precious one at that.

Savaric then stopped, dropped her to her feet, and walked her backwards until her back was touching the stone wall behind her, so they could be hidden beneath the shadow of the gatehouse. He leant forward and tugged her hood over her head, without uttering a word. Marguerite blinked in surprise as he pulled her close into a tight embrace, holding her so that his tall powerful build could further shield her from view of guards manning the stone gatehouse and anyone else who might happen upon them.

She knew that words were needed at this moment. If Savaric had not used his quick wits, and even quicker actions, she may well have been discovered by Anais and the man she had met.

'Thank you.' She tipped her head up, meeting Savaric's unfathomable gaze. 'I do not know what would have become of me if you had not…'

Marguerite swallowed down the remainder of her words as Savaric bent his head and covered her mouth with his. He growled low, kissing her deeply, much to her astonishment. What in heaven's name was he doing at such a time? Even now Anais de Montluc could be on their trail returning from her rendezvous. They needed to move now. They needed to go back through the city gates and hope that they were not missed.

And yet Marguerite was helpless to stop him from devouring her mouth hungrily, not that she actually wanted him to stop. Instead, she went on her tiptoes and kissed him back with the same fervour, the same passion that he ignited in her. It was a kiss that was vastly different from any that they'd shared before.

Her whole body came alive, with the touch of his fingers grazing up and down her spine and then settling on either side of her hips, pulling her even closer, her breasts pressed against the hardness of his chest. Marguerite reached up, her hands brushing across the wide expanse of his shoulders, her fingers curling around the base of his neck, holding on to him, in case her knees buckled.

God, but that just might happen...

Her blood heated through her veins, rushing across her body and down to her toes. And unlike the kiss on the skiff where Savaric had refrained from touching her and was so controlled in every manner, this one was wild, intense, and oh so demanding.

He softened the kiss as he drew one hand towards the back of her head, holding her firmly but gently to him.

'Keep still,' he whispered against her lips before kissing her again, pulling her hood firmly over her head.

It was then that Marguerite heard it...the muffled sound of footsteps drawing nearer. She tried to pull away but Savaric kept a firm hold of her, giving his head a little shake.

He enveloped her even more within the folds of his cloak, so that she was completely concealed from view, before he began to sway, moving her with him. He began to whistle and sing a bawdy ditty intermittently between pressing kisses to her lips, face, neck and was doing everything that he could to give the impression that they are having an assignation.

'Sir Savaric?'

Marguerite stiffened in his arms as they heard Anais de Montluc behind them. But once more, Savaric held her against him, as Marguerite dipped her head and pressed herself even closer against his chest.

'Sir Savaric, is that you?'

'Ah, the fairest of the incomparable Precious A's, Lady Anais.' Savaric slurred his words and swayed a little more, over Marguerite's head, giving the woman an inane grin. 'I find that I am not in a fit shtate to be in your eshteemed company.'

'I can see that, sir,' Anais muttered in a clipped tone.

'And I can see that I have offended your sensibilities, my lady. Pleashe…pleashe accept my apologies and avert your eyes.' He chuckled softly, swaying his head. He truly was a marvel at acting the inebriated drunkard fool.

'Not in the least, I do understand that…that men have certain needs.'

'Indeed, but you should not be here alone, my lady. Pray what brings you outshide here?'

'Not a thing, sir. I find that I took the wrong turn and found myself outside the city walls.' Anais had resumed her usual persona of a giggling, empty-headed maid.

'Then allow me to eshcort you back,' he mumbled. 'I can send this doxy on her way with a silver or two between her teeth and she'll be happy for it—won't you, sweetheart?' Savaric slapped her backside and laughed.

Marguerite wondered whether Anais du Montluc's face had flushed as much as hers with Savaric's lewd behaviour.

'That is very…er…good of you, but there is no need.

Good evening, sir.' Anais could not seem to get away quickly enough.

'And a verra, verra good evening to you, my lady,' he bellowed after her before dipping his head, and resuming to sing a tawdry line or two loudly between pressing more kisses on her face.

Marguerite listened for a long moment at Anais de Montluc's retreating footsteps as the woman walked back inside the gatehouse and into the city. Once certain that Anais was no longer nearby, Marguerite threw her head back, exhaling a deep sigh of relief. That had been a very close thing.

'Doxy?' She chuckled softly.

'It was the first thing I could think of.'

'And I am glad for it, thank you. Anais has gone.' She sighed deeply. 'Well done for thinking so quickly.'

'*That* is my job, mistress.' Savaric straightened, pulling away and releasing her swiftly, dropping his hands to his sides. He took a deep breath in, and looked away for a moment, his hands on his hips, before turning back around. Oh, dear, the man did not seem very pleased.

'And a job well done,' she added quickly, hoping to dispel the tension. 'Even I was taken in and believed that you were a drunkard wastrel.'

'That is because it was a performance, Marguerite, nothing more,' he said in a clipped tone. 'All of it. And one that I would not have had to do, had you not behaved so recklessly.'

Marguerite knew the truth of what the man was saying, had known all along, yet it still stung that even the kiss they shared had all been a pretence. That it was *nothing more*. She also knew that her longing for Savaric was something she had to overcome. Marguerite opened her mouth to respond but no words came out.

Savaric spoke for her. 'Now, would you care to tell me what in God's name you think you were doing?' He glared at her.

Chapter Eleven

Savaric tamped down his frustration at the small maddening woman in front of him. 'Well? Care to explain?'

'Explain?' She looked up at him innocently. 'I am not certain I comprehend you.'

'Allow *me* then, Marguerite,' he ground out between clenched teeth. 'You nearly got yourself captured at best in those woods, or killed at worst!'

She waved her hand dismissively. 'I think not. And thanks to you, I managed to avoid such a fate.'

His nostrils flared at her flippant remark. 'And what if I had not reached you in time? What if whoever that man was got to you first? Have you considered what your fate might have been then?'

'I believe you are familiar with the skills I possess with a dagger.'

She lifted her head in that proud, defiant manner, challenging him to refute the statement when all he wanted to do was cover her mouth with his to stop her from chattering this nonsense. Did she not understand how scared he had been for her safety? Did she not appreciate that it could have ended in disaster, as it once nearly had? He shuddered, looking down at the woman and in particular those swollen lips of hers. Damn but he should not have kissed Marguerite.

'Well, are you not?' she murmured.

Savaric had realised that he had to get Marguerite away from Anais de Montluc and her accomplice or else be discovered. So he had carried the aggravating woman, running as fast as he could in woods that he was very familiar with and forming a scheme, which he devised the moment they reached the gatehouse into the city.

Yet he should have refrained from kissing Marguerite. That had not been part of his plan. How many times did he need to make the same mistake over and over again? The woman had him tied in knots, his head reeling.

'I am, yes. But that is not the point, as you well know, Marguerite.'

'You are making far too much of it, Savaric.'

'I assure you I am not.' He dragged his fingers through his hair irritably. 'What in the world possessed you to throw caution to the wind and follow that woman on your own? It could have led you to an unforeseen situation and put you in unnecessary danger. In truth, it very nearly did.'

'Just as *you* did, if I remember correctly, when you found yourself in an alley by the docks. Or have you conveniently forgotten that?'

'That was entirely different.' He glared at her.

'Of course, it was.'

'Indeed. And after getting over the shock of seeing *you* there that night, I decided to turn back and get you.'

'How considerate of you. But as you later found out, quite an unnecessary act. I can look after myself, Savaric. I have been doing so for the past two years.'

'That might be so,' he muttered through gritted teeth. 'But you were not doing so tonight. I spotted you in the distance and decided to follow you. Not only had you not noticed me coming upon you but you stood motionless, as if you had turned to ice.'

'You have already mentioned that.'

'Have I? How careless of me. I had intended to remind you at least another half a dozen times, mistress.'

Marguerite bristled. 'Have you quite finished scolding me?'

'God's breath, woman, but you need to start trusting me. You need to start telling me of your plans before you march headfirst into danger.' He closed his eyes tightly and rubbed his forehead.

'I do trust you,' she whispered, her shoulders sagging in resignation. 'I do. But we have more pressing matters to discuss, Savaric.'

True, they did. For as much as he was scared for Marguerite's safety, he had to admit that she had unravelled something on this night. The woman certainly had courage as well as tenacity. And he could not help but admire her for that.

Savaric signalled for them to move away from the gatehouse and somewhere a little quieter so that they would not be overheard.

'Tell me exactly what Anais de Montluc said as my

focus was on you and getting you far away before her accomplice found you.'

She snapped her head up. 'Then you did not hear their discourse?'

'No, I did not.'

'Oh, Lord. The events that unfolded in those woods were far more significant than I could ever have imagined,' she said excitedly. 'She is one of them, Savaric. Anais de Montluc is either a member of or is closely associated with The Duo Dracones.'

'Lady Anais de Montluc?' He muttered an oath under his breath. 'How can you be so certain?'

'Apart from the woman being so different in manner to the one she usually presents, her accomplice whom she met in the woods referred to her as *la femme immaculée*.'

'He called the maid that?' Savaric's eyes widened in shock. 'You distinctly heard him utter those very words—that name?'

'Yes.'

'Dear God, then that must mean…'

She nodded. 'That Lady Anais de Montluc is the one the young apprentice was referring to.'

'The implications of this are huge.' He grabbed her by the shoulders and smiled. 'Because if Anais de Montluc is *la femme immaculée*, then she is also the one who aspires to be consort to Henry, and Queen of England one day.'

'Yes, precisely.'

'Did you hear anything else?' he asked urgently.

Marguerite nodded. 'I watched as Anais gave the

man a leather pouch, filled with what I assume to be clippings of silver coin.'

'So based on what we now know, it must have been Anais de Montluc who misplaced the silver clipping that was found in the garden at the Palace of Westminster.'

'So it would seem.'

He shook his head in disbelief. 'By God, Marguerite, we are finally getting somewhere, and it is all because of you!'

'And you. I could not have done any of this without your help, Savaric.'

'I did say that we worked well together.'

'Yes.' She dropped her gaze. 'So, what now? We need far more irrefutable proof of her involvement.'

'And we shall get it. We must continue to watch everything she does and everything she says, without letting on that we are aware of our suspicions.'

'Yes, agreed.'

He frowned. 'Did you by any chance see the man she was meeting?'

'Not clearly.' She shook her head. 'Although…although I had initially thought him to be a member of The Duo Dracones.'

'Did you happen to see his face?'

'No, I saw the exchange with the pouch as the man knelt in front of Anais. And I heard a litany of words that she chanted under her breath. It was like a strange incantation, unlike anything I had ever heard before.'

Interesting…a muttering of some strange recitation was fitting with everything they had known about The Duo Dracones.

'God's bones, but Lady Anais de Montluc.' He shook his head.

Marguerite worried her bottom lip. 'I would never have believed it myself, until I saw her. It was odd, Savaric. It was as though I was observing a different person altogether. Her manner, the way she spoke, and even the way she moved were all so different to how she usually presents herself.'

'Mayhap what you saw in the woods is the real woman behind the mask of the flirty, simpering maid.'

She nodded. 'Yes, I believe so too.'

'And *la femme immaculée*, who is by virtue an immaculate woman and refers to someone who is typically pure, seems like another adopted name within The Duo Dracones.'

'In that they defer to their rank and position within the organisation?'

'Indeed. So far there has been *agneau*, or lamb, given to members who are dispensable.' He grimaced. 'Such as Ned Lutt and others like him.'

She nodded. 'Then there's…there's Renaisser, whom we know to be high up in their organisation. And now the immaculate lady, who I would also assume is upper ranks just by having such a name bestowed on her.'

'Yes.' He flashed her a brief smile. 'Hubert de Burgh will need to be informed of these findings, as well as the rest of the Knights Fortitude.'

'Will we apprehend Anais de Montluc for further questioning?'

He frowned, shaking his head. 'No, I believe de Burgh will want to proceed with due care and caution. He will not want any mishaps, unlike the times before,

when members of The Duo Dracones who were appre-
hended fell on their sword before being interrogated.'

'That is good reasoning.'

'Besides, he will want us to watch and follow her in
the hope that she might lead us to other members of The
Duo Dracones. And he will also want to know, before
apprehending her, whether there are others at court who
are involved.' He lifted his head and frowned, pondering on another matter. 'Do you believe that you might
be able to recognise the man you saw conferring with
Anais de Montluc?'

Her throat worked as she swallowed. 'Yes, I think
so. Not that I saw his face.'

'Could it have been de Vars?'

Marguerite shook her head. 'As much as I know you
would dearly wish for that, he was not Lord Richard
de Vars. Of that I can be sure. Although de Vars might
still prove to be a traitor and still a member of The Duo
Dracones.'

'The man is a pompous ass, Marguerite, but all I
am interested in is the truth and catching the bastards
once and for all.'

'As am I.'

'Yet you believe the man who met Lady Anais in
the woods to be someone you might have encountered
before?'

'I… I thought that the man might possibly have
been… Renaisser.'

Damn…

Now he could comprehend the reason Marguerite
stood so still, as though she had seen an apparition.
Savaric did not miss the way her throat worked as she

swallowed uncomfortably. It made him uneasy, contemplating that the bastard who had had hurt her two years ago might have had the opportunity to do so again— if, indeed, the man in the woods had been him. God, it did not bear thinking about. It was hard to consider that she had seen Renaisser in Paris recently, let alone this.

'Are you certain, Marguerite?' He tried to steady his voice in order to hide the concern creeping in.

'Yes. No.' She shook her head. 'I cannot be sure, either way,' she muttered, her body visibly trembling. 'I thought that mayhap it might have been him because of his…his stature and even his voice. But it might have been my imagining.'

Christ…

He rubbed his hands up and down her shoulders and arms as she exhaled a shaky breath.

'I want you to know this, Marguerite. I want you to know that I would rather die a thousand deaths than allow that bastard to hurt you again,' he said in a low quiet voice.

She nodded. 'I know and I appreciate your concern. But I must face this myself. I must face him.'

Alone. She had not said the word, but it was implied nevertheless.

'Must you? Why?' he sighed as he bent his head and pressed his forehead to hers. 'You do not have to face him, as you say. Not on your own. I will be beside you, Marguerite, whenever you need me. Always, Marguerite. Never forget that.'

'Thank you,' she said on a soft whisper as he reached out and wiped away a rogue teardrop that had fallen onto her cheek.

'You do need to rely on me, sweetheart.' He murmured gently. 'I know… Indeed I realise that I have not always served that purpose. And for that I apologise. But in this, at least let me help. Let me be the one who you can turn to.'

Marguerite stepped back, looked away, and wiped her face before turning to face him, as if nothing had happened. Once again, she was as impassive and reticent as ever, as though she had not just shown him her vulnerable side. But what she did not appreciate was that her feelings were both understandable and remissible. Every man, woman or child had fears and obstacles beyond their control that they had to conquer. And there was nothing weak about acknowledging or wanting to overcome them.

'Thank you, but there is no need.'

The stoic manner in which she looked so lost and alone as she wrapped her arms around herself made him want to pull her back into his arms again and never let her go. Which of course Marguerite Studdal would never welcome.

'I know I give you no reason to truly trust me. I know I have made so many mistakes in the past, but promise me that you will try, Marguerite. Promise me that you will try and accept that you are not alone,' he whispered, tilting her head up with a finger beneath her chin. 'We can do this together. Remember I once told you to fetch me when you need me. I will come to you. Any time, day or night. You have me…'

She nodded and opened her mouth to say something but closed it instead. Savaric knew the moment her eyes filled with something akin to longing that he had made a mistake. Had he even understood what he had just said in his garbled, asinine manner? Either way he needed to make himself clear.

Savaric cleared his throat and dropped his arms by his sides. 'So, the next time you wish to follow someone you will send for me? And for the love of everything that is holy, you will not do it alone.'

His words seemed to jolt Marguerite out from her dazed fervour.

'Yes.' She blinked and whatever emotion had been there in those lovely blue eyes of hers was starting to fade. 'Yes, you are right of course. But it is not easy for someone like me to trust another completely when I have only had myself to rely on.'

Savaric closed his eyes, knowing the truth of those words. 'I can imagine that these past two years have not been easy?'

It was a question that he had plagued him since the moment he had found out about Marguerite not only working for de Burgh and the Crown but also that she had done so alone and in a foreign land. What must it have been like for a young woman like Marguerite, who had been striving to gain justice for her family honour and for her young brother?

'No, it was not.'

'Yet you were resilient and steadfast, Marguerite, both of which are admirable qualities.'

She shrugged. 'All I knew was that I needed to continue with what was expected of me and do my duty by Hubert de Burgh.'

'Which you have done admirably.'

'It is not done yet.'

'No, but with the grace of God, it will be. Soon.' He reached and removed a stray leaf from her shoulder. 'And what of your life in Paris? How did you find the French Court?'

'Difficult, relentless…lonely,' she muttered, frowning. 'Having to be careful with what I said and how I behaved around maids such as Anais de Montluc was difficult. As well as constantly having to be someone I was not. That was tiresome. So, yes, mostly lonely. I had forgotten what it was to be *me* again.'

This was a sentiment that he could wholly relate to, the relentlessness of it all. And the loneliness. But unlike Savaric with his Knights Fortitude brethren, Marguerite had had no one, not while she lived in another kingdom. It seemed like a miserable existence.

'I am sorry for it.' He reached for her hand and laced his fingers through hers. 'And wish that matters could have been different.'

'It was not all bad to own the truth but it was never easy. Not for me. And yet, it was the only way for me to prove myself to de Burgh, in the hope that I would gain everything that I needed to.'

His chest clenched knowing that however much she tried to make light of it all, Marguerite had been forced into a situation that was not of her making. One that she was doing everything she could to readdress now. But it should never have come to this. It should never have been this young maid who had to be the one to reclaim her ancestral lands or gain the pardon for treason for her father that she so longed for. It should have been someone else.

'My father, as you know, had been wrongly accused

of conspiring against the Crown, Savaric. And with many false allegations and damning evidence presented against him by a clever, vociferous man, who had paid for and gained support from my father's own men— well, his fate had sadly been decided. It mattered very little how many times we, along with his vassals and other defendants, pleaded my father's innocence, he was still tried for treason and hanged. There was no one, save me and my brother, Godfrey, who was too young and of a sickly disposition. And well, the King's bench was hardly going to listen to the two of us.'

She sighed before continuing. 'I can be thankful of one thing, and that is that the man, whose name I refuse to utter, who had plotted against us, who brought about my father's execution and had wanted to force my hand in marriage, died suddenly and unexpectedly one day while riding on horseback. In the end the bastard had done it for naught because Studdal Castle and all our ancestral lands had been taken by the Crown then anyway. I was at court when I learned of this and knew it was my one chance—my one and only chance to right all the wrong that had been done to my family name, which is what I have pursued ever since.'

God, but Savaric hated their cruel and unforgiving world at times.

'Oh, Marguerite,' he whispered against her forehead. 'You have endured much. Tell me, though, why you are doing this by yourself?'

She gazed up at him and searched his eyes for a moment before taking a long shaky breath. 'Because there was no one else, Savaric. There was no one who would take on the mantle and my cause. No one to take on the fight on my behalf. There was no one to be my champion.'

He screwed his eyes shut and felt as though his heart was ripped out from his chest. And in that moment, he felt nothing but Marguerite's despair and anguish.

Dear God...

Savaric had always known this to be the truth from everything he had surmised about Marguerite before and ever since she had come back into his life. Yet to hear it acknowledged openly that she had no one was far more gut-wrenching than he had ever thought possible.

It should have been me...

He wished that he had been the one to have taken up arms and defended Marguerite's honour. He wished that he had been the one to hold her and protect her from harm. He wished he could have been *her champion*.

And in that, Savaric had also failed her. He had cut her out of his life, believing it to be best for both of them—which it was. He still believed that in his bones. To that end, he had made Marguerite believe his indifference towards her so that they could separate for good, yet all he had done was to cause her further pain. He had never intended for such an outcome but that did not assuage his guilt.

Yet Marguerite had endured. She had overcome her misfortune and had gone to Hubert de Burgh, unwavering in what she sought, and after she had received the necessary training she had left for Paris, with no one to rely on but herself.

Not unlike Savaric himself...

He could recall how he had pushed himself to the absolute limit so many moons ago, when there had been so many obstacles in his way. Marguerite too, he realised, had faced just as many challenges.

And while Savaric had not been there to protect her when she had fled for the French Court, even though she had managed, he could now.

'We are all but trying to find our way in this world. The only way we can,' he murmured softly and lifted her fingers to his lips. 'But let me help you in this. Let me be your champion. I would gladly do it.'

'You would?'

'Yes...'

Marguerite's head dropped, gazing at their entwined hands. The moment stretched as the breeze whipped up her cloak and, in the distance, he could hear the faint murmur of the gatehouse guards' chatter and laughter as they changed shifts.

'You kissed me...' Marguerite whispered, lifting her head and meeting his eyes. 'After you carried me here from the woods.'

'Yes,' he muttered inanely, unable to elaborate more.

'Why?' she asked.

It was indeed a good question and one that Savaric did not have a ready answer to.

'Why did you kiss me?' she murmured, her eyes glittering with an emotion he could not fathom.

Savaric should tell her that it was inconsequential. That it was a ploy, in which he could make his ruse of a drunkard even more believable. He should say any number of things rather than the truth—that he wanted to kiss her again, desperately. And he wanted to do more than just kiss her mouth. He wanted—nay, needed—to lose himself inside her.

But he could not do it. He could not continually lie about his feelings for her.

'I am drawn to you, Marguerite Studdal, I am drawn to you in a way that I do not seem to comprehend myself.' He shook his head slowly. 'I have tried so hard but alas, I seem unable to resist you.'

And he was unable to stop wanting her.

She stared at him for a long moment before moving a little closer, tipping her head up, and gazing into his eyes.

'And must you? Resist?'

'*Marguerite…*' he hissed through his teeth, as his heart started to pound in his damn chest.

Savaric touched her bottom lips with the pad of his thumb, dragging it back and forth.

Hell…

He was tempted to kiss her again and would love nothing better than to touch her, hold her, make it all go away. He wanted to be the man that she deserved.

Everything then seemed to happen slowly. The flame-coloured lock of hair that had slipped out from beneath her hood dancing in the breeze. The fluttering of her lashes before she closed her eyes, and the soft gasp that escaped from her mouth as she tilted her head higher just as he lowered his. But just as their lips were but a hair's width apart, the bells from the cathedral chimed, breaking this moment crackling with so much unfettered desire and longing.

Marguerite took a step back as he raked his fingers through his hair, watching her flushed face, biting down on those lips that he had almost kissed again.

'We should leave…' he muttered.

She nodded, unable to say more.

'Come, allow me to escort you back to into the city.'

'Yes.'

Savaric walked beside Marguerite as she began to march towards the gatehouse. Needing to break this growing awkwardness between them, he brought their discourse back to the reason why they were both there on this royal tour. Why they were here outside the city gates. And why he had been forced to go after her in the woods.

'Keep a very close eye on Anais, and ingratiate yourself with her to find out more, Marguerite. Thanks to you, we now know that the woman is obviously not who she seems, but you must be vigilant, and watchful,' he murmured from the side of his mouth. 'Do not, however, betray that that you are aware of anything, most especially not what happened tonight. I shall do the same. Anais de Montluc, better known as *la femme immaculée*, is almost certainly part of The Duo Dracones and will be just as dangerous as they. So be on your guard.'

Marguerite nodded. 'Yes, I shall.'

'You spoke of chances earlier. Well, here it is—the one we have all been waiting for. I shall inform de Burgh on your excellent findings tonight and send missives to the rest of the Knights Fortitude. Now, we shall allow Anais to lead us to uncovering more about The Duo Dracones herself.'

'Yes, and how they intend to use the silver clippings, melted down or otherwise, against the Crown.'

'Precisely.' Savaric frowned. 'And remember what Ned Lutt muttered before breathing his last?'

'He seemed agitated that…that time was against us.'

'Precisely. *Redimentes tempus, quoniam dies mali*

sunt. Whatever evil they are planning to unleash will happen very soon and mayhap once we reach Dover.'

'Dear God.'

'But we shall be ready.'

She swallowed uncomfortably. 'We shall have to be.'

'Indeed. And Marguerite?' He stilled her by the arm. 'On my honour, I meant it when I said that I will be your champion.'

Chapter Twelve

Marguerite pasted a smile on her face as she reached out and grabbed a handful of dried fruit and nuts that the Dowager Queen Isabella had brought from her native Angoulême. The lavish repast had been laid out on the blanket under brightly coloured canopies for the Dowager, her ladies, and some of her personal guards and retainers who had also journeyed to England with the King's mother and who would soon escort her back.

Marguerite languidly reclined against a jewel-coloured bolster cushion in an attempt to appear more like an indolent courtier, as she swept her gaze in every direction, surveying all around her. In particular she watched Anais de Montluc and everything the traitorous maid did.

Yet the woman had retreated to being just the same as she was before the incident in the woods the previous night. Indeed, it was as though Marguerite had imagined the whole thing, with Anais's mask of a giggling simpleton firmly back in place. But it did not fool her. No, beneath that exterior lay a cold, calculating heart and one that Marguerite needed to expose.

And in the same vein, Marguerite knew that she must also pretend to be someone she was not, while biding her time until Anais revealed herself. Which she was confident the traitorous woman would do, sooner or later, despite Savaric's caution.

Savaric…

Every time Marguerite thought of the man, she flushed remembering how he had come to her rescue in the woods and brought her back to safety after she had stood frozen, gripped with an inexplicable fear of the possibility of whom the man Anais had met might be. And whom he might be.

Yet when Savaric had held her in his arms, Marguerite had never felt so safe, so protected. It had felt wonderful, even if he had only been trying to conceal and hide her. But the strength and heat from his body, as well as his masculine scent, had sent her head reeling. And then he had covered her mouth with his and everything changed.

Heavens, but that kiss—well, it was nothing like a courtly kiss and it had all but melted her into a puddle against him. But what had meant far more to Marguerite were the words he had said to her afterwards. The surprising truth that Savaric was concerned for her, had wanted her to trust and rely on him, was something that she had not expected. Indeed, he had mentioned 'trust' only a few weeks ago but last night he had truly meant it. He had been regretful and everything he'd said had been laced with so much tenderness that it had left her breathless.

Let me be your champion…?

He had shocked Marguerite when he had asked this.

No one had ever uttered such sentiments to her before and it touched her deeply, more than he would ever know. Not that Marguerite had disclosed her feelings to him, which were all a muddle in any case. She knew that however much she had tried to resist and push him away ever since she had returned, she nevertheless desired and wanted him in a manner that confused her. Yet one thing was for certain—Savaric Fitz Leonard did care for her…mayhap he always had. Just not in a lasting way that promised more.

She sighed and pulled her mind back to the scene before her.

'It was truly an unbecoming, unchaste sight, Ann, but I could hardly look away,' Anais Montluc said not too discreetly to her friend Lady Ann, both of whom sat opposite to Marguerite.

'Oh, you must say more, I implore you.'

'Very well, I shall divulge all, but you must promise not to say a word.' Anais giggled to her friend, loud enough for all the ladies to listen in on.

'You have my word. Now tell me all.'

'Well, I was just coming back inside the city when I happened upon him—a knight of the realm, I dare say—with a camp whore wrapped around his…his taut body.'

'Oh, my word.' Lady Ann tittered. 'I wonder whether he pretended not to see you, being caught in such a predicament.'

The other maid shuffled closer excitedly as all the Queen's ladies listened.

'Not a bit of it. He was sotted and carried on with his whore, as he smiled, flirted, and spoke with me, unashamedly and without a care. As though it was the most natural thing in the world to hold a conversation with a lady of my standing, while being in a…in a disgraceful carnal state with a woman not fit to be seen.' She laughed, flicking her head imperiously.

'What impudence, my dear. And such a shock to your sensibilities.' Anais now held the attention of the Dowager Queen, who had placed the palm of her hand against her chest and shook her head in horror as the other ladies giggled behind their hands. 'You say this person, whom I could hardly call a man of good breeding, *a knight*, actually had the audacity to speak to you when he was otherwise…otherwise preoccupied?'

'Yes, Your Grace.' Anais looked up innocently and took a small bite of an apple she had been slicing carefully. 'Indeed, I was quite shocked.'

The young woman looked anything but, yet all the maids including Marguerite murmured words of sympathy at her difficult ordeal.

'But why were you outside the city gates?' Lady Alice raised a brow and shrugged as Anais snapped her head around and glared at her. 'Apologies, but you said you were coming through the gates when you were met by this scene, and you know my curiosity in such matters.'

'That is hardly the point, my dear. What matters is that I do not expect my innocent, virtuous ladies to be thus insulted,' Isabella, the Dowager Queen said, putting an end to Lady Alice's curiosity. 'I shall have words with my son as well as Lord de Burgh about this ignominy, if you will supply me with a name?'

'Oh, that is not necessary, Your Grace. The young

man was behaving as all young men do, so I have been told.' She chortled, setting Marguerite's teeth on edge. 'And besides, he was, as I said, quite inebriated.'

'That is not the point, my dear. It will not do and I simply will not have such flagrant disgraceful displays in front of my ladies. A name, if you will.'

'As you wish, Your Grace. It was Sir Savaric Fitz Leonard whom I saw.'

Amid all the gasps, Marguerite's head was reeling. What was Anais de Montluc about, other than wishing to cause trouble for Savaric—which would come to nothing even at the Dowager Queen's insistence that he atone for such lewd conduct.

No, the only reason that Marguerite could think of, was that this outburst of Anais's stemmed from jealousy, even of a camp whore, as she had put it, since the woman had made it plain how much she desired Savaric's favour based on how she had singled him out with her outrageous flirtations. Marguerite felt a wave of guilt knowing that it had been *her* actions, which had inadvertently brought this attention to Savaric, when all he had done was come to Marguerite's rescue.

God's bones, but she had to find a way to warn him.

'I can see that you do not approve of my informing our lady Queen, Mistress Marguerite?' Anais had been evidently watching her and had noticed her frown.

'On the contrary, you have every reason to, my lady,' she retorted quickly. 'I am only shocked and outraged as everyone here, by such untoward behaviour to a lady of your standing.'

'Yes…but then what do you expect from a man like him?' Anais de Montluc shrugged, helping herself to one of the soft bread rolls piled high on top of each other. 'He is after all a barbarian, being of such questionable origins. And such men have unnatural needs, or so I have been told.'

'Yes, I wonder at my Lord de Burgh keeping him on in such exulted honour. Even having his presence here offends me.' The Dowager Queen grimaced.

'There is a ferocious wildness about him that I do not like. Not that he isn't a fine masculine specimen. But the man certainly needs more refinement. He needs taming...'

They all began to laugh at this statement and yet Marguerite felt sick in her stomach at the manner in which these women were discussing Savaric. It was disgraceful and unpleasant, especially the way that Anais wetted her lips, as it appeared the woman was actually considering the Dowager Queen's words. It seemed that the woman had carnal thoughts herself when it came to Savaric but could quite easily talk so dismissively about him.

Lord but Marguerite's gut twisted in disgust at how vile these women were. It was astonishing but ever since she had returned to England and been thrust once again into Savaric's company, she had been exposed to the abhorrent contempt that he often faced in his daily life. It was as though her eyes were beginning to open to what was constantly directed at the man. She was also starting to see how the world viewed him and from what she could grasp, it was shameful. Even when Savaric was not present, his person, his character, and even his honour were questioned and all because he was different.

He is after all a barbarian, being of such question-able origins.

God, but Marguerite wanted to scratch Anais's eyes out for even speaking his name, let alone inciting such hateful vitriol. And yet she had to sit there on that damn blanket with those damn vicious women nodding and agreeing with them as they besmirched and denigrated Savaric's good name. It would not do. Her heart clenched tightly for Savaric as she considered what it must be like for him. Did he find it difficult to constantly have such baseless aspersions made about him? Or did he merely endure such intolerance and view it as something he just had to accept and live with? After all, he was still a Crown Knight working for one of the most powerful men in the kingdom.

Yet it mattered not. Marguerite had an inexplicable need to defend and shield him from anyone who wanted to harm and cause him pain. Which was a ridiculous notion since the man was a powerful knight and quite used to protecting himself. Something which he was extremely proficient at and had years of experience doing. Yet why did she want to go to him at this very moment and speak with him, to ensure that all was well?

Because I care for him…just as much as he cares for me.

This realisation hit her in the pit of her stomach, as she understood what this all meant. That she had never stopped caring for Savaric, had never stopped thinking about him, had never stopped wanting him…

Dear God.

It was not exactly a good moment for Marguerite to acknowledge her feelings for Savaric Fitz Leonard, especially with what was at stake. Nevertheless it was there—the stark reality of her futile feelings. And yet were they futile? Were his feelings the same as hers or was she once again trying in vain to convince herself of something that did not exist? Just as before...

All this time she had believed that while Savaric may have desired her, and even kissed her, he had viewed his brief yet inexplicable connection with her two years ago as a mistake. This was what he had explained to her, again and again, until she had finally accepted that he did not want her.

My heart is not engaged, Marguerite, but I wish it were not so...

God how those words had tormented her these past two years. They had twisted her up and shattered her foolish heart, strengthening her resolve against him... just as Savaric had wanted it. She could see that now. Looking back through the passage of time, Marguerite could now recall more than just her own heartache. She could remember his anguish, his despair... his pain. It was as though he had invited her scorn, her dislike, and had done everything he could to turn her away from him. Did she have the right of it? And if so, why? Why had he behaved in that manner? It was a question that had plagued her all this time. It made so little sense unless she was mistaken about Savaric. Yet it was difficult to know how he truly felt. The man had erected such an impenetrable wall around himself, it was hard to know either way. But she would. One way or another Marguerite would find out the truth of why Savaric Fitz Leonard had rejected her and pushed her out of his life two years ago.

But not yet. Marguerite could not get distracted by her conflicted feelings towards Savaric and had no choice but to put this to the back of her mind…for now. Until this mission was resolved and she had, God willing, managed to secure everything she hoped to gain. Even then, Marguerite had to tread carefully, not fully trusting that she could risk her heart again. Besides, her plans had always been to be by her brother Godfrey's side at Studdal Castle, once it was hopefully restored to him. That was all that had mattered to her. It still did. Nevertheless, Marguerite wanted to know the reasons for Savaric's behaviour two years ago.

However, until then there were more pressing matters to discuss, such as Anais de Montluc, her possible involvement with The Duo Dracones and the reason she had just turned against Savaric.

The royal party reached the magnificent fortress castle of Dover, perched on a hill and looking down the cliffs, by nightfall. The King, along with Hubert de Burgh, his courtiers, retainers, the Dowager Queen and her ladies reconvened in the grand King's Hall after mass, to partake in the evening's banquet that the royal kitchen had prepared. The hall had already been beautifully decorated by the time the court had entered, with freshly strewn scented rushes, and richly decorated red and gold tapestries of the royal standard hanging from the ceiling, reaching down to the floor. The long tables were simply dressed with plain linen cloth, embroidered with the colours of the Angoulême standard. The fare was not as lavish as usual but entirely satisfying after many long days of travel. They had plenty of meat,

game, and fish dressed in many sauces and herbs accompanied with harvested fruits, cheese, and bread.
This was all washed down with rich Burgundian wine
and local ale.

While they sat in the large, cavernous hall enjoying
their meal surrounded by a hum of noise and chatter,
Marguerite kept an eye out for an opportune moment
so that she could arrange to speak with Savaric without
gaining notice. Yet the man was nowhere to be seen.
Where on earth was he? She hoped that he had not
been reprimanded for his behaviour in front of Anais
de Montluc in Canterbury but then for the sake of ap-
pearances and knowing that the Dowager Queen had
made a point to complain about him to de Burgh, that
might just account for it. Marguerite looked across at
the main table set on a dais, where the King sat with
his mother, Hubert de Burgh, the Archbishop of Canterbury, and other senior courtiers as they tucked into
choice cuts of the delicate meats and fish served on silver trenchers. She sipped wine and watched the courtiers, while biding her time until she could leave the hall
and go in search of Savaric. And the fortuitous moment
came when the musicians who had only just arrived at
the castle began to play their buoyant, melodic music.
Marguerite, along with the others sat on the wooden
bench, stood and clapped. With all the ladies', especially Anais de Montluc's, attention fixed on the musicians, Marguerite slowly stepped back until she was
able to slip out of the hall undetected. She quickly descended down the spiral staircase and made her way
outside, blinking, and adjusting to the inky darkness of

the night with the opalescent moon providing the only glimmer of light.

Why had he not come to the banquet? Where could he be?

Marguerite looked in every direction of the bustling inner bailey, a hive of activity even at such a late hour. With the royal party newly arrived, servants were dashing about carrying chests, bedding, fabrics, and other commodities.

She grabbed a young page on his way towards the buttery and asked whether he knew of where knights, and squires, arrived recently with the royal party might go, if they had forgone the delights at the great hall. The lad looked at her as though she had sprouted two horns, possibly because anyone who would choose to forgo the delicious offerings in the King's Hall was likely not to be of sound mind. However, he had seen many of the young guards and squires slope to the tavern just yonder in the outer bailey.

Marguerite pulled the hood of her cloak over her head and continued through the guarded gatehouse, over the barbican and out through the gates and onto the busy outer bailey that spilled out over the rolling hill.

Marguerite made haste once she assessed that the noisiest lone dwelling near what looked like stables might be a tavern and approached it. She entered the establishment and noted that not only was the place crowded with pilgrims en route to Canterbury but that there were very few women present. After scanning the room, she finally located Savaric sat in the corner surrounded by squires and local men. She wove her way around the tables before reaching Savaric's side.

'So, this is where you have got to?' she said wryly.

'Mistress, what a pleasant surprise. To what do I owe this pleasure?'

Marguerite was evidently not going to be asked whether she wished to sit or not, so did anyway. 'Since you failed to attend the banquet, sir, I came out to enquire after you.'

'I am well as you can see, Marguerite.' He smiled before muttering under his breath, 'What in heaven's name are you doing here, woman? Do you want to be mistaken for a working moll again?'

'Not in the least, but that is precisely the reason that I came to speak with you.'

'Save your breath, mistress, for I have already been reprimanded for my misdemeanours by de Burgh.'

Her brows shot up. 'He admonished you when you were only doing your duty? When...when you had come to my aid?'

'I was doing a lot more than that, Marguerite.' He winked. 'Besides, what could he do, when the Dowager Queen demanded I was made an example of for my unseemly behaviour in front of a lady.'

'I had wondered whether Anais de Montluc might be the reason why you are here. I am so sorry, Savaric.'

'There is nothing for it. Besides, I am far more comfortable in a place like this with the common folk than in the grand hall with courtiers and ladies who look down their noses at me.' He shrugged, making light of it, but there had been a quick flash of hurt before it was masked over. She would happily throttle Anais de Montluc for causing this. Not that she could comprehend the woman's reasons for doing it in the first place. 'But you should not be here, Marguerite. You belong there in the splendour at court, while I do not.'

'I would rather be with you,' she murmured.

She noticed a short intake of breath before he quickly shook his head. 'No, that will not do, you must leave. After all, you are the ears and eyes, remember, while I shall ascertain information here,' he whispered in her ear. 'We have much to do, unless you have forgotten.'

'Of course I have not forgotten. In truth that is the reason I have sought you out,' she lied.

'Oh, and what might that mean?'

'Gawd, what is it 'bout you, Savaric, that have the women folk in a dither?' A big burly man with a huge beard and huge belly chuckled from the next table, as he slapped Savaric on the back. 'She be the second wench who comes lookin' out fer yer.'

Another woman came looking for Savaric? Here? How unexpected, not that Marguerite was surprised. Savaric was not only handsome, appealing, and desirable but was also honourable, kind, and caring. She knew that she was not the only one who appreciated these qualities in him. And yet why did such information send darts of jealousy coursing through her? She did not like it one bit, nor these feelings stirring within her.

Savaric threw him a tight smile. 'I am evidently one lucky man, but call her that again and I shall gut you from here to here.' Savaric pointed his knife from the man's neck down to his pelvis.

'Beggin' your pardon. Yer knows I'm only jestin' with yer, me ol' Savaric.'

'Less of the old, if you will, and remember your manners in front of the lady, Connacht the Big, or there will be no more silver for you.'

'Connacht the Big?' Marguerite's lips twisted despite herself. 'I take it there is a Connacht the Small?'

'There is, missus, but he prefers Connacht the Ugly as his moniker, even though he be a wee slimy bastard,' the bearded man replied, taking a huge gulp of ale. 'And there's also a Connacht the Foul but we donna speak about him since he ran off with one of my crewmen's woman. Bad form, that.'

Marguerite hid a smile behind her hand. 'Yes, it is. You might say that he lived up to his moniker.'

Connacht the Big chuckled and turned to Savaric. 'I like her, more than the other one who came 'ere.'

'So do I.' Savaric grinned. 'Connacht here is a well-respected seaman and believes he might know the whereabouts of the captain of the vessel we seek.'

'If yer can supply me with the ship's name, I might be able to see what I can find out, like.'

'I can help there.' Marguerite smiled. 'It is the *Draco Marinus*…or the *Sea Dragon*.'

Connacht the Big smoothed down his long beard and made a single nod. 'Aye, I knows the cap'n of the *Dragon* all right and tight. He's known as the Ghost, 'cause one moment he's there, next he's vanished—as has the *Dragon* along with him.'

'That is most interesting, Connacht.' Savaric reached from his pouch and handed over a couple of silver coins to the man, who took them eagerly. 'And if you remember anything more or have further information for me, you know where I am.'

'Aye, that I do. But one thing, Savaric, from what I be

hearin' the cap'n is mixin' with some dangerous folks, so watch yer step.'

'Oh, believe me, I shall.' Savaric rose and held out a hand to Marguerite, indicating that this discussion was over.

Once they were outside, Savaric pulled her around the corner to hide under yet another shadow.

'Christ in heaven, Marguerite, but what made you come here tonight?' He exhaled through his teeth before continuing. 'A woman of your standing in a tavern full of rowdy men.'

'I went to The Three Choughs tavern on the bridge, did I not? And that tavern was also frequented by rowdy males, if I recall.'

'The difference being that you are here as part of the entourage with the court. And as such you do not belong outside the castle, on your own.' He leant a little closer. 'And we cannot be seen together, Marguerite. Not alone like this. Indeed, it might be best to ignore and disregard one another if we want to maintain the pretence of being recently acquainted. You are to act the aloof lady, and with that you should be within the castle keep.'

'I know and I am sorry but when you did not attend the banquet, I had to…to find you.'

'Why?'

Marguerite could hardly tell him the truth, that she was concerned for him and wanted—nay, needed—to see him. So instead she said the only thing that she could.

'Because I needed to ascertain something that has been troubling me since we last spoke.'

His brow lifted in surprise. 'And this could not have waited until the morrow?'

'No, I am afraid it could not.'

'Very well.' His brows furrowed in the middle as his eyes darted in every direction.

'Are you looking for something?'

He gave her a sheepish smile. 'Only my hat, which I must have misplaced in the tavern.'

'Then let us return to retrieve it.'

He pulled her back as she turned back to the tavern. 'Let's not. The tavern owner, nay, every man present, will recognise that hat to be mine.'

'That distinctive?'

'Indeed.' He grinned. 'Come, it's of no matter, I shall fetch it in the morn.'

Just then, a handful of seamen stumbled out from the tavern, sotted and singing loudly. Savaric looked over her shoulder and shook his head. 'There are too many people here, too many strangers, Marguerite, and as I said earlier, we cannot risk being seen together. So, unless you want to speak privately in the chamber that I have acquired here, let me fetch my squire to escort you back to the castle.'

'No.' Marguerite lifted her head and before she could assess the wisdom of what she was about to do, she said, 'I shall follow you to your chamber, if you would be so obliging.'

Chapter Thirteen

Savaric was still in shock that Marguerite Studdal had insisted on speaking with him in the privacy of the bed-chamber that he had acquired in one of the outbuildings belonging to the tavern. He had been lucky to get a private room, especially since the port of Dover was so exceptionally busy at this time, but it was amazing how easily the seal he carried from his liege lord opened doors that might otherwise shut in his face.

Now he wished that he had secured a flea-infested pallet in a communal chamber rather than having Marguerite here alone with him. It was not a good idea for them to be together alone like this and Savaric could see a myriad of potential problems that might arise as a result. Namely that he was finding it difficult to concentrate on anything other than the tempting woman who sat on the pallet bed, as if it was the most blessedly ordinary thing to do.

He dragged his fingers through his hair and stared at her. God, but he was alone in a chamber with Marguerite, whom he desired and wanted badly. And from fear that he might go to her, he made certain that he stood with his back pressed against the wooden door, putting as much distance as he could between them.

'So, you wished to speak with me about a pressing matter that has been troubling you?' Savaric prompted so that he could get this over with and usher Marguerite out of this chamber and back inside the castle where she belonged.

'I did, yes.'

'Well?'

'Mmm…well?'

Her restlessness puzzled him. Why on earth was she here if it made her feel so awkward? 'Marguerite?'

'Yes?'

'I believe you wished to expand on some matter?'

She frowned. 'Expand on…?'

Damn but she really did seem a little uncomfortable.

'What is it that is troubling you?' he murmured, crossing his arms over his chest.

Marguerite blinked and all at once seemed to realise why she was here in his chamber. And that somehow made her appear a little more at ease.

'I have been pondering on our last discourse, Savaric, and there is something that is not quite right. That just does not make sense to me. And the annoying thing is that I presently cannot think what it might be. Only that it concerns Anais de Montluc.'

'I see.' In truth he did not see. Not in any capacity did he comprehend the reason why this woman had come to the tavern this eventide and then insisted on coming here for this, when she should be at the castle watching the goings on at court. Watching Anais de Montluc as she should be.

'It is only that I cannot fathom why Anais would need to implicate you in the way she did, with the Dowager Queen.'

'It could be a number of reasons.'

'Yes, it could be that she was annoyed that you did not respond to her furtive advances, or that she wanted to ingratiate herself with the Dowager Queen more in the hope that she would promote a match between herself and the King…or that she simply wanted you away from court. I do not know. Presently, it makes little sense to me.'

Savaric shrugged, considering the observations that Marguerite had made. 'I do not know but mayhap we shall learn more in the coming days'

'I feel that there is something that we are missing. But what, I cannot fathom.'

It was indeed a mystery and one that piqued his interest. And while he was being forced by Hubert de Burgh to maintain discretion and keep away from King's Hall, especially the Dowager Queen and her ladies, Marguerite was not.

Savaric rubbed his jawline. 'You make good points, mistress, and it seems to me that since you are so concerned about Anais de Montluc, you should be at the banquet and observing her more closely.'

She sunk her teeth onto her bottom lip and nodded. 'You are right, it is foolish, mayhap a mistake to single you out and come here. I should go.'

Savaric pinched the bridge of his nose and hoped that he had not insulted her. Not when they were beginning to be get along on much better terms with one another. However, those terms were still rather precarious given the intensity of his desire for Marguerite and how he needed to maintain an absence of feeling while still allowing himself to openly care for her. And to be her champion, as he requested just a few days ago. It was quite a feat having to balance it all. Yet at this moment as she sat on the pallet, looking a little bewildered and yet utterly alluring, he could feel his resolve slipping.

'No, wait.' Savaric took a step towards her and caught himself before he reached her. He would surely be lost to her once again if he got too close, just as on the previous occasions, when he had given in to his desire and touched her, kissed her. He closed his eyes and exhaled a shaky breath.

'Now that you are here, it might be prudent to wait until the banquet is over before you rejoin the merriment, otherwise you might be missed?'

She smiled and nodded, evidently quite happy with his nonsensical explanation. It would have been better if she left now, bringing an end to this strange, awkward meeting.

'So...'

'So?' he repeated, wondering what else the woman wanted to say.

She lifted her head. 'Did you manage to partake in a meal?'

'I did, and before you ask it was quite satisfactory.'

'Ah, good.' She dropped her head and looked at her entwined hands on her lap.

'And you? Did you enjoy the banquet food at the King's table?'

'Yes.' She nodded. 'The veal dressed in a delicious rich sauce was particularly tender.'

'I am happy for you. Ours was sadly lacking in flavour and our two-day-old pottage far too watery for my taste. Still, I suppose it was filling enough.'

Were they actually conversing about their evening meal now? It seemed so, and it seemed that their mundane conversation was actually masking the tension growing within the chamber.

'Ah, good,' she muttered, her eyes darting around the chamber, everywhere except in his direction.

Savaric raised a brow and sighed. 'Was there something else you wanted to ask me, Marguerite?'

She hesitated for a moment before speaking. 'Actually, yes. If I may ask, which lady had come to seek you before I had?'

'Ah, that…it might come as no surprise for you to learn that it was Lady Anais herself.'

And yet it was. It had been wholly unexpected for Anais de Montluc to seek Savaric out and even more so for her to make him such a shocking offer.

'Anais Montluc came to visit you here?'

'Indeed. It was as much of a surprise for me, when you regard the degree to which the lady claimed to be insulted by me.' He added wryly, 'She had been so outraged and upset when she encountered me in Canterbury that she naturally had to seek me out immediately upon our arrival here.'

'What could she possibly want with you after everything that she caused?'

He shook his head. 'I would rather not say.'

Marguerite scowled, incredulous. 'She disabused you and took you to task? To your face?'

'No, not quite.'

'Then what?'

'I would not like to offend your sensibilities, mistress. Let us just say that the woman came here and she behaved…quite predictably.'

'Tell me, Savaric. I assure you that my sensibilities will not be affronted, other than on your behalf, of course.'

That made him smile. God, there was something so endearing about this proud woman who wanted to defend him so fiercely. It made his chest tighten. It made him want to go to her and pull her into his arms.

'Tell me.'

'The woman as good as propositioned me and said that if I would…if I would take her to my bed then she would inform the Dowager Queen that it had all been a mistake.'

'She *what*?'

'Really, now, Marguerite, you are going to put me to the blush.' He raised a brow. 'Let us just say that the woman made me an offer and leave it at that.'

'She wanted you…you to bed her?'

'Yes.' He shook his head and chuckled. 'Can you believe her audacity?'

Savaric was not a vain man but knew of his appeal and attraction to some women who were curious about him, with his huge stature, unusual mien, and foreign looks. Indeed, he had been told by some that they wanted a taste of the forbidden. And in Anais de Montluc's case it was that and more. The lofty woman wanted to exercise her dominance and superiority over him, while getting a sense of perverse gratification. And yet, in one form or another, this was something that he was quite used to.

'Yes, I can quite easily believe her audacity. The woman is a viper.'

Marguerite was, however, different from anyone he had ever met before and it had always puzzled him. Why had a woman like her not treated him with the same disdain as others had? The usual response was to treat him as an oddity, with a barely disguised contempt. He glanced at Marguerite sitting on the bed, so outraged on his behalf, and smiled inwardly. She, like his Knight Fortitude brethren, did not see him the way others did. No, she regarded him in a manner that he wished to be seen—as the man he truly was.

And it was this that had terrified him from the moment he had laid eyes on her two years ago. That Marguerite Studdal saw him as someone worthy of her when he could never be that. She blatantly refused to see what was right in front of her. Their difference and disparity. Despite every ill and harrowing event that Marguerite had experienced she still carried with her that very sentiment that he could not comprehend or even accept in the harsh world they lived in. *Hope…* and it was a dangerous thing to believe in when one had lived in Savaric's boots and seen the many terrible things he had.

Marguerite blinked several times before she spoke again. 'I… I take it that you declined her generous offer?'

'You need to ask?' He raised a brow.

It was astonishing that on the one hand a woman like Anais de Montluc viewed Savaric as an aberration, someone she felt beneath her, yet the revolting woman desired him all the same. It was frankly as insulting and disrespectful as it was contemptuous.

'No, I suppose not.'

'Would you care for some wine?'

'Please,' she said, nodding, as Savaric strode to the trestle table in the corner and poured wine into two mugs and turned back to face her.

'I admit I was taken aback with her brazen request, but I told her that while it was indeed a flattering offer, there was a woman who had already arrested my attention.'

He had a woman? A woman Marguerite had never been aware of?

She felt like her heart might shatter into a thousand pieces.

Oh, God above. In all the years that she had known Savaric she had never once thought that there might have been *a woman*. Of course, she had been so foolish. So incredibly foolish. Why had she not thought that a man as attractive as Savaric would already be taken? Already promised to another. God, she felt as though she had received a punch in the gut.

'I see.'

'No.' Savaric's small, wicked smile made her stomach flip over itself. 'I really don't think that you do.'

He held out the mug and as she reached to take it, their fingers touched briefly. Her pulsed hitched as she felt it immediately, the strange frisson that passed between them.

Savaric pinned her with his gaze, making it difficult to breathe. 'It's you, Marguerite. It has always been you.'

The feeling of elation that rushed through her made her feel a little dizzy. And altogether breathless.

God in heaven.

Marguerite held his gaze and watched him take a small sip of wine while he kept his eyes fixed on hers. She followed his lead and drank the wine, licking a dark red droplet from her lip and hearing a soft groan pass from his mouth.

They stood there a moment transfixed, still, looking deep into each other's eyes. She could not move, could not breathe, her heart pounding so fiercely that she felt it might rip through her chest.

'Kiss me.' Her request was so sudden, so unexpected, that his brows rose a fraction.

And yet he did nothing. Instead, he continued to gaze at her with a look that was impassive and so composed, it made Marguerite feel a little uncomfortable. She realised that this unpredictable man had been shocked by her bold request. But then he had been propositioned already tonight by another woman who had hoped to lure him to his bed by attempting to bribe him. God, but did he believe her to be the same as her? Did he believe her to be cut from the same cloth as Anais de Montluc? Why indeed why not? After all, she had also behaved just as wantonly.

But she was wrong. Savaric was not nearly as composed as he seemed. It might be the small visible twitch in the muscle of his jaw or the flicker of light from the torch held inside the metal sconce that mirrored the same spark of intensity in his golden eyes, as though there was a fire raging within Savaric, one that he was trying to control.

'Kiss me.' She repeated.

He reached out and took the mug she had been holding and placed both mugs on the small threadbare rug on the floor and stood again, towering over her. His gaze slipped from her eyes to her lips and back again. And just when she thought he might lower his lips to hers, he grabbed her hand and caressed her palm before pressing a kiss on the inside of her wrist. He sucked on that delicate skin where a pulse was jumping wildly before teasing it with a swipe of his tongue and small kisses up and down her arm.

'You should have left this chamber, Marguerite,' he whispered against her skin as he nipped on it gently.

'No, I... I want to,' she muttered. 'Stay.' It was with great difficulty that she was getting any words out.

'That might not be such a good idea, love.'

She gasped at his use of such an endearment—one he had never ever said before. *Love?* But Marguerite would not think too much of such a thing. Not when Savaric was now grazing the shell of her ears with his lips, tongue, and teeth.

'You need to leave.' He cupped her jaw and pressed a kiss to the corner of her lips.

'No.'

He licked along her bottom lip, making her tremble. 'Yes.'

'You are not giving any inducement for me to want to leave you,' she said on a rasp. 'Not by the things you are doing to me. Not by any means.'

'Then mayhap I should stop.' He pulled away.

'No.' She shook her head as she backed against the pallet and sat, her knees giving way 'Do not dare.'

He raised a brow and smiled faintly. 'Is that a demand, mistress?'

Her chest rose and fell as she removed her veil from her hair. And then unbound her hair slowly, letting her unruly hair cascade over her shoulders and down her back, and watched as his eyes filled with a potent unfettered desire that melted her insides.

'And if I said that it was?'

He reached out and brushed his hands down her hair, and groaned softly, bringing a lock under his nose and inhaling deeply. 'I would say that you are mad.'

Catching her bottom lip between her teeth, and keeping her gaze pinned to his, she began to untie her kirtle dress and allowed it to fall down her body and puddle at her feet. Before her courage deserted her, Marguerite took a deep breath, removed her boot, hose and rose, lifting her eyes to his, feeling a little self-conscious that she now stood in front of the man dressed only in her cream tunic and the lace tie that she always wore around her neck.

His eyes raked her from her head down to her toes and back again before shaking his head slowly. 'Quite, quite mad.'

Savaric wrapped a length of her hair around his hand over and over and gave it a little tug, making her stumble forward and straight into his arms. His hands skimmed up and down her back before settling on either side of her hips.

'Pray what happens now, mistress?'

'Now?' She encircled her arms around his neck, clinging on to him. 'Now you kiss me.'

He dipped his head and smiled against her lips. 'So demanding.'

And then he caught her mouth in a kiss that was just as demanding and urgent. He brought one hand around her neck to hold the back of her head in place and deepened the kiss, tasting her mouth, his tongue sparring with hers.

He pulled away on a gasp and undid his leather gambeson and threw it on the floor before pulling his linen tunic over his head and tossing this aside as well.

Dear God...

She shivered, and not from the cold but from the magnificent man in front of her. His shoulders, wide, his whipcord muscly chest, hard. His arms... Good Lord but his arms were huge. He exuded a raw masculinity that made her want to touch him. Desperately. Of their own volition, Marguerite's hands reached out, her fingers trembling as she felt the contours of his taut chest, grazing down the narrow line of crisp hair along a flat toned stomach that disappeared under his hose and braes.

He cupped her jawline and his fingers fumbled to untie her lace necktie but something in her gaze stilled him.

'May I?' he murmured and when she gave the smallest shake of her head his hands dropped away.

This was Savaric, the man she cared for and trusted above all others. Yet for some reason this was harder than divesting her kirtle dress. His finger softly grazed her neck, touching the lace necktie around her throat, backwards and forwards.

'You still wear this?'

Yes, she wanted to say but the word was caught at the back her mouth.

He glanced up and smiled, softly. 'You have nothing to hide from me, love.'

Marguerite returned his smile knowing his words to be true. And yet that wasn't the reason why she wore it.

'It is not the ugliness of the scars that I hide, Savaric, but the reminder of the time that this happened.'

He pushed a lock of hair away from her face, curling it behind her ears and sighed. 'I do understand, Marguerite, more than you know.'

She frowned. 'How?'

He took her hand in his and exhaled slowly. 'There is a reason why I am rarely seen without my hat, despite misplacing it this evening. The one with the wide brim and colourful plumage that in truth is a little ridiculous.'

'Is it because on you it looks quite dashing, per chance?'

'Thank you but no, not quite.' He pressed a quick kiss to her fingers. 'It is because it makes me accept that in this kingdom, I shall always remain an outsider. I shall always be viewed as different, foreign, beneath others. And by wearing something so distinctive, so unusual, so damn outlandish it makes me—nay, forces me—to embrace that difference even more because I am not shying away from declaring that this is who I am.'

A lump formed at the back of Marguerite's throat as she slowly began to comprehend what he had shared with her.

'So can you not see?' he asked gently. 'That you should not hide your scars any more than I should hide myself away? This scar is part of who you are, Marguerite, a reminder of all that you have endured, as well as being a reminder of your strength and fortitude.'

No one had ever said such words to her. No one…

Marguerite pushed away the threat of tears at the intensity of his words, since she knew they were real, and honest. It forced her to comprehend the truth of all that had happened to her in the past two years and how she had become stronger and yes, how she had endured.

Taking a deep breath, she raised her eyes to his and what she saw almost made her swoon. There was so much longing, so much warmth and tenderness in his eyes. Indeed, she could feel the strength of his support and encouragement ripple through him.

Before Marguerite could change her mind, her fingers curled around her neck and she untied her lace necktie herself, throwing it onto the floor, on top of the pile of her clothing.

Savaric took in a small intake of breath as he brushed his fingers gently along the long jagged scar that ran horizontally across her throat and then leant in and pressed soft kisses against it.

'So brave, so beautiful,' he murmured as she tilted her head up, allowing him an easier path for his fingers to graze across the scar.

'As are you.'

Stripped, uncovered, and without the walls that he had carefully built around himself, this was who Savaric had always been. A man who cared for her so intently, so tenderly. A man who was honourable, steadfast, and tended to people and things that mattered to him. And he was so much more than he believed himself to be. It was, after all, why she loved him. She pulled away on a gasp and stared at him, as if seeing the man for the first time.

Love?

Marguerite loved Savaric? The question was something that took her by surprise but not strangely the answer... Because it had always been hovering inside her. It had always been there. It had always been Savaric...yet she had never truly wanted to acknowledge it to herself. Not until now.

Marguerite reached out and cupped his jawline as he turned his head and pressed his lips to her palm. She went up on her tiptoes and kissed him with as much passion as she could muster, wanting to show this beautiful man the extent of her feelings.

'Easy, love.' He chuckled softly, his golden eyes glittering with warmth and affection.

'Hush, Savaric, and kiss me.'

He shook his head and smiled. 'Indeed, very demanding.'

She nipped his neck. 'This is what you do to me.'

'What I do to you?' He raised a brow as his hands grazed up and down her back. 'Pray what do you think you do to me?'

Marguerite pressed a quick kiss to his lips and before she could change her mind reached down and pulled her sheer linen tunic over her head and threw it onto the floor. She now stood in front of him with nothing but the sound of her heart thumping in her chest and the fire crackling in the hearth. She resisted the urge to cover her breasts and her sex with her hands and allowed them to fall by her sides instead. They were shaking uncontrollably.

Savaric stilled as his eyes widened at her audacity. He expelled a slow breath through his teeth, his eyes devouring her nakedness. 'Dear God…you are a temptress, Marguerite Studdal.'

Emboldened by his words she stepped forward and pressed against the hard wall of his huge chest. She tilted her head up, allowing him an easier path for his fingers to graze up and down her jaw and face. His lips, tongue, and teeth then followed suit before trailing a pattern down the curve of her neck. Savaric walked her back until her legs met the edge of the pallet, making her sit. She then swung her legs around and lay on the pallet as he followed her. She arched up as he cupped her breast, circling his thumb over her nipple before he took it into his mouth and then moved to the other. He moaned or was it Marguerite who had done so? It was difficult to say, difficult to think.

What in heaven's name was happening to her?

This, with Savaric, was unlike anything she had ever experienced, not that she had any such experience to compare—only whispers at the French Court of tantalisingly illicit intimacies.

Savaric's big powerful body was supported by his arms bent on either side of her, so as not to crush her beneath him. But it mattered not, she wanted to feel him pressed against her, skin to skin, as close as possible. She entwined her fingers around his neck and pulled him towards her and raised her mouth to his, kissing him in just the same manner that he had. Ravishing and claiming his mouth. He growled deep in his throat as he responded by deepening the kiss, slanting his lips over hers, again and again.

He pulled away only to lick and nip along the shell of her ear.

'We should stop,' he said, his voice hoarse and raspy.

'Please. We cannot...'

Marguerite could not finish the thread of what she was saying but knew that this, between them, could not come to an end now.

His hands circled around her ankle before moving up and skimming over her legs, moving up slowly towards her thighs, as his mouth travelled down her neck along her collarbone, nipping and pressing open-mouthed kisses.

'We cannot? Tell me, is that what you said?'

'No...yes.'

He licked and sucked her nipples again, flicking his tongue around each sensitive nub before moving to the other.

'Does that mean you wish me to stop?'

'No. Do not dare to... *Please*.'

He smiled against her skin. 'Oh, I aim to please.'

Marguerite's chest rose and fell as he kissed, licked, and nipped the underside of her breast and moved down her belly. And then moved even lower down her body. Her breath hitched inside her throat as his fingers reached her thighs with his mouth, tongue, and teeth following the trail left by his hands.

He lifted her long leg and placed it on his shoulder and turned his head, pressing small kisses along the inside of her thigh before surprising her by lowering his head between her legs and kissing her sex. Marguerite nearly jolted off the bed as he slowly, languidly gave her such sweet, exquisite pleasure in the most unimaginable way she could ever have thought possible.

Dear Lord, what on earth was he doing to her?

She felt overwhelmed by the thrill of this wanton, wicked sinfulness. Yet it was delicious, gloriously so. Marguerite turned her head and bit down on the edge of a bolster cushion to stifle a scream, squeezing her eyes shut, as these unfamiliar sensations rippled over her body, building tighter and tighter before shattering into a thousand and one pieces.

Chapter Fourteen

It was one of the most incredible feelings to be there, lying on the pallet bed holding this beautiful, fiery woman in his arms after watching her come undone so spectacularly. Never had Marguerite been so vibrant and vital as she had giving into wild, sensual abandon. Indeed, it had been a gift to elicit such a rapturous response.

Savaric held her close, stroking her back as he felt her body ease from the release of such heightened pleasure. He would forgo his own, as this would have to be enough. It had to be. He could not risk more intimacy with Marguerite when he could not offer more, especially a future together. Despite everything that had changed on this night, that could never change, however much Savaric wished it were otherwise. She deserved so much more than someone like him.

Yet it had been extraordinary. Marguerite had been so receptive to his touch, to his kisses…

'Savaric?' she murmured, her head resting on his chest, with her glorious red hair spilling all around her.

'Yes.' He kissed the top of her head, his hand brushing through her soft locks.

She lifted her head and peered at him. 'Are you well?'

'Indeed.' He smiled against her head. 'I feel extremely well. And you?'

'Unlike anything I have ever felt before.' She tilted her head to look at him. 'However, I am aware that there is more, Savaric. The carnal act between a man and a woman, that is.'

God's bones...

'Yes,' he said as she rolled away from him and onto her front.

Her arms bent, she leant up and cradled her head between her hands, watching him for a moment or two before speaking again.

'Must I ask why we...we stopped?'

Because continuing down this path would mean that he would lose some part of himself to her, as she would lose a part to him. And Savaric could not do that. He had to desperately hold on to a semblance of restraint, even though it was killing him. He would love nothing more than to be sheathed deep inside of her warmth but as much as he wanted Marguerite, cared for her, damn it, he knew, had always known that they did not belong together. They never could...

And this was all that Savaric could allow himself to take—this one small moment of pleasure that he had given her. His hand skimmed down her spine, along the dip in her small back and along her firm round bottom, feeling her shiver under his touch. This was all they would have. Now. Tonight.

'Savaric?' She frowned.

'There is more. Much, much more but… I cannot, we cannot.'

'We can do whatever we choose.' Her fingers went to the ties around his hose and braes, untying them when his hand shot out and covered hers, stilling them. 'Savaric?'

'No. No, I'm afraid we cannot,' he murmured.

'Why?'

'Allow me to be gallant.' He gave her small smile, brushing his fingers along her cheeks. 'Besides, I could get you with a child, Marguerite. Have you considered that?'

Savaric could tell from her surprised look that she had not and hoped that this explanation would suffice. Please let it be. He could not bear the thought of saying something that might offend or worse, cause Marguerite pain. Even more than he had caused before… She had come to mean more to him than anyone he had ever known. And it was for this reason he had stopped.

It made his chest ache just thinking about how soon, very soon, they would have to part ways, and as much as he wanted to make this one night of intimacy be the real carnal act between a man and woman, as Marguerite so eloquently put it, he would not be that selfish. He would not bind himself to her when he had nothing to give. When he was not worthy of this beautiful, wonderful woman.

Marguerite sighed and sat up on the bed, reaching down to retrieve her clothing from the floor, and began to dress. And with this growing silence, a wall seemed to be erected between them. He hated it. He hated that the warm glow of intimacy was ending in this coolness. And so soon afterwards.

'If I ask of you something, will you honour me by telling me the truth?' Marguerite said, finally breaking the silence as she tied her kirtle dress behind her before turning around to face him.

He grabbed her hand and pressed a kiss on the back of it. 'I will endeavour to, yes.'

'Good, because I have often wondered, Savaric, all these years why…why did you make me believe that you cared little for me, when I now know the opposite to be true?'

His heart sank knowing that this had been the question he had been dreading ever since he had clapped eyes on Marguerite again and one of the many, many reasons why he'd not allowed himself to get too close to her. He had told himself over and over that he needed to keep her at arm's length and maintain just enough of a level of civility since they had been forced to work with one another. But no more than that.

And he had failed. Spectacularly. There seemed a nice evenness to it all. That he had come full circle from where he had cut off ties with Marguerite Studdal two years ago, and now. Once again, he was back at the same crossroads, as before. With the same question hovering over them again.

Marguerite frowned and stood before him, her spine straight and with her hands on either side of her hips. 'Unless I am very much mistaken about your regard for me.'

God, she was magnificent. And in that moment, she was the embodiment of strength, courage, and fortitude—the same fortitude that Savaric and his knight brethren were honour bound to. How could he ever have believed otherwise? Even two years ago, that resilience and determination had been there, evident under the surfeit of doubt and insecurity, and all it had taken was a small grain of confidence that had bloomed and grown. For Savaric there would never be another woman quite like her. But with that came the pertinent question of whether he would answer Marguerite with the same falsity as before or tell her the truth about his *regard for her*.

He sat on the edge of the pallet, dragging his hair back with his fingers, and lifted his head to meet her quizzical blue eyes, so cool and impassive now.

'You are not mistaken in my regard for you, Marguerite.' He noticed that she had been holding her breath, which she expelled once he made his declaration. He reached out and caught her hand in his. 'I believe you are the loveliest woman I have ever met, and yes, I care for you…deeply. I always have.'

The words were true but somehow not enough to express the raging storm of emotion he felt within the walls of his chest. God, but it hurt.

'Then why did you make me believe the opposite was true? Why did you convince me that it had all been a tawdry attraction between us and nothing more?' She swept her arms around the pallet at what had just occurred between them. 'Even though we had never succumbed to *this*.'

He screwed his eyes shut for a moment before opening them. 'Because I could not risk for us to become more attached to one another than we were becoming. I needed to sever ties between us once and for all. And if that meant that I needed to make you believe that I was a bastard, in every way, well, then so be it.' He swallowed uncomfortably before continuing in earnest. 'But it was wrong of me to have done it. It was wrong for me to have hurt you, Marguerite. Forgive me?'

Marguerite did not respond, but continued to study him, gently prising her hands out of his. 'I am glad that you are being forthright with me, Savaric, but what I want to know is why you would purposefully deceive me? Why would you want to define yourself as…as a…?'

'A bastard?' He sighed. 'Because that is exactly what I am, as you are well aware.'

'That still does not explain why you needed to push me away then, as you are also doing now, by the by.'

'What I am doing is right—as it was before. But I know that the way in which I did so two years ago was wrong and for that I am sorry. I should have told you. Expressed myself better.'

'Do not tell me that you are already bound in marriage?'

'No.'

'Or that you have half a dozen children scattered about the kingdom?'

His lips quirked a little at the corners at that. 'Not that, no.'

'Then you have an incurable affliction? Or some strange incurable malady?'

'No, not that either.'

'Then what?' She sighed, shaking her head slowly. 'What could possibly have been the reason for you to sever ties between us and make me believe that you didn't care?'

A good question and something that Savaric had never ever reconciled himself to, nor did he talk of it to anyone. But then Marguerite was not just anyone. Indeed, she needed to know this about him, along with everything else.

'Will you not sit? Please. Allow me to explain my sorry tale,' he murmured as Marguerite sat on the edge of the pallet. 'The man who sired me was a powerful landed knight by the name of Sir Roger Leonard of Bewdley, who was on the crusade to the Holy Land when he met a local woman. He got this woman with child—*me*—and returned when I was an infant of three or four years, demanding that the woman hand me over to him. And do you know what the woman who birthed me did?'

Marguerite was now sitting opposite him, with her hands laced through his, without his even realising it. How had that happened?

'I can imagine that she resisted parting with you.'

'Ah, but you have a soft and generous heart, love. No, in truth she could not get rid of me any faster than she did.' Savaric shook his head and laughed bitterly. 'The silver she received from Sir Roger of Bewdley made the decision so damn easy. And before I knew what had happened, I was given to a stranger without a backward glance.'

She closed her eyes and shook her head. 'I am so sorry, Savaric.'

'No more than I. And I became very poorly on the journey back from the Holy Land. I remember that there was even a conversation of leaving me at an infirmary in France, but somehow I recovered and I survived the long, long journey to this far-away kingdom that would soon be my home.' He exhaled and lifted his eyes to her. 'I shall not bore you with any more of this morose tale of woe that is so damn pitiful.'

Marguerite of course ignored this. 'And did you live with Sir Roger? What happened on your return?'

'I was unceremoniously dumped on a local maid in Bewdley near his manor house, where I believe more silver exchanged hands. And then I did not see the man again until I was ten and four.'

'That must have been so devastating for you. So unbearably hard.'

'What was unbearably hard, Marguerite, was that the woman he had left me with thought nothing of meting out punishment, at times with great severity, at every opportunity, or calling me a heathen for being different. I recall one memorable time when she would scrub my body so hard, making me bleed, while plunging my head into the river, so that she might somehow wash off the objectionable dark colouring of my skin.'

'Dear God, that is a vile, despicable thing to do, especially to a poor displaced child.' She slipped her hand in his. 'I am so sorry you had to endure such treatment. It should never, ever have happened.'

'No, it should not have, and yet it did. Indeed, such experiences are hardly unusual.'

'Damn that woman to hell and anyone else who treated you ill.'

Savaric was slightly taken aback by the ferocity of Marguerite's defence of him as a young child, even though it was gratifying. At least he had that and not her pity. And he had to admit that it was humbling to have her support and understanding. 'Indeed.'

'And what of your father? What of Sir Roger?'

'By the time he returned, he found that not only had I lived but I was a strapping lad, and of the same height I am now. He decided that he would put me to good use and train me as his squire, to be thus promoted to be a knight, if and only if I worked and toiled from dawn to dusk. It was hard, gruelling work but at least it gave me purpose, which I grabbed with both hands.' Savaric rubbed his forehead, wanting an end to this discourse. 'It was not long after that I caught the eye of Hubert de Burgh, who offered me a chance at being a Crown Knight and then eventually what I have become now, a member of the Knights Fortitude. So that is the extent of my sorry tale, which, when all is said and done, is not so very bad. Not now that I have the esteem of one of the most powerful lords in the land and the support and friendship of Warin and Nicholas, my fellow knights who are as close to me as brothers.'

Both of whom were now bound to others, with families of their own. He flicked his gaze to Marguerite, who was now silent, her lips pressed together as she waited. Ah, yes, she was waiting for him to expound further. To enlighten her on those decisions that he made two years ago and again tonight.

He sighed deeply and cupped her jaw, caressing her cheek. 'So, now do you see, love, that because of who and what I am, it would be impossible for you and I to have a future together? It would be doomed from the start.'

'Would it?' she whispered. 'That much you have surmised, without any explanation or indeed ever conferring with me?'

'Marguerite...'

'No, Savaric, no.' She moved out of his embrace and shook her head. 'You want me to forgive you for what came to pass between us two years ago? Very well, you have it. But you fail to comprehend that while you are now being truthful with me, you are still the one making decisions that affect us both. And these decisions are wholly based on assumptions that you have made and are still making.'

'Assumptions that I have made and am still making?' he repeated, striding towards her. 'That is because you have never lived in *my skin*, Marguerite. You know none of what I have faced and still face, to this very day, despite being a Crown Knight and a member of the Knights Fortitude.'

'I realise that...' She gazed into his eyes, cupping his jaw. 'And I wish to learn and comprehend more. I want to be by your side, Savaric. I... I love you.'

Savaric froze and felt as though every drop of blood had drained from his body. Love...? Oh, God, no... this is what he had always wanted to avoid for both of them. He had never been one to inspire such feelings as a child, since no one bothered with him then, showing him only cruelty and unkindness. But to care for him...to *love* him? These were sentiments that would cause Marguerite undue pain...pain that he would not have her endure.

'Have you not been listening to what I have said?'

he said, feeling unsteady, unsettled by her words. 'You cannot love me.'

'Ah, so now you are to determine how I feel about you, Savaric? And what would you have me do? Deny my feelings? Deny that I hope for a chance to be with you? A chance at happiness because of what others may or may not think of us?' she scoffed.

'Can you not see, Marguerite, that it will be…it will be unsafe for you to even entertain such feelings?'

'Unsafe?' she whispered, shaking her head. 'At least when I am miserable and lonely, I will be content in knowing that I have at least been *safe*. That will certainly keep me warm at night.'

'Hell and damnation, woman, do you not comprehend that I am trying and have always been trying to protect you from the scorn which we will no doubt arouse if we were ever to become attached in any manner? It can never be—not a woman like you with a man such as me.'

'A woman like me?' she said sardonically. 'Alas, I believe you forget the very reason that I came back to England. You forget why I implored Hubert de Burgh to give me this chance to absolve my sire's name. Lest you forget, I am the daughter of a condemned traitor. My name carries nothing of worth, Savaric. I am no one.'

'Don't ever say that!' He was outraged that she could even contemplate such a thing about herself. 'Your worth is measured by far more than who your father was. It is beyond measure.'

'But not in the eyes of the world.' She wrapped her arms around herself. 'Can you not see that you too are worth far, far greater than what others might measure you against?'

'It is not the same. Not by any means.'

He glanced up and noticed Marguerite's eyes welling up and a single solitary tear dropping to her cheek. His gut wrenched as he reached out to wipe it away. How had this night managed to descend to this? How? His heart ached so badly that he felt as though it might crack and break into tiny pieces. Mayhap it would have been best to keep all of this from her rather than causing her more distress. But that would have been inevitable whatever he had done. He hated having to voice all of this to her. He hated it! And it was one of the many reasons he had refrained from doing so in the past.

'I see...' she muttered in a cold, sad voice filled with resignation. 'It seems to me that mayhap your regard for me is not the same after all. If it was, Savaric...you would try and fight for us.'

'Would I?'

'Yes, as would I.' Marguerite leant towards him and laced her fingers with his. 'Because I care not one jot for the opinions of others. And neither should you.'

How was he going to make her understand? How was he going to make her comprehend that their differences were so great that it was more than just fighting and resisting unkindness and intolerance that would be directed their way. Far more than that. 'It is not merely the opinions of others that is objectionable. By God, it is far more than that.'

'Oh, yes, as you reminded me earlier, it would also be their scorn, would it not?' The disdain was almost dripping from her lips.

'It is insurmountable.'

'Nothing is insurmountable. Surely you know that?'

'I wish I had your confidence, Marguerite, but having lived in this world as I have, I know it will not hold true. I know we would be doomed from the very outset. There are far too many differences for us to overcome, love,' he added gently.

'But there are also many, many similarities.'

Savaric raised their entwined hands in front of her, wanting desperately for Marguerite to see the difference between them. 'It is not enough and sadly it never will be.'

Marguerite's gaze was pinned to their entwined hands and their different skin tones before she nodded. 'Yes, I see. But tell me, what is the colour of your blood and mine, if I were to make a cut against my skin and then yours? Would we then be as different as you suggest?'

Savaric had never had anyone so willing to risk everything for the sake of being with him. It was as humbling as it was futile, since by the same virtue he would never be willing to risk any harm coming to the woman he loved. He would protect her with every sinew, every muscle, every fibre of his being. He would…

Love? He loved her? The answer was as clear and bright as the day's first ray of sunlight.

Dear God, he was in love with Marguerite Studdal. In truth, if he examined his heart, he would find that he always had been, even though he had resisted it from the first. Yet he could never let her know. Not if he wanted to convince her that they must part ways when all of this was over. Even though it would break him.

'I comprehend what you are saying but it changes

nothing. People see what they want to see.' Savaric hoped that the turmoil of emotions was not evident on his face. He hoped that he had somehow managed to school his features into a mask that revealed nothing.

'And I suppose that is all that matters.' She let go of his hand and picked up her cloak from the floor, giving it a shake before putting it on. 'I comprehend that you are afraid, but I would fight for a chance at real happiness with you.' She gave him a single nod. 'I would. Even if you would not.'

Marguerite turned on her heel and walked away, ready to leave.

'It is not that I would not fight for you as well as the chance at happiness, but that I cannot and will not allow anyone to insult you, scorn you, hurt you, all because you…you love me. Nothing is worth that.'

'Oh, I quite disagree,' she said softly over her shoulder. 'It is worth all of that and more. After all, without love, what is left?'

Nothing…

Marguerite continued to dress quietly, leaving Savaric dishevelled with his heart in tatters, running through everything that had happened. Everything that they had said to one another on this night.

He lifted his head and watched Marguerite as she adjusted the hood of her cloak.

'Wait, Marguerite, if you allow me a moment to dress, I shall escort you back to the keep.'

'That will not be necessary.'

'But…'

'I thank you but no, I need a moment with my own contemplations if you will.' She strode to the door.

Marguerite stopped and turned to face him. 'I am glad that you are no longer shying away from who you are, Savaric. I am glad that you have accepted the man you are and were always destined to become.' She sighed deeply before continuing. 'But then you should also accept that I love you and that I want to be with you, regardless of anything else.'

With that Marguerite turned and quietly let herself out of the chamber.

Chapter Fifteen

It had been a vile morn that had bled into a vile day and an equally vile dusk. With the gloomy, forbidding grey skies and the relentless rain, Marguerite should have foreseen how this day would come to pass. And not just with the dark musings and heartache that had gripped her since the previous night in Savaric's chamber, but with the imminent danger around them. Yet she had not. She had not predicted the extent of the disaster they would all find themselves in by the end of this day.

She had decided after a fretful night's sleep that she would honour Savaric's wishes and keep away from him as much as possible. To that end, she knew that she must reconcile herself to the fact that it was over between them, before it had truly begun…just as before. Even if it made her heartsick. But until they could separate and go their own ways, they had no choice other than to see this mission through to the end. Which Marguerite had done by throwing herself into the pleasantries and pleasures of court that morn, accompanying the entourage that included the King as well as his mother and her ladies on a hunt in the nearby demesne land and woods. That was when everything had gone perilously wrong.

Marguerite had been keeping alert to anything that might provide more information regarding The Duo Dracones, the silver coin clippings that they had been stealing from the coffers of the treasury, and their intended use. And in that she had kept a very close eye on Anais de Montluc, *la femme immaculée*, and the Dowager Queen. Marguerite knew that she had to find something soon with time against them, as this was their one and only chance of finally apprehending the traitors.

And yet, despite having much to do, her mind constantly returned to Savaric and everything he had revealed the previous night. God, but Marguerite had been so dazed after she had left him that she did not know how she had even got back within the castle gates. Their discourse kept turning over and over in her head, so she had not noticed the strange, eerie mood that had enveloped them on the hunt. She had not noticed that the drizzle of rain had made the ground sodden, making progress on horseback slow and unyielding. She had not noticed that the mist, rising from the English sea, was making visibility precarious. And she had certainly noticed far too late that their party had somehow splintered away from the main hunt.

It had been because of Anais de Montluc who, after fawning and flirting with King Henry with the approval of the young man's own mother, had then sought the company of Lord Richard de Vars and led him ahead of their group, slowing the progression on their mounts by their incessant chatter. Marguerite should have known that all of this had been part of the woman's schemes.

She should have known but had not noticed that this was all very, very wrong and completely out of place. No one who attends a hunt chatters incessantly and so loudly, for fear of frightening away the prey. And by the time Marguerite had snapped to attention, it was far too late.

By God, it had happened so fast. Marguerite had seen the lone masked rider on horseback from the corner of her eye, in the distance, as they took aim at the Dowager Queen with a crossbow. She had screamed as loudly as possible, alerting all and one to the danger they faced, which had also scared the Dowager Queen's grey palfrey. It'd bucked its hind legs and jolted skittishly in distress but thank the heavens, the arrow had missed its mark, piercing into the trunk of a nearby tree. Yet, with her horse in awry, the Dowager Queen had managed to lose her grip of the reins and had been thrust to the ground, and onto her back.

Marguerite had turned her horse around, quickly dismounted, and gone to the aid of the Dowager Queen, who'd been shaken, hurt, but thankfully unharmed. In the midst of the mayhem, half a dozen guards chased after the lone rider, who had seemingly vanished. And by the time the guards had returned, the King, Hubert de Burgh, and the rest of the Crown had gathered around the Dowager Queen and her ladies, fussing over her and attempting to come to terms with what had happened, arranging a comfortable conveyance back to the castle. The lone rider who had made an attempt on the Queen's life had, indeed, vanished into thin air, but in his haste to get away, he had left something in his wake—his hat, or rather Savaric's distinct signature hat, adorned with the large brightly coloured feather plumes…

The uproar that resulted from this finding was breathtakingly quick. And it had not been long since guards had been dispatched to go in search of Savaric and arrest him. Marguerite had wanted to go to him immediately and forewarn the man of what had occurred. But she had been taken aside by Hubert de Burgh, who forbade her to go, insisting on a meeting in his privy chamber at the castle instead.

Damn de Burgh for preventing her from warning Savaric, who might even at that moment be caught and even killed in the skirmish. What was he about? Why was he not doing all he could to help one of his own men?

'I want to know how, how this has all happened?' the man blustered, pacing back and forth in his small chamber. 'How in heaven's name was Savaric so easily implicated?'

Marguerite knew she should not exasperate the great man but his response was beyond her. 'Should you not be more concerned with getting him out of this predicament rather than why or how he was implicated? Unless, that is, you believe Savaric to be responsible, my lord?'

'Do not take that tone with me, mistress,' he bellowed before rubbing his forehead irritably. 'This is about far more than just Savaric Fitz Leonard now. It is about all of us! With Savaric implicated in this attempt on the Dowager Queen's life, even those barons who have always objected to the woman, and believe me, there are many who have an enmity with Queen Isabella, will now feel quite differently. They will use the situation to influence the King against *me*. After all, Savaric was one of my men and by extension I shall also face the full threat of hostility, with my many enemies sharpening their swords as we speak.'

Dear God...

'Then you believe what happened earlier to have the hallmarks of The Duo Dracones then?'

'I do.' He grimaced. 'First and foremost, this group of traitorous conspirators are against the English Crown and see me as a huge obstacle in their way to get to the King.'

She nodded. 'Then you must also believe this to be mediated then? To incriminate Savaric.'

'Yes, but what I want to know is how they managed to get to him, mistress. How in heavens did they manage to claim this?' The man threw Savaric's hat on the table and glared at her knowingly. 'Because the Fitz Leonard that I know would never be so distracted with his duties to misplace his damnable hat.'

Indeed, Savaric had been distracted the previous night, but then so had she. And in truth their discourse had nothing to do with Hubert de Burgh, The Duo Dracones, Anais du Montluc or any of the many other reasons they had been thrust into each other's company and forced to work with one another.

Instead it had everything to do with Marguerite declaring her love for Savaric, only for him to explain that they could never be together. And his rejection had been far, far worse than before because Marguerite now knew that he had never been indifferent to her as he had made her believe. Indeed, he esteemed her and cared deeply for her, but saw no future for them for fear of the intolerance they might face. She wanted to weep at that. She wanted to scream and shout her frustrations at the injustice of it all. But at that moment, none of it mattered. There was a far greater injustice at stake here. Whatever the future held for them once they parted, she could not allow Savaric to get caught up in all of this.

'He might have been distracted but I know for certain that Anais Montluc went to see him last night and obviously took his hat at the tavern he was staying in, when he least expected it. She did it to incriminate him.'

'And how, pray, do you know this?'

She flushed, pushing away her irritation at the implication in his voice. 'Does it matter?'

'I believe I should have all the facts, mistress, before answering that.'

She felt her colouring deepening. 'Because I too went to see him in the tavern, whereupon he told me himself.'

Hubert de Burgh gave her a hard glare but did not pass a comment. Yet she knew all the same what he must be thinking. That she, Marguerite, had been the cause of his distraction and had made him forget his duty as a Crown Knight. In truth, if she had not gone to him the previous evening none of this would have happened in quite this disastrous way. Savaric would have ascertained that Anais de Montluc had taken his hat to use against him for nefarious reasons, and known exactly how to act.

'I see.'

'Then you will confront Anais de Montluc about her presence at the tavern last night?'

'Confront one of the Dowager Queen's own ladies at this sensitive time? Are you mad?'

'But my lord, please consider. You are aware that Lady Anais was the one who stole the hat, to implicate Savaric. You are aware that she is part of The Duo Dracones and was referred to as *la femme immaculée* within their organisation. And you are aware that she is more than likely involved in the plot to steal silver clippings from the treasury for a plot that will manifest itself very soon.'

'I wish I could do more but at this time, there is nothing I can do. The maid was clever enough to pass judgement on Savaric's character in Canterbury, which put a mark against his name from then on.' He sighed deeply. 'And hence why I've begun gathering information regarding Anais du Montluc since then.'

'Oh and what have you found, my liege?'

'The maid is the youngest of three daughters to the Baron du Montluc, and with her two eldest sisters making advantageous marriages at court, I assume Anais was keen to follow in their footsteps.'

'Yes, and I witnessed first-hand her ambitions at court in Paris.' She nodded. 'However, what I still cannot fathom is how and when she became involved with Renaisser and The Duo Dracones.'

De Burgh shrugged. 'It is hard to say, but all it would have taken was a chance meeting with Renaisser in Paris, possibly even at court. The man would have promised her something that surpassed even her lofty aspirations—a consort, a crown, and the chance to be the mother of a future king—in exchange for her involvement. All heady stuff for an ambitious daughter of a mere baron, who would love nothing better than to rise above the expectations of all whom knew her, do you not think?'

'Yes, I can certainly believe that of her. Anais is nothing if not shrewd and calculating.'

'Which is why we cannot accuse her of wrongdoing. Not presently, when we might lose whatever ground we have made in capturing all members of The Duo Dracones. Remember, the maid is not aware of everything we know about her.'

'But my lord, you cannot allow Savaric to get caught in this web of lies that Anais de Montluc and The Duo Dracones have devised, to get through to you?'

The man had the grace to look uncomfortable. 'Savaric is… He is an easy mark to be singled out and blamed in such a situation. As well as this, he is also much maligned of late, with the Dowager Queen herself passing judgement on him so publicly.'

Marguerite expelled a breath. 'Then what do you suggest?'

He shook his head slowly. 'There is nothing that we can do for him now. Not when my own position is so precarious and under threat.'

'Are you telling me that you would allow one of your own men who has sworn fealty to you to perish?'

'Of course not!'

'So, you are saying that we shall sit idly by and wait for Savaric to be arrested? Or worse, executed for an attack on the Dowager Queen that he had no part in?'

The older man paled. 'I have never declared thus.'

'Then you must act, my lord.'

Marguerite wanted to scream at the man as she watched de Burgh murmur to himself, hardly taking in what she was saying. He slumped onto a chair and shook his head. 'I had feared something like this might befall Savaric and tried to protect him by sending him away from the machinations at court. And still they managed to get to him and through him—to me.'

'My lord, please, we must do something more for him. Please, I implore you.'

He rubbed his brow and shook his head. 'I have sent word in Canterbury for Warin and Nicholas to come as soon as may be, since I feared the worse. However, other than that, there is nothing more I can do at the moment, Marguerite. My hands are tied.'

'It cannot be so,' she pleaded. 'You are the most powerful magnate in the kingdom.'

'Mistress, an attempt, or a supposed one, was made on the Dowager Queen's life and made to look as though it was one of my own trusted men. Thus, my position is no longer assured. Indeed, it is under threat even now, when the King can no longer lend his support to me.'

'There must be something we can do?'

He shook his head. 'There is nothing I can do for Savaric at the moment but he is one of my best men. He can look out for himself.'

'And if not? If he somehow cannot fight against the many, many guards who are even now on their way to arrest him, despite being one of your *best men*? What then?'

He slammed his fists hard on the table. 'If you want to help him, then find out more, mistress. Find the evidence against Anais du Montluc, otherwise we have nothing.'

'I shall endeavour to do all that I can but know this,

my lord.' She leant forward, her hands gripping the edge of the wooden table. 'I will not stand by for the crown to execute another innocent man for the crimes of another, as it did my own father. I will not stand by and let that happen to Savaric.' She straightened her spine and glared at the man. 'And if that might bring about my own arrest or should we *lose ground*, as you so eloquently put it, then so be it. I cannot in good conscience allow Savaric to meet such a fate. And as he is a member of your Knights Fortitude who has given you his continued fealty, you should do the same. He deserves better than this.'

And with that she stormed out of his privy chamber, her skirt flapping behind her, knowing she had to put some distance between herself and the man, lest she might actually throttle him. She stopped in her stride and took a deep breath into her chest. God above but had she just spoken to Hubert de Burgh in that manner, argued and challenged him? It was because she felt so desperate. It was a perilous situation that they now found themselves in, which was the reason why she had to do more. She had to find information that might aid and support Savaric in some way. And there was only one way in which she could do it. Yes, her best chance to find something potentially incriminating was in Anais de Montluc's chamber.

Marguerite continued through the myriad of hallways and spiral staircases, grabbing a flaming torch as she reached the Dowager Queen's solar. She entered the small chamber that she shared with a few of the other ladies, and after checking she was alone, changed her garments to the male ones she wore at the Port of London that first night she encountered Savaric, grabbed her set of daggers, and strapped them onto a leather belt around her waist, then topped this with a long dark woollen cloak. It was time to play the part of a young squire.

As all the Dowager's ladies would, at that moment, be tending to her after the attack in the woods, this was Marguerite's one and only opportunity to try and gain more information and evidence that could be used against Anais de Montluc.

She crept into the woman's chamber and began searching everywhere as expediently as possible, throwing a brief glance at the entrance every so often, in case someone was coming. Marguerite looked among Lady Anais's possessions in the wooden coffer, in her chest, her large saddlebag, under her pallet, and even beneath her bedding. But there was nothing—nothing at all except for the usual items one would expect a noblewoman to have with her on such a journey.

Marguerite rubbed her clammy forehead. There had to be something here that she was missing. There had to be. It was imperative that she exposed Anais de Montluc for the scheming traitor she was, but there was nothing. The chamber seemed to be devoid of anything that might be construed as evidence. Once again, the woman was one step ahead of her. Once again Marguerite had failed. As she moved to leave the chamber a sliver of light, from the last vestiges of the day, beamed through the wooden shutters and across the chamber, and caught a glint on the floor. Intrigued, Marguerite lowered herself to the floor and brushed the rushes aside but there was nothing there. It was not an item among the rushes but something beneath the wooden flooring.

This could be what she was looking for, and without further ado Marguerite used the sharp edge of one of her daggers against the wooden slats on the floor, trying to prise it open. Little by little the wood began to gape open and reveal what lay beneath, which seemed to be a block of something shiny and metallic. She reached down under the flooring, brought up the item, and gasped. It was a silver bullion and there seemed to be more hidden under the floor. Her heart pounded in her chest as Marguerite turned it around in her hands and noted the small emblem of The Duo Dracones in the corner. This was what she had been looking for—this! This had to be what all those silver coin clippings which had been stolen from the Crown treasury were intended for—to be melted down and made into bullions for The Duo Dracones. And she could only imagine what they would need to purchase with the bullion, if they intended to take the Crown by force—a mercenary army.

'Have you found what you have been looking for?' a voice from behind her—a woman's voice—muttered. Anais de Montluc…

'I believe so.' Marguerite gripped the hilt of her dagger from beneath her cloak. She had to be patient, calm and, when the time came, decisive. 'May I get up from the floor?'

'Yes, but I bid you to put your arms in the air and turn around slowly to face me.'

Marguerite did as she was commanded and turned around to face Anais de Montluc, who was pointing a dagger in her direction. 'Well, you have been busy, my lady, or should I call you *ma femme immaculée*?'

Anais's eyes widened. No, the woman had not expected Marguerite to know the other name she was known by.

She looked her up and down. 'It seems to me that you have been feigning, mistress.'

'No more than you, *my lady*, but even I had not thought you capable to attack the Dowager Queen and blame it on another.'

'You take a vested interest in Fitz Leonard but really, he was an easy target to pin the attack onto. After all, he stands out from other Crown Knights, does he not?' She jabbed the dagger closer. 'I take it that was you, whoring yourself to that mongrel that night in Canterbury?'

'Do not call him that.' Despite having a dagger pointed at her, Marguerite could feel her anger rising.

'Or you shall do what exactly?' The woman's lips curled into a sneer. 'I must say that it is rather touching, your defence of such a man.'

'Of such a man?'

'I can see the attraction of such a virile, handsome man—indeed I would have enjoyed the pleasure of his bed. But he is still a mongrel nevertheless.'

'I warned you to refrain from calling him that.'

'And if I don't?' The woman chuckled and shook her head. 'You are pathetic, Marguerite Studdal.'

In one quick move, Marguerite stepped forward, bent her knee and with her other leg swung it around, catching the woman off guard and disarming the dagger out of her hand. She then kicked the dagger out of the way before reaching down and claiming it.

'And you are a traitor, Anais de Montluc.' Marguerite raised a brow as she held the weapon out in front of the woman. 'Now, this is what we shall do. You are going to oblige me by accompanying me to confess to Hubert de Burgh. And if you are very accommodating, my liege lord might even be at ease to grant you a pardon, not that I would. I am not so forgiving, *my lady.*'

'What a rousing speech, but unfortunately I am not in mind to be as accommodating as you want me to be, mistress.'

'Oh, so you wish to fight it out then?' God, but the woman was a fool. Still, she needed to have her wits about her. 'I warn you that in this I shall prevail.'

'Oh, I think not...' The woman's smile should have alerted her to the ominous presence in the chamber and yet she had failed to register it. She had wanted so badly to outmanoeuvre the woman that she had been a little careless and not heard him enter the chamber via a secret opening through the panel on the floor.

'We meet again, mistress,' a cold voice said from the shadows in the chamber, making her blood run to ice. It was a voice that came from the depths of Marguerite's worst nightmare. 'What an unexpected pleasure.'

'Renaisser...' she whispered as the dagger slipped from her fingers, and she grasped the lace necktie around her throat. No, it could not be. It just couldn't...

Chapter Sixteen

Savaric's instincts had not deserted him, despite his mind still reeling from everything that happened the night that Marguerite had come apart in his arms. The night she had told Savaric that she loved him...

He had been tossing and turning in his pallet all night, the scent of her still clinging to his bedding, his mouth, and even his body. He wished things could be different between them. He wished he had had more time with her. He wished he could just hold her. He wished for so many things that he could not have.

Hell's teeth, but he had to stop his mind from constantly returning to Marguerite Studdal, otherwise he might run mad. Mayhap he already had. But the way she'd looked at him when he had explained that they could never be together... It had tormented him all night.

Without love, what is left?

The words that Marguerite uttered before she had left him churned over and over in his head. They were slowly stripping him bare. Everything he had once held true was beginning to unravel and with it his firmly held beliefs. In truth she had shaken the very foundations of his reasoning and found it wanting. By God, but she challenged him and made him look at the situation from an altogether different perspective.

You should also accept that I love you and that I want to be with you, regardless of anything else.

Could he be the man whom she believed him to be? The man Marguerite deserved? Savaric loved the woman but was that enough?

The following morn he had resigned himself to push the matter out of his mind. For now. It simply was not the time for such musings, even though he desperately wanted to see Marguerite.

Instead, he had to turn his mind to more pressing matters, namely the nagging feeling that there was an intangible danger permeating Dover Castle, the demesne land, and its shoreline. He had risen early just before dawn, broken his fast in the tavern, and gone to find his hat, which he had misplaced the previous night. Something he had never done. But then with Marguerite's visit and her insistence on coming to his chamber last night, it was a wonder that he hadn't lost his mind, let alone forgotten a damn hat.

Yet it was only after he had been informed that no one had found such a thing that he started to wonder whether he had even misplaced his signature item of attire. His leather hat was as ridiculous as it was distinctive, and could even be considered an extension of him in many ways. And it was not something that Savaric left lying about. And while someone could have taken it from the tavern, it seemed a little coincidental. As was the visit by Anais de Montluc before Marguerite's the previous night. In truth the woman would have had ample opportunity to take the damn thing, but why? The more Savaric considered that she might have done so, the more he began to consider the reason why Anais de Montluc would. A sense of foreboding wrapped around him. If his misgivings were correct then he had to leave the tavern with much haste. And just to stay on the side of caution, he decided to take that course of action. Savaric returned to his chamber, packed his meagre belongings, and turned to leave.

'Goin' somewhere, sir?'

'Ah, Connacht, yes, my good man.' Savaric wondered why the man was seemingly keeping an eye on him as he strolled along through the courtyard as though he hadn't a care in the world. 'Here, allow me to give you the monies I owe for your chamber.'

'Thank ye, sir, but me thought you'd be stayin' a while longer.'

'I shall return soon enough.' He rubbed his chin and watched the old man from a hooded gaze. 'There is a grave matter that needs my attention.'

The man clung to his cloak. 'Well, in that case, I best tells ye that I found the information you sought 'bout the captain otherwise known as the Ghost.'

'Oh, and what might that be?'

'If ye would like to return to the tavern with me, then we can discuss it better. Over a nice mug of ale. On the 'ouse, as well.'

Savaric's senses were heightened immediately but he masked it with a wry smile. 'I would love nothing better but alas, I have a prior engagement.'

'With who, sir? Only I'd like to know how I can locate you like, if I needs to.'

There was something not quite right with this strange exchange. 'Worry not, Connacht, I shall come to you anon, here at the tavern, and you can let me know all that you have learned regarding the *Ghost* and his cog the *Dragon*.'

'Very good, sir.' He gave him a singular look and turned to leave. 'Until later.'

It was a very odd exchange indeed and one that roused Savaric's suspicions as well as his mistrust. Why the hell was Connacht, whom he had known for a few years, so adamant that Savaric met with him now? It was not only strange, but the man had also been agitated. Yes, there was something amiss there.

But then, there was something amiss everywhere here in Dover. Savaric did not know what it could be but felt it in his bones, nevertheless.

Without his hat, and concealed under the hood of his cloak, he felt more inconspicuous as he ambled through the fortified barbican of the castle and walked through the inner bailey. He knew about the hunt that the royal party had been engaged in earlier that morn from listening to the many conversations in the tavern but it seemed that it was returning to the castle. And it was as he was ambling through the cobbled square of the inner bailey that the fine hair on the back of his neck rose. Something seemed very, very wrong here. There was a sense of confusion in the uneasiness as guards readied themselves in groups to leave the castle and the uncertainty was pierced by a palpable tension. He heard whispers of the Dowager Queen being hurt on the hunt as he passed through and an ominous feeling seeped through him. What the hell was going on?

He pulled his hood over his face and made his way to the stairway that led to Hubert de Burgh's set of chambers.

With the commotion and clamour of guards and hearth knights beyond the main keep and the inner bailey, there were very few in this part of the castle, which in itself alerted Savaric to the sudden trepidation surrounding the keep. He slipped inside Hubert de Burgh's antechamber and strode towards the middle wall of the chamber, darting his eyes all around before sliding a panel aside, allowing him to enter the secret passage that de Burgh had installed himself, when he was the constable of the castle during King John's reign.

Savaric pulled the panel back into place, plunging him into complete darkness as he continued along the long, dank passageway, feeling his way until he came to a dead end. He then crouched low and felt his hand along the bottom left-hand side and pushed the loose stone in, making the narrow panel spring open. He slid this across and squeezed his body through the opening, noting in amusement that de Burgh had evidently not designed this with someone of Savaric's stature in mind.

Only a stone wall now separated him from de Burgh's privy chamber and Savaric strained to hear the muffled voices within. He silently opened the small door that led within de Burgh's curtained storage closet and listened as the door within the chamber opened and closed.

Savaric peeped around the thick dark curtain expecting to find an empty room but was surprised to see

Hubert de Burgh himself perched against the edge of the small wooden table, rubbing his hand up and down his face in agitation.

Savaric walked around the curtain and stepped into the chamber, startling the older man.

'Oh, good God!' He stood and crossed the chamber. 'What are you doing here, Fitz Leonard?'

'I had to see you, my lord.'

'The risk was too high, Savaric.' The man ushered him back into the curtained closet and lowered his voice to a whisper. 'You cannot stay, my boy, the situation is now even more dangerous than before.'

'How so?'

'The Dowager Queen was the target of an attack on the hunt by a man on horseback wielding a damn crossbow.'

Dear God...

'Is the Queen hurt? What happened?'

'No.' The older man shook his head. 'The bow failed to hit its mark, yet the horse she had been riding threw her off so yes, she was hurt but not badly, thank the lord. However, there's more, Savaric... When the assailant was given chase, a hat was found on the ground. Your hat.'

He screwed his eyes shut and shook his head.

'You are not as surprised as I believed you might be at such news.'

'No, I am not, as I had foreseen such an outcome.'

'Then why in heaven's name had you not warned me?'

'Because I had only just found my hat to be missing myself, which is by the by, something that has never occurred, and why I came to the conclusion that something was afoot.'

'Well, you are too late.' The man threw his hands in the air. 'It's now extremely dangerous for you, and I can no longer extend my support, nor protect you.'

'I have ascertained that.'

'And can you also see how this will now undermine my position as well?'

'Yes.' He made a single nod. 'I can.'

'My enemies will use this to tear down everything that I have tried to achieve ever since I helped secure the throne for King Henry, when he was just a boy of nine years.' The man stood erect with his hands behind his back, staring out in front of him. 'It was in this very castle that I fought a siege, defending this kingdom against becoming a vassal for a foreign king. And I would do it again, if I had to, Savaric.'

'You shall always have my fealty, my lord. I will stand by you.'

Indeed, as the man had been more than a mentor and had always believed in him, Savaric would always owe Hubert de Burgh his continued loyalty. Just as a certain fiery woman had the strength to put her faith in him…

Marguerite…

Lord knew how Savaric wanted to be the one who would rise to that challenge and shield her from the unpleasantness of the world. He wanted to be that man for her.

De Burgh turned his head. 'I was reminded of your fealty only moments ago, not that I have ever been in doubt.'

If only he had more time with Marguerite to smooth

their rocky path. If only he had more time to be, to talk, to love.

Time?

Savaric was suddenly alert, pondering on something that had plagued him for some time…

Indeed, before he had died Ned Lutt had voiced his caution about how little time there was. About how evil would be soon be unleashed.

Of course…it all made sense. It all fell into place.

'This has been about *you*, my lord. All of it.' Savaric turned and addressed de Burgh. 'From the first, The Duo Dracones plotted to crush you in every manner, in every way, again and again. Thomas Lovent uncovered the group and then later, Warin and Joan, then Nicholas along with Eva stopped each attempt that they made. But now they grow impatient, they grow desperate. This time The Duo Dracones want to bring about your downfall at the very place of your triumph, as you mentioned earlier.'

'Dover!'

'Precisely. And we have walked straight into it.' Savaric shook his head. 'The danger is far more imminent than we perceived. Even as we speak, they are mobilising under our very nose. They attacked the Dowager Queen, whether real or otherwise, earlier and blamed it on me, a Crown Knight, thus creating a diversion. Creating chaos. A perfect time to attack an unsuspecting garrison on English soil, with a group of mercenaries paid with stolen silver clippings from the Crown treasury, no less.'

'Dear God. You mean they think to attack us, now?'

De Burgh rubbed his forehead. 'Here, in a mighty fortress such as Dover Castle? They shall never prevail.'

'We shall need to act decisively without alerting them of this knowledge,' Savaric said. 'Then we strike the bastards when they least expect it.'

Hubert de Burgh nodded. 'And for that to succeed, I need you to take care, focus your attention to the task at hand, and get out of this castle in one piece.'

'I shall endeavour to, my lord.'

'And from within, Marguerite Studdal will help me placate the Dowager Queen as I shall do the same for the King Henry.'

At the mention of Marguerite's name Savaric looked across and asked the question that he had desperately wanted to since the previous night. 'And how does Mistress Marguerite fare?'

'She is extremely worried for you, and gave me a set-down for not appearing to do more.'

The corners of Savaric's lips twitched and he felt himself flush. Christ, when was the last time such a thing had happened to him? When had a woman ever felt the need to defend him? 'I can imagine you were not too pleased by her…er…impudence?'

'No, but I believe I comprehend her feelings.' The man shook his head. 'In any case, she stormed out of here on a mission to find evidence that might absolve you of any involvement in the attack on the Dowager Queen's life.'

Savaric stilled. 'What did you say, my lord?'

'I believe that Marguerite has gone to Anais de Montluc's bedchamber so that she might find something to prove the woman's involvement with The Duo Dracones.'

'God's blood. When was this?'

'Just before you arrived.' The older man frowned. 'What seems to be the problem?'

The problem was that her anger and annoyance might have made her, inadvertently, walk into danger. 'You say she has gone to Anais de Montluc's chamber?'

'Do not think of doing anything as asinine as going to find Mistress Marguerite in that part of the castle. If you are seen anywhere near the Queen Isabella's quarters, it would be assumed that you have returned to finish what you started, Savaric. And attack her again.'

'I will ensure that I remain unseen, my lord.'

'But the castle is swarming with guards and knights.'

'And I shall take due care.'

'You are playing a dangerous game, Savaric.' The man sighed deeply. 'Very well, but you must understand that if you get caught, there is very little I can do for you. Your guilt is assured the moment you step foot in the Queen's ladies' chambers.'

'I know.'

'And you also know the best route to that quarter, I assume?'

'Yes, my lord. I remember it well.'

'Good. Take care, my boy.' The older man clasped his arm as Savaric bowed. He then left the small closet and went back the same way he had come.

Savaric made his way through the secret passageway which led to the antechamber, flipped his hood back and bent his head low, walking with purpose along the hallway. He quickened his pace and rushed down the spiral staircase but did not leave the building. Standing still for a moment, to avoid a group of castle guards nearby, he expelled a breath after they turned to walk further into the bailey. After checking there was no one in his vicinity Savaric moved to the back of the stairwell, opened a trap door, and slipped inside another secret passage. He rushed along the long passageway that bought him up to another trap door which he climbed out of, and after checking around the area, he moved up the spiral staircase that led to the royal apartments. With his heart thumping against his chest and his head lowered as he passed a few guards standing near the entrance of the Queen's apartments without pausing or slowing his pace, he entered the lady's empty antechamber with two bedchambers off each side. Sighing in relief, Savaric's next task was to look for Marguerite in either chamber. She was not present in the neatly arranged bedchamber that he entered, nor the second.

Damn…

He had been convinced that this would be the first place that Marguerite would have looked, unless…unless he had missed her again. It was quite possible since Savaric had entered this part of castle through secret passages, where he would not have encountered her. Mayhap she found something before moving on. Mayhap she had…

Savaric's eye caught something on the ground crushed amongst the rushes. He bent down to pick it up and found it to be Marguerite's lace necktie. That indeed was unexpected as she never ever took it off. Even during that night of intimacy they shared, she had doggedly wanted to keep it tied around her neck, covering her scar, until he had persuaded her otherwise. Strange…unless she had taken it off on purpose. Unless she was somehow trying to convey a message to him. Savaric continued his search of the chamber as he pondered this, knowing he was running out of time. Someone was bound to enter the chamber soon and encounter him, so it was imperative he made his search as expediently as possible.

He looked beneath the pallet and apart from the strewn rushes there was something glinting in the far corner. He stretched out to reach for it but just as he grabbed hold of it, he heard footsteps and a murmur of voices from outside the chamber. Before they entered the room, he quickly dived beneath the pallet to hide from view.

He kept totally still as two women, two of the Precious A's came in and chatted for a long moment.

'I do not know where Anais was going with Marguerite, dressed in such sombre attire. Do you?'

'No, I am not concerned with that woman's movements. I find Anais de Montluc to be quite unpalatable.'

'You're only irritable with her because of her awful chatter. But that aside, I did find it strange that they had a man with them—do you suppose it could be the notoriously handsome Savaric Fitz Leonard?'

'You must not talk of him,' the other woman hissed. 'He could be a traitor. And no, the man accompanying Anais was certainly not him, as he had not been tall enough to be Sir Savaric.'

'Do you suppose he was the assailant who made an attempt on the Queen's life?' one of the women muttered.

'I doubt it. I never took him for a fool. Come, Alice, we must get back to the Queen.'

And with that, the women's footsteps retreated away from the chamber. Savaric waited for a moment, ensuring that they had left before dragging himself out from under the pallet, standing, and rubbing his jaw. From what he had just heard he was now convinced about what had happened to Marguerite—she had been taken. He opened his palms to glance at her dagger, realising that she must have kicked it under the pallet as well as untying her lace necktie moments before she was forced to go somewhere with Anais de Montluc. And in Savaric's mind, both items that had been left here were a desperate attempt from her to send a message to him about who had taken her. It stood to reason that if she was seen by the Queen's ladies accompanying Anais de Montluc, then the man they had seen with them must be no other than Renaisser.

Christ Almighty! Savaric needed to get to Marguerite as soon as may be. He could not think about what she might be going through in the company of that bastard. And if the man even touched her...

He pushed that thought away...for now. He had to have his wits about him, unless he wanted to get captured. Savaric tucked Marguerite's possessions away under his cloak and went back the way he came. He needed to get back to the trap door that he had crept out of earlier, which would in turn connect him to de Burgh's network of secret passages that would lead to the north side of the castle and a tunnel beneath the curtain wall of the fortress. He managed to get to the spiral staircase unseen but as he was halfway down the wooden stairwell, he heard murmurs above him.

'You there, stop,' a voice ground out from above.

'Who, me?' Savaric altered the pitch of his voice but did little to slow the pace. 'Can't stop, sir. I 'ave an urgent message from one of the Queen's ladies for my lord Hubert de Burgh himself.'

'No, wait. I said halt!' the man bellowed.

Hell and damnation. Savaric had little time for this—he could not stop and allow guards to stall or even arrest him. He had to get to the woman he loved. Marguerite needed him and while there was breath left in his body he would do just that, even if he had to raze this damn castle to the ground to get to her. He just hoped that she was somehow safe and unharmed.

Savaric rushed down as the guards followed him and shouted, trying in vain to get him to stop in order to conduct whatever interrogation they had in mind, but naturally Savaric kept on going. When he reached the bottom, he kicked the wooden door open, and swung back around, moving to hide in the shadows behind the back of the stairwell. The guards reached the ground level and ran out into the bailey. Savaric did not have long until the inevitability of the guards coming back inside the building. He quickly opened the trap door, looking around before making his way down the small entrance and turning back to close it on himself. As soon as his boots hit the uneven surface of the ground beneath him, he turned to move but stopped in his tracks as he faced the unwelcome sight of Lord Richard de Vars with one of his men.

'Ah, Fitz Leonard, finally. I have been expecting you.'

'I am honoured, my lord, but sadly I have neither the time nor the inclination to stay and converse at this moment,' he said as his hands clenched around the hilt of his sword.

'You impudent filth! You dare to address me thus, after your vicious attack on Queen Isabella?'

'I suppose you are disinclined to believe that I had nothing to do with the attack?'

'Strangely enough, yes. You might not be surprised to learn that I always believed someone like you to be capable of turning.'

Someone like you…

God, but how many times would he have to hear such damning words?

'Duly noted.' Savaric had little time for this or Richard de Vars, even if he now no longer believed the man to be involved with The Duo Dracones. He stepped forward and punched de Vars hard, swinging around and delivering a similar unexpected blow to his man. 'And duly dealt with.'

He stepped over the men and began to run down the narrow passageway, grabbing a flaming torch along the way. He could hear the two men giving chase to him after seemingly getting back on their feet. Savaric picked up his pace and moved down the winding passageway.

The further Savaric raced down from the fortress castle, the closer he was now getting to the sea, with the passageway becoming damp from the stonewalls and sludge on the ground. Yet Savaric continued forth, feeling his chest burn from the exertion of the run. He reached the end of the secret passage, which opened outside the castle walls and far below the sloping hill, down towards the shore. He ran out and stopped a moment to catch his breath when he looked up to find the sharp metal tips of three swords pointing straight at him and behind them the men wielding the swords, wearing capes and shrouded in darkness with masks over their noses and mouths.

God's blood!

Savaric screwed his eyes shut and muttered a long curse under his breath, knowing he needed to think and needed to do it quickly.

'Ah, so glad that you have encountered a few of my men,' Richard de Vars retorted almost gleefully from behind, having now evidently caught up with him. 'You did not think I was going to leave your capture to chance, did you?'

Savaric couldn't resist a shrug. 'Ah, but there was always the hope.'

The man slapped him hard with the back of his hand, his gold signet ring catching Savaric's cheekbone. 'You insolent mongrel! Lady Anais had the right of you, Fitz Leonard. She had always suspected you of conspiring against the Crown and if I did not have to take you back to the castle for interrogation, I would gladly run my sword through your worthless body here and now. I would finish you off here, I would…'

Savaric heard a thud and lifted his head to find the man's eyes widened in surprise and shock before he slumped in a heap onto the ground. And behind him stood one of the masked men who had drawn his sword out to him earlier. He tore off his mask, as did the other two, and Savaric almost wept with relief to find Nicholas D'Amberly and beside him Warin de Talmont, with one of the Knights Fortitude's squires grappling with de Vars's man.

'Your timing is as impeccable as always, D'Amberly,' Savaric drawled as he inhaled a shaky breath. 'But by God, I am happy to see you, and you too, de Talmont.'

He stepped forward to clasp his friends by the arm.

'See here, Warin, I told you Savaric would miss us.'

'No one ever misses you, D'Amberly, and especially not your incessant prattle. I swear you belong in a lady's bower chamber.' De Talmont shook his head and glanced at Richard de Vars and his man, both incapacitated on the ground. 'And what are we to do with these two?'

'Tie them to a tree,' Nicholas D'Amberly muttered. 'No one shall miss them, especially Richard de Vars who, as I have always said, is an arse.'

Savaric smiled as Warin shook his head and turned to him. 'And are you well, my friend?'

'I am now thanks to you both. But they have Marguerite. And I need to get to her.'

'Who has her?'

'Lady Anais de Montluc and Renaisser.'

'Renaisser is here?'

Savaric nodded. 'I'll explain our findings en route but we need to make haste now. We have little time.'

'Are you saying that you know where they might be?'

'Here in Dover. The Duo Dracones plot has now come down to this very moment.'

'And where are they now?'

'I do not know but I know a man who does—Connacht the innkeeper.'

Nicholas D'Amberly ran his fingers through his hair. 'Shame, I always liked the man, but I suppose he now reeks too much of betrayal.'

Savaric nodded. 'That he does.'

'And so it begins.' Warin rubbed his jaw.

'No, this is where it all ends.'

'This is where we shall prevail. We shall get The Duo Dracones once and for all.'

'Aye,' Nicholas said as each man clasped the others' arms in solidarity and in unity.

'Pro Rex, Pro Deus, Pro fide, Pro honoris.'

They said the motto of the Knights Fortitude of the Order of the Sword together in unison, as an apt reminder of their pledge to fight for King and country, binding them together as they stepped into the unknown.

Chapter Seventeen

Marguerite had been taken out of the castle numb, dazed, and in state of shock at having the man who had haunted and terrorised her dreams for so long walking beside her in the flesh. She was unsure how she had so easily been cajoled into walking alongside Renaisser and Anais de Montluc straight out of the inner and then outer bailey, which led them through the formidable barbican of Dover Castle, but she offered no resistance, no struggle. Not in any way.

Her limbs and her body complied with their demands and iron will, following where they led in silence, while inside she was screaming, needing and wanting to take action, but her fear and terror of Renaisser made it impossible to do so. It was as though she had no control over herself, debilitated and weakened by her deep anxiety for this man.

And yet slowly, slowly this feeling of trepidation that had gripped itself so tightly around her began to wane. Marguerite started to wake from this horror as they made their way down the hill in the cloak of darkness, and she realised that she needed to do something if she wanted to live. She could not allow this to happen to her again—for Renaisser to dominate and overwhelm her. If she did that then it would only allow him to hurt her once more. Marguerite had to stand up to him and find a way out of this. But for now, she would gather herself together, gather her resolve and strength, and learn more about what the situation actually entailed. As well as what Renaisser wanted with her—not that it could be good.

They continued to walk along the shoreline, putting the castle far behind them. But as they neared a hidden cove, Marguerite realised why they had come here. She was shocked to find an army of men who had arrived to these shores by many different vessels and had mobilised together here, awaiting their leader. Oh, God, so *this* was what it had all been about—the conspiring of The Duo Dracones against the Crown. A Crown that even at that moment would be chasing its tail on a heedless search for a man—an honourable, chivalrous man—it believed to have made an attack on the Dowager Queen. It all made sense now—the clipping of coins, stolen from the Crown and the melting the silver down to fund all of this, presumably. The treacherous bastards!

Marguerite had to find a way out of here and warn Savaric and Hubert de Burgh before it was too late.

'I see now what your intentions are,' Marguerite murmured, finding her voice at last.

Since they had dragged her to the shore, her hands and feet had been tied together and she had been forced down on the ground. And while they had left her, Marguerite had been trying to loosen the ties around her wrists for some time to no avail. Her arms stretched behind her, reached down to the back of her tied ankles where she had hidden her smallest knife strapped to her leg. Now if she could only grasp it and use it to cut through these bindings…

Renaisser had been conferring with a few of his men, as well as the man Marguerite recognised to be the captain of the cog ship.

Renaisser turned and tilted his head to the side. 'How very observant of you, Marguerite.' He gave her a smile that sent a chill through her. 'And may I say how delighted I am to be reunited with you again.'

She needed to keep him talking as her fingers touched the knife and slowly dragged it from behind the back of her leg. 'And I presume your plans are to see the downfall of the Crown?'

'No, just your master, the faithless coward Hubert de Burgh, and all his supporters. And once he no longer has the ear of the King, we shall endeavour to penetrate the heart of the Crown. And then my beautiful *belle immaculée* will even become Queen to the hapless King Henry.'

'You are quite mad.'

'No, just driven to rid this land of all the false, corrupt, and immoral men such as your master, Marguerite. The young King will soon come to our way of thinking—he will come to serve *us*.'

The man truly was mad. 'And what of me? What use to your big schemes am I?'

He raised a brow. 'I have yet to decide your fate, my beauty, but mayhap I shall keep you for myself or use you in whatever manner might further our cause. Who knows? Your anticipation in this will surely heighten the excitement, do you not think?'

She looked away lest the man witness her revulsion and continued to drag the small blade into her hand. Just a little bit more and she would have it.

'I think that this is a lost cause. I think in the end you shall fail.'

The man lifted his hand to strike her but then allowed it to fall to his side. 'You do amuse me, Marguerite. Mayhap I shall keep you after all.' He chuckled as he reached down and yanked her chin up. 'Tell me, sweet, have you dreamt of me all this time, as I have of you?' His lips curled at the corners into that vile sneer.

God, he was detestable. And yet after that initial shock of seeing the man so close and in the flesh, Renaisser had seemingly lost his power over her. He was no longer as terrifying as she had imagined him to be. And this gave her a courage that she grasped with both hands. Mayhap it was the memory of the words Savaric had uttered the last time she had seen him that somehow gave her the hope and belief. He had told her to accept the visible scars she had. To remember that she had endured and overcome.

Marguerite tipped her head up and glared at him. 'No, I have not given you a moment's thought.'

'You lie,' he murmured, running a finger slowly across her neck. 'You think of me often, my sweet.'

No, Marguerite refused to allow the man to have such a hold on her ever again. She would think of Savaric, his struggles, his strength, and his belief in her.

Indeed, it mattered not what Renaisser thought. He was nothing to her now.

She watched the man walk away as she finally had the blade in her grasp. She clenched it in her fist, tipping it upwards between her two fingers, so that she could start to work the rope ties digging into her wrists, without it being visible. And then what? What could she possibly do when she was surrounded by Renaisser and so many of The Duo Dracones? Apart from a few of her daggers still strapped to her, Marguerite had little else.

No matter, she would continue with the task at hand and think of her next move anon. Suddenly a clamour alerted her attention. She looked up to find a lone man making his way towards Renaisser and wringing his hands together.

'What do think you are doing here, Connacht?' Renaisser was evidently not happy to see this man.

'I'm so sorry, me lord, but there's a bit of a problem to the plans you laid out.'

'If you presume to tell me that you have failed, then know that I shall carry out the threats I made to you and your family.'

'I 'ave not failed yer, me lord Renaisser. I would not do that. But the man you wished me to keep at the tavern, so he gets arrested—Savaric Fitz Leonard. He's still not caught. He's a wily one and no one knows where he is gone to hidin', like.'

'Go back to your tavern and await further instructions, Connacht. The whereabouts of a lone Crown Knight who has a price on his head do not interest me.'

A man stepped out of the shadows and strode with

purpose towards them. Marguerite's heart missed a beat as she realised that it was Savaric Fitz Leonard himself.

'Mayhap you should care, Renaisser,' Savaric drawled sardonically, raising a brow.

Marguerite continued to work through the rope ties, her heart swelling for Savaric. God, how she loved the man.

'Well, well, well, this really has become a reunion, has it not, Marguerite? Welcome, Sir Savaric the Crown bastard,' he spat as Savaric bristled. 'I take it you have considered joining us, since I cannot think you fool enough to come here alone?'

Savaric looked magnificent as he stepped forward and stopped with his legs apart. He shook his head slowly. 'No, I have not come to join you.' He drew out his sword from its scabbard and held it in the air. 'And nor have I come alone.'

Warin de Talmont stepped forward and stopped beside Savaric and then Nicholas D'Amberly did the same on Savaric's other side. The three men stood side by side and Marguerite's jaw dropped slightly at how powerful and intimidating they looked together.

Renaisser had seemingly been shocked into silence for a moment before shaking his head at them. 'Ah, I see you have all come, together as one. How touching. But you are far too late.'

'I think not,' Savaric bellowed for all of them to hear. 'Throw down your weapons and we might spare you.'

There was a murmur among the men of The Duo Dracones before their leader silenced them. 'You think you can defeat me? You think to defeat me when I have all these men and there is just the three of you?'

'I believe that I would enjoy proving how we can defeat the bastard with just the three of us,' Nicholas said as he and Warin also drew out their swords.

'But let not us not give him that satisfaction.' Savaric's eyes flicked to Marguerite's for a moment before he fixed them to Renaisser's and smiled ruefully.

Marguerite gasped, mesmerised as a dozen or so men stepped forward from the shadows and stood behind the three Knights Fortitude, and then another twenty or thirty men stood behind them in formation in another line.

'We…we still outnumber you,' Renaisser muttered, sounding unconvinced even to his own ears.

'Mayhap, but would you take that chance against a *bastard Crown Knight* as well as all the men here?' Savaric pointed his sword blade at him. 'What say you?'

'I say that we shall still succeed.' Renaisser's voice rose in an attempt to whip his men up so they did not lose faith.

Nicholas D'Amberly also pointed his sword. 'And I say that you are merely wishing for that to be the case.'

'Indeed. As it is, you might want to take a look behind you.' Warin raised his sword up and another line of men stepped forward at the rear of where The Duo Dracones had amassed on the beach, effectively hemming them in. 'And mayhap take a look up there.'

Marguerite lifted her head and saw there up on the white cliffs many men on horseback, and swore she could see Hubert de Burgh in the centre, and even Sir Thomas Lovent—a fellow Crown Knight and brother-in-law to Warin—there beside him.

'I shall repeat.' Savaric's voice rose as he addressed

The Duo Dracones and their mercenary army. 'Throw down your weapons and surrender.'

One by one the men around Renaisser threw down their weaponry and stuck their arms behind their heads in surrender.

It was the end for them and Renaisser knew it, which meant that now, at this moment of vulnerability, he would also be at his most dangerous.

Renaisser came and pulled Marguerite to her feet, yanking her in front of him and grasping on to her from behind, with a dagger placed at her neck. She froze, recalling the sense that she had been here before with this man, and was suddenly taken back to the time two years ago when Renaisser threatened her in exactly the same way.

'I seem to recall that you were rather fond of this woman,' Renaisser jeered, pulling her tightly to him as Savaric took a step forward. 'If you would rather not have her throat slit more permanently than the mark I left her last time, then I suggest you call off your dogs. Do you hear me? Call these men away.'

She could hardly breathe but she just about managed to respond. 'Do not dare, Savaric. I am not worth whatever this man wants to bargain me with.'

Savaric kept his eyes pinned to Renaisser's as he stepped slowly towards them. 'Oh, I quite disagree, love. Your worth is more than you can ever imagine.'

'What a touching declaration. Now as I said, call these men off and do not come any closer, Fitz Leonard.'

'Alas they do not answer to me.'

'Then tell whoever it is that they do answer to!'

Marguerite could feel the sharp edge of the blade

digging into her neck, knowing she had to stop this now or it might be too late.

'Ah, you must mean King Henry, who is there atop the cliffs watching you, and all you traitors, Renaisser? And that includes you, Lady Anais. Your part in all of this shall not be forgotten. Now let Mistress Marguerite go.'

'I have not done anything, sir.' Anais de Montluc, who had conspired with Renaisser and others only moments ago, now pathetically dropped to her knees. All completely for show. 'Have mercy on me. This man forced me to do his bidding. I am blameless… I am innocent of wrongdoing… I am…'

'Shut your mouth!' Renaisser bellowed at her.

It was in that moment when Marguerite finally managed to cut through the bindings that tied her wrists together behind her back. She let them fall to the ground and in a single motion, jerked her head back with so much force that it made contact with Renaisser's nose, surprising him. And then just as quickly she brought both arms back and hit the man in the stomach, making him drop to the ground.

Marguerite ran towards Savaric, as Renaisser got back on his feet and managed to launch himself towards her. Savaric ran to her aid but as he reached her, Renaisser grabbed a lance from the ground and struck it towards Marguerite and Savaric. Without thinking Savaric pushed her behind him, effectively becoming a human shield to her, as Marguerite pulled out her dagger and threw it at Renaisser, who was advancing towards them. He fell to the ground with the dagger hitting its mark, just as Savaric struck the lance with his sword, propelling the weapon away from them.

They both froze in that moment, unable to move, unable to breathe. But it was over, thank God. It was all over.

Savaric glanced at Renaisser lying motionless on the ground and then at Marguerite. He dropped his sword before stepping towards her, as she ran towards him and into his arms.

'Did he hurt you?' he murmured against her ear, holding her tightly against him.

'No.'

'Did he touch you?'

'No.'

His shoulders seemed to sag a little. 'My God, Marguerite, I do believe you just saved my life...again.'

She smiled against his chest, as tears streamed down her face. 'You are worth saving, Savaric Fitz Leonard, and do not allow anyone to tell you differently.'

He smiled. 'As are you, my love.'

Marguerite pulled away from him and looked up. 'And you saved my life as well by and by. He was aiming that lance at me.'

He cradled her head with both hands, his thumb wiping away dirt and the small grains of sand from her face. 'I would rather have died than allowed him to hurt you again.' He touched his forehead to hers. 'God, when I found out that he had taken you, I wanted to tear everything down in my wake, from the castle to the trees, and every damn thing until I could get to you. But in the end, it seems that you didn't actually need me, my brave woman.'

'Oh, quite the contrary, Savaric Fitz Leonard.' She

raised herself on her toes and reached up, pressing her lips to his. 'I need you more than I can say.'

Savaric pulled her tightly into his arms and returned her kiss so passionately that Marguerite thought she might melt into a puddle at his feet. Somewhere behind them, she could just about make out the roar of approval from the men assembled at the beach, clattering their weapons and stomping their feet.

'I am sorry,' she said a little breathlessly, pulling away, and felt herself blushing at such a public display.

'I am not.' He grinned, coaxing her back into his arms. 'And never will be.'

Chapter Eighteen

Marguerite looked around King Henry's privy chamber, with Hubert de Burgh, the Dowager Queen, and a handful of courtiers present, took a deep breath to steady her nerves and waited until she was beckoned forth. She saw the three Knights Fortitude, standing together to the side, attired in all their finery, having just been highly decorated by King Henry for their services in finally catching and apprehending The Duo Dracones, and ridding the kingdom of the threat that they had posed. Renaisser's death certainly assured them of that. And Lady Anais de Montluc was fortunate that King Henry had not handed out a harsher sentence after her treachery. Instead he had secured an agreement with the lady's father, Baron de Montluc, that his youngest daughter would enter a convent in France and never set foot on English soil again.

Marguerite felt a swell of pride in her chest for what they had all achieved together. Every single one of them had played their part, especially Savaric, who was now once again reunited with his infamous hat and had also been rewarded handsomely by both King Henry and Hubert de Burgh, which he thoroughly deserved. Savaric glanced across and winked at her, making her feel more at ease.

Suddenly the buisine trumpets heralded that Marguerite's turn had come. The moment had arrived. She walked down the aisle until she reached the dais and stopped, lowering herself into the most graceful curtsy she could muster, and knelt in front of the King and his mother.

Hubert de Burgh then decorated Marguerite for her part in helping capture The Duo Dracones. And for theirs, the Crown of England pledged to retract her father's name as traitor, return her family's confiscated lands as well as returning Studdal Castle back to her family, or rather her young brother. And as a way to show their gratitude, they presented Marguerite with a symbolic key to Studdal Castle and a rolled vellum, for which she received applause from all who were in attendance.

God above, she had done it! Marguerite felt somewhat overwhelmed with gratitude and a huge sense of relief, as if a weight had suddenly been lifted off her shoulders. She felt the sting of tears and realised that she was now finally able to restore her family's name and honour. Marguerite now hoped that with her father's name absolved, she could live again—that she could finally breathe again.

Marguerite willingly accepted the key and vellum from de Burgh and kissed the hand of King Henry, just as servants arrived with goblets of wine and small dainty pastries filled with cheese, spiced meats, and dried fruits, on top of ornate silver trenchers. She was joined by Nicholas and Warin, who both kissed her hand, and their wives, Eva and Joan, who gave her hugs, congratulating her.

But there seemed to be one person missing.

She frowned, looking around their small assembled group. 'Does anyone know of Savaric's whereabouts?'

Warin looked at Nicholas, who shrugged, looking a little uncomfortable. 'He extended his apology but declared that he had to leave.'

'Leave?' She shook her head, unable to believe that he had gone. 'What could possibly be so pressing that he had to leave now, at this very moment?'

'I do not know, Marguerite, although I should add that Savaric is not always very comfortable at court functions such as this,' Warin said with a sigh. 'Even so, I should follow him and ask him directly, if I were you.'

Yes, she would do just that. Marguerite could not comprehend that after such a public display on the beach, he would now just leave, mayhap depart from the castle itself without even bidding her farewell… *just like last time.*

Would he even do such a thing?

Without a further glance she picked up her skirts and turned on her heel, striding out of the chamber, and quickly made her way down the spiral stairwell and down into the inner baily, the chilly breeze sending a shiver through her body. She did not care…she did not register it. All she wanted was to get to Savaric and find out what he was about. Marguerite pushed ahead, running through the outer bailey and through the barbican, down the hill to the village and finally reaching the tavern. She stopped to catch her breath in the courtyard before climbing her way up the wooden steps and there in the doorway was Savaric Fitz Leonard. The shadows masked his features, but his tall, taut frame was unmistakable. He leant against the wall and when he saw her, pushed away from the stone and stepped out of the darkness.

'You came?' He held out his hand to her.

'I was not aware that I was being summoned.'

'And yet here you are anyway.'

She took his hand, his fingers wrapping around hers. 'Yes, I am here anyway. Not that I know why you left so suddenly?'

'Does it matter?'

'Yes, no… I do not know.'

He kissed her fingers. 'Would you prefer it if I said that I wanted you to myself? Or that I could not wait any longer to be alone with you?' Her pulse quickened at his unexpected words.

'Only if that is true.'

'Oh, it is.' He smiled slowly, making her stomach flip over itself. 'Come.'

Savaric led her inside and stopped as they walked through the threshold, giving her a moment to look her fill around his chamber.

Marguerite gasped, taking in the changes, unable to fathom what it all meant. There was a roaring fire in the hearth providing a warm glow throughout the chamber and a small trencher of the same pastries they had in the King's privy chambers, as well as a handful of red apples, some chicken legs, and a wedge of cheese, with two silver goblets and a jug of wine. She looked across the pallet, which was covered with a beautiful cream-and-blue coverlet, and pink flowers and petals strewn all over. A bubble of laughter rose inside her as she shook her head in disbelief.

'Pink?'

He shrugged and grinned sheepishly. 'I really am partial to pink carnations.'

The corners of her lips twitched. Her eyes darted around the room before returning to his. 'I see…or at least I think that I do.'

'There is really nothing complicated here, Marguerite. Not in how I feel about you. And after the declaration I made at the beach, I wanted a more private one, just the two of us.'

'Oh, and what declaration is that?' She turned in his arms as she waited for his answer, her heart hammering in her chest so hard, she felt that it might tear out of her skin.

'That I need you.' He smiled tenderly. 'That I want you. As I believe or rather hope that you want me.' His hands wrapped around either side of her hips.

True, and yet she needed more answers than just this. 'But I thought that you said that this connection between us could never be?'

'I did, but that no longer holds true, Marguerite. Especially after I almost lost you…again.' He tipped her chin up to meet his gaze. 'I could not bear that.'

She swallowed hard. 'You…you couldn't?'

'No.' He shook his head. 'It is mayhap because I love you.'

'You do?' Why was she continually questioning him inanely again and again?

She took in a shaky breath, knowing it was because she was unable to believe that this was truly happening. That Savaric was saying words that she had longed to hear for so long.

'I do, yes.'

'And I love you.' She looked up and smiled. 'So what happens now?'

'Do you really need me to answer that?' he murmured, glancing around the chamber and raising a brow.

She pulled away slightly. 'I need to know why, Savaric? Why this change of heart?'

He inhaled deeply as though he needed to ready himself for what he was about to say. 'In truth, I realised that a woman who would so readily stand and defend me in the fierce manner that you did at the beach was one who might also be prepared to face the many challenges that life would throw at us. And there would be many, Marguerite.'

She gazed into his eyes to see the absolute truth there. The intensity, the heat, and the love. Oh, and there was so much love brimming in his golden eyes that it made her heart soar.

'I am ready to face them. As long as you are by my side.' She smiled. 'Besides, you also saved my life.'

'I will always be there for you, Marguerite Studdal. Surely you know that.'

'I begin to, yes,' she murmured softly. 'Although I still cannot believe that it is me whom you want.'

'Can you not, when it is you who has accepted me as the man I am?' He clasped her hands, pressing a kiss in the centre of her palm. 'You see *me*, Marguerite, just as I am, and surprisingly you somehow still accept me.

I doubt that I shall ever fully reconcile myself to how astonishing that is.'

Oh, God!

Marguerite swallowed, trying to dislodge a lump that had formed in the back of her throat. 'I do see you and what I see is a man, who is kind, honourable, and extraordinary in every way. But above all I see a man who speaks to my heart.'

He smiled, brushing his fingers down the column of her neck. 'Ah, but that is because you have ruthlessly captured mine, as you have my body and soul.'

'I have?'

'Indeed.' He tipped her chin upwards. 'Be mine, Marguerite Studdal?'

'I already am,' she whispered before Savaric swooped her up into his arms and shut the wooden door with his heel.

He carried her to the pallet and laid her down among the carnation petals, and began to divest his clothing, never once taking his eyes off her. And then when he stood in all his naked glory, he smiled that knowing smile which never failed to send a shiver through Marguerite and slowly, carefully, breathlessly undressed her, showing her again and again the endless measure of his love. And in every possible way.

Epilogue

Six months later...

Savaric Fitz Leonard sat atop his black destrier and gazed out into the distance over the white cliffs of Dover and watched the fathomless blue sea that stretched along the vista. He dragged the salty sea air into his chest and exhaled, turning to face the two men who were beside him on their horses, also looking out to the English sea. Two men who had always been there for him and had always been more like brothers than mere associates— Warin de Talmont and Nicholas D'Amberly. Together they had been through many, many difficult trials over the years, through conflict, through hardship, through personal tragedies, and through the challenges of finally managing to apprehend and quash their adversaries, The Duo Dracones, here at Dover.

It had been so damn hard, so incredibly arduous, and had taken many, many years to foil every attempt they made against the Crown, but they had endured and overcome it together, as one, as the Knights Fortitude. Yet they had not done it alone.

Savaric glanced sideways beyond his friends at the women who had captured each of their hearts completely, sitting on their mounts looking regal with all their court dress fineries.

He noted Nicholas smiling at his wife, Eva, who had only recently come out of her confinement after the birth of their firstborn—a healthy daughter named Beatrice, after Nick's beloved mother. Her hand wrapped around the necklace that had been gifted by her husband.

Savaric's gaze turned to Warin, who planted a furtive kiss on the top of Joan's head when he believed no one was watching them. Warin's spirited wife was in his arms, together on the horse, and while Joan's failing sight had progressively worsened, it had never diminished the strength of their unity, care, and devotion to one another. Indeed, Warin and Joan had taken more young lost children into their care along with their adopted daughter Ava, adding to their ever-growing brood.

His gaze fell to the woman sat on her grey palfrey, with the most beautiful burnished red hair dancing softly in the breeze under a thin veil. His chest constricted as he watched his wife, Marguerite, laugh at something Eva had said to her. God, but even after all this time she still managed to stir his blood and steal his breath.

Savaric had swept Marguerite away after the last time they had all been here at Dover. After the peril and adversity, they had endured at the hands of The Duo Dracones, when he had almost lost her. God, but Savaric had never before experienced such fear as during those agonising moments when her life had once again been threatened. He had promised Marguerite that he would not dwell on it, not when they had so much to live for, but even now after so many months had passed, he would sometimes lie awake at night pondering on his immense good fortune and how different it could all have been. Indeed, there were moments when she was asleep when he would watch her in disbelief, knowing that she was his.

Savaric had taken Marguerite back to Studdal Castle, to be reunited with her brother. And it was there under her favourite tree beneath the moonlit sky that he had asked her to marry him. He knew that it meant a great deal to Marguerite and was glad to be able to make such a public avowal to her, even if it was to be against the backdrop of possible hostilities to their union. But he had been relieved to find no such thing among her people at least. And there was more good fortune that was to be bestowed on them as Hubert de Burgh had granted them a manor with its own demesne lands, for all their work in finally bringing about the downfall of The Duo Dracones.

It had been beyond their expectation. Beyond all imagination. And it had been the same for all of his Knights Fortitude brethren.

Savaric was immensely proud of their achievements. All of it…the good, the bad, and even the danger they had faced, since it was through the hardship, strife, and difficulties that they endured that made their triumph all the sweeter. They had overcome it all. Each and every single one of them.

Savaric had never known his friends to be as happy and content with their lives as this, but then he shared in this unadulterated happiness. He too had found it, had felt it, had tasted it, and wanted to cling on to it for dear life.

In truth, none of them were ever meant to have found this newfound happiness. Even now, after all this time, it was bewildering that the likes of Warin, Nicholas, and Savaric had found such a precious thing.

Indeed, they were meant for a hard life of servitude, bound by the oaths they had sworn to King Henry, their liege lord, and nothing more. Yet, despite it all, they had each found women who had seemingly been fashioned just for them.

They had found love.

Yet they had come perishingly close to losing what they had found. But somehow, they had managed to prevail and thwart a common enemy, every time it posed to attack the Crown. They had managed to overcome it all through the strength of their loyalty, friendship, and love…

Savaric flicked his gaze to Marguerite and winked at her, which in turn made her smile, a smile that he felt all the way down to his toes. God but his wife gave him a sense of peace that he could never have known he would need or want. He was still learning to accept her love and that he was worthy of it. Indeed, Marguerite was his anchor, his heart, his home…

Savaric pulled out his sword from its scabbard and raised it in the air as Warin and Nicholas followed suit.

'Pro Rex,' he ground out.

'Pro Deus,' Warin said solemnly.

'Pro fide,' Nicholas added

Before they all bellowed, *'Pro honoris!'*

Indeed, their Knights Fortitude motto was a timely

reminder that until each man drew their last breath they would always be bound together as Protectors of the Crown.

'And for love.' Marguerite's eyes were pinned to Savaric's.

'Yes.' Joan nodded. 'You cannot forget *that*.'

'As if we ever could.' Nicholas chuckled.

'I sincerely hope not.' Eva raised a brow.

'After everything that has happened,' Warin muttered. 'I rather doubt it.'

'Then for love.'

Savaric returned Marguerite's smile as they repeated the same words.

'Always, for love.'

* * * * *

*If you enjoyed this story, make sure to read the other books in Melissa Oliver's
Protectors of the Crown miniseries*

A Defiant Maiden's Knight
A Stolen Knight's Kiss

*And be sure to pick up her
Notorious Knights miniseries*

The Rebel Heiress and the Knight
Her Banished Knight's Redemption
The Return of Her Lost Knight
The Knight's Convenient Alliance

Get 3 FREE REWARDS!

We'll send you 2 FREE Books plus a FREE Mystery Gift.

FREE Value Over **$20**

Both the **Harlequin®** Historical and **Harlequin®** Romance series feature compelling novels filled with emotion and simmering romance.

Get 3 FREE REWARDS!

We'll send you 2 FREE Books plus a FREE Mystery Gift.

FREE Value Over **$20**

Both the **Harlequin® Desire** and **Harlequin Presents®** series feature compelling novels filled with passion, sensuality and intriguing scandals.

YES! Please send me 2 FREE novels from the Harlequin Desire or Harlequin Presents series and my FREE gift (gift is worth about $10 retail). After receiving them, if I don't wish to receive any more books, I can return the shipping statement marked "cancel." If I don't cancel, I will receive 6 brand-new Harlequin Presents Larger-Print books every month and be billed just $6.30 each in the U.S. or $6.49 each in Canada, a savings of at least 10% off the cover price, or 3 Harlequin Desire books (2-in-1 story editions) every month and be billed just $7.83 each in the U.S. or $8.43 each in Canada, a savings of at least 12% off the cover price. It's quite a bargain! Shipping and handling is just 50¢ per book in the U.S. and $1.25 per book in Canada.* I understand that accepting the 2 free books and gift places me under no obligation to buy anything. I can always return a shipment and cancel at any time by calling the number below. The free books and gift are mine to keep no matter what I decide.

Choose one: ☐ **Harlequin Desire**
(225/326 BPA GRNA)

☐ **Harlequin Presents Larger-Print**
(176/376 BPA GRNA)

☐ **Or Try Both!**
(225/326 & 176/376 BPA GRQP)

Name (please print)

Address   Apt. #

City   State/Province   Zip/Postal Code

Email: Please check this box ☐ if you would like to receive newsletters and promotional emails from Harlequin Enterprises ULC and its affiliates. You can unsubscribe anytime.

Mail to the **Harlequin Reader Service:**
IN U.S.A.: P.O. Box 1341, Buffalo, NY 14240-8531
IN CANADA: P.O. Box 603, Fort Erie, Ontario L2A 5X3

Want to try 2 free books from another series? Call 1-800-873-8635 or visit www.ReaderService.com.

*Terms and prices subject to change without notice. Prices do not include sales taxes, which will be charged (if applicable) based on your state or country of residence. Canadian residents will be charged applicable taxes. Offer not valid in Quebec. This offer is limited to one order per household. Books received may not be as shown. Not valid for current subscribers to the Harlequin Presents or Harlequin Desire series. All orders subject to approval. Credit or debit balances in a customer's account(s) may be offset by any other outstanding balance owed by or to the customer. Please allow 4 to 6 weeks for delivery. Offer available while quantities last.

Your Privacy—Your information is being collected by Harlequin Enterprises ULC, operating as Harlequin Reader Service. For a complete summary of the information we collect, how we use this information and to whom it is disclosed, please visit our privacy notice located at corporate.harlequin.com/privacy-notice. From time to time we may also exchange your personal information with reputable third parties. If you wish to opt out of this sharing of your personal information, please visit readerservice.com/consumerchoice or call 1-800-873-8635. **Notice to California Residents**—Under California law, you have specific rights to control and access your data. For more information on these rights and how to exercise them, visit corporate.harlequin.com/california-privacy.

HDHP23

HARLEQUIN
PLUS

Try the best multimedia subscription service for romance readers like you!

Read, Watch and Play.

Experience the easiest way to get the romance content you crave.

Start your **FREE TRIAL** at
www.harlequinplus.com/freetrial.